THE RUNAWAY SISTER

DAISY CARTER

Copyright © 2023 Daisy Carter
All rights reserved.

This story is a work of fiction. The characters, names, places, events, and incidents in it are entirely the work of the author's imagination or used in a fictitious manner. Any resemblance or similarity to actual persons, living or dead, events or places is entirely coincidental. No part of this work may be reproduced, stored in a retrieval system, or transmitted, in any form or by any means, without the prior permission of the author and the publisher.

CHAPTER 1

The West Country, England - 1853

MAISIE GRIFFIN HITCHED up the skirt of her dress and cautiously stepped forward. The mud felt soft between her toes, making sucking sounds as her feet sank into it, and air bubbled up from where it was trapped, popping with a faint whiff of sulphur and briny seawater. Gaining confidence, she walked faster, ignoring the way the mud seemed to tug at her ankles as if it wanted to hold her fast.

Something caught her eye at the water's edge, glinting with promise. Was it a coin? Or perhaps a diamond brooch. There were rumours aplenty that thieves in Gloucester sometimes threw their ill-gotten gains in the river to escape the constables if they were being chased. Her pulse quickened, and she glanced nervously across the estuary. The tide had already turned, that much she knew. But mudlarking was still quite new to her, and she didn't have the casual understanding of the powerful waters that the other children possessed. The mighty river seemed to be a law unto itself, changing from month to month under the influence of the equinoxes. And then there was the Severn bore, a powerful surge of waves on the days following the new and full moon, which could drag an unsuspecting person away to a watery death in an instant.

"What 'ave you seen, Maisie?" A gap-toothed boy with a tousled shock of ginger hair stood further along the river bank, watching her closely.

"Nothing much. I expect it's just a piece of old clay pipe." She wasn't about to give up her treasure so easily.

"Best hurry up then. The water's running fast today." The lad jumped down from the tussocky marsh grass and started heading towards her. He seemed to have an uncanny knack for avoiding the softest mud, which could trap a person in seconds and was closing the gap faster than she wanted.

"I said it's nothing." Maisie hitched her skirts higher, not caring if her ragged petticoat might show.

THE RUNAWAY SISTER

Modesty was a luxury her family couldn't afford. "Stay back, Fred. I saw it first, so it's mine."

"Not if I get there first. Them's the rules, Maisie Griffin, and you know it." Fred Piper sniffed loudly and chuckled. He knew when he was onto something good. "Just because you'm older than us doesn't mean you get first dibs on things. It ain't as if you've been doing it long, not like us proper mudlarks."

Maisie could feel her frustration rising, but she bit back the retort that was on the tip of her tongue. Fred had been kind enough to let her onto their patch just downriver from Frampton Basin, and she didn't want to get on the wrong side of him. Even though he was only nine years old, his cocksure demeanour made him a natural leader of the raggle-taggle gang of children who scavenged for old trinkets and bits of rubbish in the mud to sell.

"Please, Fred. Ma hasn't been well." She lunged forward, desperate to grab whatever it was, but she hadn't accounted for the way the mud dipped away in front of her. In a split second, the icy cold water from the incoming tide was eddying around her knees, making her gasp with surprise. "It's just there, I saw it sticking out of the mud." She thrust her hands into the water, groping blindly. "It's a brooch, I'm sure of it. Worth a few bob...enough to pay the rent and a few hot dinners to help get Ma's strength up."

Her skirt ballooned up around her for a moment,

3

floating on top of the water, before the cotton became waterlogged and stuck to her legs, suddenly weighing her down.

"Come back, Maisie. It ain't safe now." Fred's voice sounded muffled and far away, as though he was fading into the background. She could barely hear it, with the blood pounding in her ears and the sound of the tide rushing past. "Maisie, turn round, it's not worth it."

"I have to. Ma said I mustn't come home empty-handed. I can almost reach it." Her dress clung to her legs, and she was surprised at how strong the river felt as it crept up to her thighs, making it hard to stay upright, but then, miraculously, her fingers closed around something hard. "I got it!" She held it up triumphantly, admiring the way the diamonds caught the weak winter sun, making them shine like facets of fire. "We'll eat like kings with this—"

"Maisie...where are you?" a new voice called. Then she heard a different sound. It started as a tiny hiccup but quickly escalated into the thin wail of a baby crying. "Maisie, can you see to our Abigail."

"Yes, Ma," she mumbled, feeling confused and wondering what her mother was doing at the river.

"Maisie!"

Her eyes jerked open, and her heart thudded

under her thin nightdress. *It was just the dream again. She wasn't at the river but home in bed.* She wasn't sure whether to be relieved or disappointed as she blinked in the darkness until her eyes acclimatised to the faint outline of grey where the thin curtains covered the window of her bedroom. There was no diamond brooch this time...or ever.

Maisie grimaced as she threw back the thin eiderdown, and her skin goosebumped in the frigid January air. Everything felt damp, and she hastily dragged her old grey gown over her head and wrapped her wool shawl around her shoulders. The crying became more insistent, and she almost stubbed her toe on the edge of her chest of drawers in her haste to get dressed.

"I'm coming, Abigail." Her voice automatically softened as she crossed the upstairs hallway of their tiny cottage. Two strides across the wooden floorboards, ducking her head under the low doorframe, and she was in her ma's bedroom.

"I'd do it myself, but I just don't have the strength. Besides, there's no point. She'll only cry more when she sees I have no milk." Violet Griffin gave a wheezy cough as she pushed herself higher on the pillows. Her cheeks looked gaunt in the flickering light from her brass oil lamp that she liked to keep lit since being widowed. It kept the sad memories away, she always said, apologising to Maisie for the extra few pennies needed for oil.

"It's not your fault you can't feed her, Ma," Maisie said stoutly. She smiled as Abigail kicked her legs excitedly in the wooden drawer they used for her cradle. "You're a hungry little one, that's for sure," she cooed, gently lifting her sister up. "I'll go downstairs and get the fire going and give her some bread and milk."

"You're a good girl." Violet sighed and pulled the blankets higher under her chin. "Six months is a difficult age. I just feel so tired all the time, and Abigail is constantly hungry." Her eyes shimmered with sudden tears. "You know what day it is, don't you? A whole year since…" The spectre of a bleak January funeral hung in the air after her words.

Maisie nodded. "We mustn't be too sad, Ma. Papa wouldn't have wanted that. I'll settle Abigail and make a start on the mending until it's light."

"And then you'll go down to the river, won't you?" A brisk breeze rattled the windows, making the oil lamp gutter, but there was no respite from work. "If you could only find something decent…if only Robert had been better paid." Her voice sounded querulous, but Maisie knew it was just the tiredness making her that way. Everyone in Frampton village knew that Violet and Robert Griffin were as much in love on the day he died as the day they first met at

THE RUNAWAY SISTER

the summer fair almost twenty years ago. That was why it was so cruel that consumption had taken him long before Violet expected to be widowed.

"Maybe today will be our change of fortune, Ma." Maisie jiggled Abigail on her hip and was happy to see the strain on her ma's face ease as her eyes slowly closed again. "I had a dream that I found a diamond brooch—"

"That dream again?" Violet's eyes snapped open. "I've told you, it's all nonsense. Chance would be a fine thing."

"I...I'm sorry, Ma." Maisie quickly backed out of the bedroom, feeling annoyed with herself. She should have known better. Ma didn't like it when she talked about her dreams, but that one in particular always felt so real. "I'll feed Abigail and make you some porridge as well. Why don't you try and get some more rest."

DOWNSTAIRS IN THE FRONT PARLOUR, Maisie put Abigail on the cushions in the wingback armchair next to the hearth and knelt down to lay the fire. Within a few minutes, the flames were crackling brightly and starting to warm the room up, so she turned her attention to the stove, riddling the embers and adding a few more precious lumps of coal.

"Bread and milk sop for you, Abigail, and a nice

cup of tea for me. How about that?" She dropped a frugal pinch of tea leaves in the pot and put the blackened kettle on the stove to boil. "We're lucky to have such a lovely home, aren't we, poppet." In reality their cottage was small, just a front parlour and kitchen and washroom downstairs, and two bedrooms upstairs, but Maisie kept up a steady stream of chatter to distract Abigail from her hunger while she hurried through her first chores of the morning.

On the whole, Abigail was a placid baby, and she loved nothing more than watching the shadows from the oil lamp dance across the ceiling. She waved her pudgy hands, fingers splayed like starfish and gurgled each time Maisie walked past, giving her a gummy smile. She had already cut two teeth, and Maisie's heart swelled with love. It was hard to imagine life without her baby sister now.

When the food was ready, she lifted Abigail onto her lap to spoon it into her open mouth. "You were our little family's special blessing, weren't you," Maisie whispered, dropping a kiss on the top of her head. Abigail had a whorl of downy hair, a little lighter than Maisie's, which was the colour of dark honey, and her eyes had just darkened to the same green they both shared.

Abigail sucked on the sop eagerly, trying to grab

to spoon, which made her smile. "Let me feed you, sweetheart. We can't afford to waste anything."

When she had finished, Maisie eyed the armchair longingly. A ten-minute rest wouldn't harm, would it? She had stayed up until almost midnight sewing for her ma the evening before, and she ached with weariness. The thought of sitting with Abigail for ten minutes in the cosy warmth was too much to resist, and she settled them both into the chair. "We'll just sit for a moment, poppet. It will be our secret."

The clock ticked on the mantel shelf, and the weight of Abigail in the crook of her arm and the warmth of the fire made Maisie feel sleepy. She looked down into Abigail's cherubic face and allowed her thoughts to drift. She was lucky to have a little sister, especially because of the age gap. Maisie had heard the other women in the village whispering that Violet was already getting on in her years when she had been born. So a second baby arriving sixteen years later was a wonderful surprise for everyone.

Her thoughts darkened as other images crowded into her mind, creating the usual fog of confusion. Consumption had killed her pa, but it wasn't the only illness to have struck their family. Maisie had suffered from a terrible chill, which had turned into a fever that left her bedbound not long after her pa had died. All she could remember from those missing months were muttered whispers outside her bedroom door and occasional shadowy figures around her bed as hands pressed on her forehead and felt her pulse on her wrist. Snatches of conversations still flickered in her mind.

"'Tis the grief of losing her pa..."

"A fever can give a person amnesia...there's no way to say if or when her memories will return from this time..."

Maisie stroked Abigail's downy hair, and her eyes grew heavy. It still felt startlingly strange to her that by the time she got better, her ma had given birth to Abigail. She had no memory of her ma's pregnancy and confinement, but she loved her new sister with all her heart, and she was grateful that somehow their family had been blessed with new life just a few months after her pa had so cruelly died.

"Just five minutes more," she mumbled. The coals shifted in the fire, and her head lolled forward as she drifted into a fitful sleep.

CHAPTER 2

"Maisie, wake up! You fell asleep, but there's no time for resting."

"Wha—?" Maisie jumped at the feel of a firm hand on her shoulder, and her eyes flew open. "I'm so sorry, Ma. I just sat down for a few minutes by the fire with Abigail. I don't know what came over me."

"It's because you've been working so hard." Violet absent-mindedly twisted her grey hair into a bun and secured it with some hairpins on the nape of her neck before opening the curtains.

Maisie blinked, surprised to see that it was daylight. She glanced at the clock and saw that she had been asleep for an hour. Fragments of her dream still held her in their grip, and she had the disorientating sense of being suspended between deep sleep and wakefulness.

"I had the dream again, Ma," Maisie blurted out. "I was standing in the river convinced I saw something sparkling in the water, but I couldn't reach it. The rain was lashing down, and the tide was rising faster than usual." She dragged the back of her hand across her eyes, wondering why the dream still felt so real. "I managed to crawl out of the water, and then someone came to my rescue. A tall man with blue eyes. He even offered me warmth and food in one of the rooms at the tavern on the riverbank—"

"Hush!" Violet's sharp retort cut across her, and she frowned as she lifted Abigail out of Maisie's arms. "You need to stop talking about these dreams of yours, Maisie. I've never heard such fanciful imaginings in all my life."

The baby looked between them curiously and stuffed her fist into her mouth to ease another tooth about to come through.

"It's just dreams, Ma," Maisie reassured her quickly. "Why do you hate me talking about them so much?"

The silence stretched between them as Violet stood at the window again, staring out unseeing with a troubled expression.

Maisie stood up, feeling a pang of hurt. They used to be so close, but since her pa had died, her ma had become more withdrawn. Friends and neighbours, who used to be welcomed into the small cottage,

THE RUNAWAY SISTER

were often turned away now, and slowly, they had become more isolated. *Was it my illness? Was it because I placed too much of a burden on Ma when she should have had some solace from Pa's death by having Abigail?* The questions and guilt swirled through her mind. It was almost as though Violet had something to hide, which made no sense. There was no point asking again. She already knew her mother would not reply.

"I'm sorry I didn't bring the porridge up for you to have in bed, Ma." She added some milk to the pan and started stirring vigorously, trying to rescue the stodgy oats that had congealed in the pan from being overcooked while she'd been asleep.

"You're still too young to understand that it doesn't take much to set tongues wagging in this village." Violet turned back from the window and put Abigail down in the small wooden cot they kept downstairs so she could sleep while they worked.

"Why would people gossip about that?" Maisie offered a smile, trying to lighten the gloomy mood. "This time, in my dream, the man said he wanted to marry me if you can believe it? He said I would make a beautiful bride, and we would have a family together, and then he swept me into his arms..." She closed her eyes for a moment, trying to recall the pleasurable details, but they were gone, as insubstantial as smoke drifting away.

"That's enough of that! We'd better get on with

our work." Violet pulled her sewing basket out and started rummaging through the bobbins of cotton.

"I wish it *would* come true, Ma." She took hold of Violet's hands, noticing how cold they were. "I wish I could marry well and take care of you so you don't have to take in sewing anymore or worry about earning enough money to pay the rent."

They exchanged a smile. "I know you mean well, but these dreams are nothing more than you getting muddled from your illness. You never had them before, if you remember?"

"Perhaps it's foretelling the future?" A warm sense of hope filled Maisie's chest. "Some folks reckon dreams are like a second sight. Fred says his granny can see the future."

"Ava Piper?" Violet scoffed. "She can no more tell the future than any of us." She sniffed with displeasure. "Don't go getting any silly ideas in your head, my girl. You just had a bad dream because today is a sad day, what with it being the anniversary of your pa's funeral."

Maisie wondered idly whether she might ask Ava the meaning of her dreams, but one look at her ma's pinched lips told her to keep that thought to herself. Violet disapproved of the way Ava earned a few pennies by reading palms and tarot cards. And Maisie had to confess there was something a little spooky about the old woman and the way her milky gaze followed her when she walked past.

After eating a hasty breakfast, they worked together quietly for the next hour, sitting in front of the window to make the most of the dim winter light for their sewing. Violet Griffin was a skilled seamstress and took on mending for the dressmaker, Rebecca Wheeler, who lived at the other end of the village. But this winter had been harsher than usual. Thick snow had covered the ground for most of December, and Violet's health had suffered. She hadn't dared turn away any work from Mrs Wheeler, which was why Maisie had been taking on some of the work so that she could keep up.

"Don't you think it would be a better idea for me to do the dressmaking all the time instead of mudlarking?" Maisie watched her mother frowning with concentration. She had noticed how she struggled to thread her needle these days because of the arthritis that was slowly twisting her fingers, making them gnarled and stiff. "I'm sure Mrs Wheeler won't care whether it's you or me doing the sewing as long as the work is done to the standard she likes."

Her mother pursed her lips but then shook her head. "I don't want Mrs Wheeler to think I can't manage. I won't have the villagers looking down their noses at me just because I'm a widow."

"They won't, Ma," Maisie cried. "There are other

women in the village without husbands. We don't think less of them."

Violet tutted to herself. "I've already had to put up with years of tittle-tattle, and I won't add fuel to the fire." She snapped her lips closed and turned in her chair slightly to indicate that the conversation was over.

Maisie stifled a sigh. Her ma had been born to a poor family who moved to Frampton when she was in her teens, but sometimes, she was too proud for her own good. People's opinions, or rather the fear of being the subject of gossip, mattered more than anything to her. Marrying Robert Griffin had been the pinnacle of her achievements because he was a scholar who earned a living tutoring children from some of the wealthier families in the area. But memories were long in Frampton village. The people who remembered Violet growing up in rags didn't take kindly to the way she had tried to better herself, whispering that she had betrayed her class while enviously wishing they had managed to do the same. Even though Violet and Robert had married for love, there were plenty of folks who were quick to assume she had been nothing other than a social climber.

If only they realised. The irony was that although Robert Griffin was a well-read man, he was also a dreamer. He taught for the love of it and allowed people

THE RUNAWAY SISTER

to take advantage of that fact, which was why they were still as poor as church mice. People assumed he had made a good living, and Violet was too proud and stubborn to tell them otherwise. Taking in sewing used to be for the little extras, but now it barely paid the rent, so there was no way Maisie could stop mudlarking. If people thought it strange that the widow of an educated man needed to work at such menial endeavours, Violet maintained that it was none of their business.

BY THE TIME the frost on the windows started to thaw, Maisie folded up her sewing and laid it neatly on the dresser to continue with later that night. The thought of scratching through the river mud for the next few hours was unappealing, but there was no changing her mother's mind once it was made up, so she pushed it aside. It was just what they had to do to make ends meet, so that's all there was to it.

To her surprise, Violet tidied away her sewing as well and reached for Abigail's soft, woollen shawl that was used when she had to go outside.

"We can't let today go by without marking it properly," Violet said decisively. "I've saved up a few pennies to pay for some flowers to put on your pa's grave. It won't be much at this time of year…some holly and ivy perhaps, but 't'will have to do. We'll go to the churchyard now before you start working at the river."

"Are you sure it's not too cold for you to be outside, Ma?" Maisie picked up her boots from where they had been warming in front of the fire and tugged them on. They pinched her toes, but new boots cost money they didn't have, and they were only to get to and from the river. A cold gust of wind blew down the chimney, but that was nothing. Standing in the estuary, the wind felt like knives of ice, cutting through her clothes to her skin, leaving her blue with cold. She shivered and looked longingly into the glowing coals, wishing she could stay inside sewing.

Violet hesitated for a moment. "I know my chest hasn't been very good, but what would people think if we didn't pay our respects? Besides, I want to. I never miss a week visiting his grave, and today is no exception." Her face was lined with grief and tiredness, old before her time. There was no question that she would ever consider marrying again. Robert had been her one true love and nobody would ever replace him, even if marrying again might make their lives easier.

THEIR BREATH PLUMED over their heads as they set off through the cobbled lanes. The honey-coloured church, with its square spire, was at the southern end of the village, close to where the fields turned into estuary marshland. It would be a brisk twenty-minute walk, but Maisie didn't mind. She hoped it might give them a chance to say hello to some of their friends and neighbours and perhaps remind her ma that being more sociable was not something to fear.

"We'll go to Mr McLean, the greengrocer first. He should have something suitable, and he's not as expensive as some." Violet marched ahead with her eyes kept firmly forward to discourage anyone from chatting.

"Why don't we treat ourselves to a lardy cake from the bakers?" Maisie pulled a coin from her dress pocket and held it up with a smile. "I forgot to give this to you yesterday. I know we have mutton stew and vegetables for dinner tonight, but it is a special day, and lardy cake was Pa's favourite."

Violet relented and slowed down. The village bakery was tucked between a toy shop and the cobblers. Usually, she would not allow such extravagance when they could quite easily make their own fruit cake, but the tempting smell of the sweet, sticky treat wafting from the bakery door was too much to resist. "I don't suppose it would harm just this once."

The sound of hurrying footsteps caught Maisie's attention before she could reply.

"Well, fancy seeing you out today, Violet. You don't often grace us with your presence in the village anymore."

Maisie's heart sank, and she groaned inwardly as she turned around to see Elsie Clatterbrook and her spinster sister, Caroline Fraser. How typical that the two women most likely to gossip and pry into their business should be out at exactly the same time as them. She wouldn't have put it past Mrs Clatterbrook to have left the comfort of her cottage to rush after them on purpose. Elsie had been sweet on Robert and had never quite forgiven Violet for snatching him from under her nose, as she had once described it.

"Good morning, Elsie," Violet said carefully. "And good morning to you, Caroline. I hope you're both well and not suffering with this dreadful cold weather we've been having." She furtively adjusted the woollen shawl so that barely any part of Abigail was showing.

Elsie waddled closer, breathing heavily through her mouth. "It ain't so bad with a nice fire in the hearth at home. My Jeffrey had a pay rise just a'fore Christmas, and he gets as much free wood as he likes from the estate. Lord Pickering gave all his favourite workers a pay rise. Not before time, I said to Jeffrey." She folded her pudgy arms across her ample bosom with a self-satisfied air.

"I'm sure that must be very welcome in hard times such as these." Violet knew that Elsie loved to brag at every opportunity that her husband worked at Frampton Manor, and had progressed to being the head gardener.

"Treating yourself to something from the bakery, are you?" Caroline was the opposite of her sister, with a thin face and wispy hair that refused to stay in ringlets. She looked at the shawl, her beady eyes alight with curiosity. "Give us a peek at the baby, Violet. We called round several times to have a look at her, but you were never at home." Her thin lips twisted into a smirk. "Or perhaps you just didn't want to answer the door to us ordinary people?"

"Abigail is teething at the moment. She's not feeling very well, and we're in a hurry." Violet clutched the baby to her chest and turned away, not caring if it seemed rude.

Maisie saw the two sisters share a glance of disapproval. "It's not that Ma doesn't want to stop and chat with you," she said hastily. "She hasn't been well these last few weeks, and we're putting flowers on Pa's grave today. It's not good for her to be outside for too long. I'm sure you understand."

Caroline shrugged, but Elsie still looked indignant as Violet edged towards the bakery doorway.

"Why don't you call around for a cup of tea

tomorrow," Maisie added rashly. "The company will be nice for you, won't it, Ma."

"I'm not so sure about that," Violet sighed. She shot Maisie a desperate look, and her narrow shoulders shuddered as she started coughing. "Why don't we wait until the weather is nicer, Elsie? There's no point coming out unnecessarily while it's still this cold. Visit us in the spring instead, and hopefully, Abigail won't be so tetchy from teething by then."

Maisie followed her mother into the baker's shop, trying to ignore Elsie's scowl at being snubbed so openly.

The two sisters turned away slightly, but she could still hear snatches of their conversation.

"...Did you ever hear anything so rude? I always said she likes to think she's a cut above us, Caroline, but she's still the same raggedy woman underneath her high and mighty ways. Robert was too good for her."

"It's them two poor girls I feel sorry for." Caroline's whisper was laden with disapproval and the envy of being a childless spinster herself. "They say she was only lucky enough to have Maisie because of that potion the gypsy travellers were giving out at the summer fair. She must have taken another dose of it to have Abigail. A woman of her age having a baby, it's not right if you ask me."

"...I heard a rumour that Robert took one of

those newfangled trains over yonder to visit the White Horse on the Ridgeway. They say you only have to step onto it, and a baby will arrive nine months later. I bet he only did it to keep Violet happy. Everyone knows he should never have married her."

John Davies, the baker, cleared his throat. "Here's your lardy cake, Mrs Griffin." He handed the parcel across the counter and gave them both a kindly smile. "I popped a couple of yesterday's jam tarts in there as well. They're not too stale if you warm them in the range for a moment." He glanced out at Elsie and Caroline, looking awkward. "It's the anniversary of Robert's funeral today, isn't it? A difficult day for you, I'm sure. He was always very kind, helping my Percy get better at his reading and writing. It was a sad loss for the village."

"Thank you, but we don't need—" Violet seemed to lose her train of thought and drifted off.

"That's very kind of you, Mr Davies." Maisie quickly picked up the parcel and shot him a grateful smile. "We'll enjoy this tonight, won't we, Ma."

"Yes…thank you, Mr Davies. I was about to say that we don't need anyone's charity, but I know that's not what you intended." She shifted Abigail in her arms and blinked back tears. "I can hardly believe it's been a year since we were standing in the graveyard, burying Robert, but it's nice to know that some people still remember how much he tried to do for the village children."

"Aye, well, don't pay any heed to those two busy-bodies," Mr Davies folded his hands across his paunch and shook his head. "I swear some of the things Elsie comes out with are sour enough to curdle milk. You're lucky to have two lovely daughters, Mrs Griffin."

"Yes...two lovely daughters," she echoed vaguely.

"Are you feeling alright, Ma?" Maisie was starting to wonder if they should head straight back home as she saw how pale her mother looked.

"Of course, dear." She fluttered her hand in front of her face. "It's just warm in here after standing outside. We must go and see Mr McLean now."

Maisie thanked Mr Davies, and they stepped out into the icy wind again. "Do enjoy the rest of your day," she said sweetly to Elsie and Caroline, knowing full well it would annoy them. She had been mistaken to think they were friends and hoped they wouldn't come visiting, what with her ma seeming so flustered and out of sorts.

"Yes, don't let us keep you." Violet allowed herself a small smile of triumph even though she knew that gloating over Elsie was meanspirited. "I was lucky enough to enjoy all those years with my darling Robert, and that's what I'm going to commemorate today with my girls." She sighed, suddenly deflated again. "You still have your Jeffrey, Elsie. Count your blessings."

Maisie took Abigail out of her ma's arms and settled her on her hip. Glancing up at the glowering grey skies, she thought they would be fortunate to make it to the churchyard before the heavens opened.

CHAPTER 3

*J*ack Piper ran a hand through his dark hair and put his cap back on, pulling it low over his eyes against the biting wind, which was blowing up the estuary.

"What I wouldn't give to be drinking a nice hot toddy by the fire right now, Duke. Never mind, a hard day's work never harmed anyone." He jumped down from the seat of his cart and patted his horse's neck. Duke was a sturdy piebald with a luxurious moustache on his top lip and feathers above his hooves, typical of his draft breed. He was good-natured, and his thick winter coat protected him against the worst of the weather. It was fair to say that he had been worth every penny that Jack had managed to scrape together to buy him from the gypsy horse fair.

"Be a good lad and wait here. I won't be long." Duke's ears flicked forward at the sound of his master's voice, and he let out a long sigh and dropped one of his back legs forward slightly, making the most of the opportunity to rest.

"Are you coming with me, Badger? If we play our cards right, Florence might have a tasty bone for you." Jack whistled through the small gap between his front teeth and chuckled as his dog bounded enthusiastically after him. Badger was of an indeterminate origin with a soft tricoloured coat and long floppy ears. Jack had found him abandoned as a pup on the side of the road, next to the stiff corpse of the collie who had birthed him, and he was the only one of the litter to survive. He couldn't leave him to suffer the same fate and had carried him home in his jacket and hand-reared him, and now they were inseparable.

"Have you got any rags for me today, Florence?" Jack strode confidently up the front path of the elegant, four-storey Georgian house where Mr Fisher, a coffee merchant, lived.

The housemaid looked up from the steps she was scrubbing, and her face split into a smile. She hastily stood up and brushed the creases from her dark grey linsey-woolsey work dress. "Morning, Jack. I wish I'd known you were coming, I would have put on my best apron." She fluttered her eyelashes and looked up at him coyly.

"I can't say I've noticed there's anything wrong with that apron you're wearing," Jack said cheerfully. He stuck his hands in his pockets and made sure to give her his most endearing smile. He could usually count on getting a few extra bits and bobs to go in the cart with that strategy.

"Oh, get away with you. You're a proper charmer," Florence giggled and twirled a lock of her hair. Jack could tell she was in the mood to chat, which was a shame because he needed to get on.

"How's everything in the big house? Are you still hoping to be promoted to become parlourmaid?" He winked. "Who knows, Mr Fisher might even promote you to become his wife…a beauty like you."

A fiery blush coloured Florence's pale cheeks, and she shook her head and batted away his words. "Don't be so silly; the master wouldn't look twice at a girl like me…would he?" There was a tinge of hope in her voice, and Jack felt momentarily guilty.

"I don't see why not, Florence. I'm sure he gets lonely since his wife died, and us working-class folk are just as deserving of being happy as the toffs, and don't you forget it. A new gown and some ribbons in your hair, and you would look just as pretty as any of them well-to-do young ladies at their coming out balls." He reached down to ruffle Badger's ears. "About those rags…if you have something for me I'd be ever so grateful. Times are hard at the moment until everyone starts doing the spring cleaning, but I do what I can to keep the family fed."

Florence straightened her mob cap on her thin, sandy-coloured hair and beamed up at him. "Don't you worry, Jack, I've saved everything that Mrs Howell, the housekeeper, would've thrown away. It ain't much, but hopefully, it will be enough to be helpful." She hurried away and returned a couple of minutes later with a bundle of rags in her arms.

"You're a saviour, Florence. What would I do without you?" He was tempted to lean forward and pat her on the shoulder but then reminded himself that It wouldn't be fair to give her the wrong idea. As much as he liked Florence and appreciated her thoughtfulness, she was not the sort of girl he would consider courting.

"And I swiped a little treat for Badger from the kitchen when Cook wasn't looking." She pulled a lamb chop bone from her pocket. It had already been stripped clean, but that didn't matter. "There you are, boy." She smiled as Badger daintily took it from her hand and darted away to crunch it up. Mind you only call when I'm here," Florence said, as Jack turned to leave. She fluttered her eyelashes again. "Mrs Howell

THE RUNAWAY SISTER

ain't as friendly as me, and Nora scarcely knows what day of the week it is since the new stable lad started working here."

"Of course. You know you're my favourite housemaid, Florence. Badger and I are always grateful for anything you can put our way. Don't forget what I said about Mr Fraser, though. A kind word and a pretty smile might be all it takes for him to see you in a different light." He winked again, making her blush, and came back out into the lane whistling cheerfully, almost crashing headlong into Violet Griffin and Maisie, who was carrying her baby sister.

"Look where you're going, young man." Violet wrinkled her nose as she eyed the bundle of old rags in his arms. "I heard you flirting with young Florence Porter just now. I hope you're not putting ideas in her head. It wouldn't be right for the poor girl to end up heartbroken just to help your rag-and-bone business."

"I wasn't flirting, just being friendly." He heaved the rags into the back of the cart, sending up a cloud of dust.

"Is this Badger?" Maisie stroked the dog, who was wagging enthusiastically and leaning against her legs with his tongue lolling out. "He was a tiny puppy the last time I saw him."

"Yes. I've had him well over a year now, and he

eats me out of house and home. But I wouldn't be without him. They keeps me company on my rounds, him and Duke, because it can get lonely sometimes, being out on my own all day."

"I suppose that's why you flirt with the maids, is it?" Violet was still frowning with disapproval. "It's that sort of behaviour that leads girls astray and ends up with them being taken advantage of."

Jack saw Maisie's shocked expression at her ma's harsh words. He thought about jumping up into the front of his cart and leaving without answering, then realised he couldn't let the comment go without defending himself. "I suppose I was flirting a little, but I only do it so that the housemaids give me better things for me to sort through and sell."

"Quite. The apple doesn't fall far from the tree," Violet said sniffily. "It's not hard to see where those sorts of dubious morals come from."

"I'm just doing what I need to look after the family, Mrs Griffin," Jack shot back. "I didn't always want to be a rag-and-bone man, but it's an honest trade." He glanced towards Maisie. "Just like Maisie, doing the mudlarking with my younger brother, Fred. We all do what we need to earn a few coins, don't we?"

"You should aspire to make something better of yourself."

THE RUNAWAY SISTER

Violet seemed to be determined to goad him, but he didn't rise to the bait. "I'd better get on, it looks like the weather is about to turn."

"Yes, we need to get on too." Violet exchanged the flowers she was holding for Abigail, taking her from Maisie and pulling the shawl tighter around her. Jack had a glimpse of the baby's dimpled cheeks and was about to say how sweet she looked, but Violet had already turned away.

He jumped up into the back of his cart to pile the rags up at the front so he would have more room. Violet's comments stung, but there was more than a grain of truth in them if he was being honest with himself. He knew he wasn't doing what he really wanted to do with his life. He had barely turned nineteen, but he had obligations.

I have to look after Granny and Fred. I was lucky enough to be able to buy Badger. Maybe one day things will change for the better. The familiar thoughts rattled through his mind, but he pushed them away. He couldn't go chasing dreams when all that mattered was earning enough money to pay the rent and feed his family. He hadn't asked to be thrust into that position, but with no parents, what choice did he have?

"I'm sorry for the way Ma spoke to you." Maisie was still lingering next to his cart as Violet walked on. "She's not usually so forthright, at least not with other people." Her ruby-red lips curved into a rueful smile of amusement that made his heart unexpectedly flip in his chest. The last time he had really taken notice of Maisie, she had still looked like a young girl, but while he had been busy building up his rag-and-bone rounds, she had blossomed into a beautiful young woman. Her honey-brown hair framed her heart-shaped face, and her eyes were an arresting shade of green edged with dark lashes. She had a way of giving her whole attention when he spoke, and he found himself staring, wishing they had longer to talk.

"That's alright," he chuckled eventually. "I'm used to forthright women from living with my granny. She soon lets me know if I do something she disapproves of, and she ain't shy of giving Fred a clip round the ear for being rude either."

"How is Ava? I don't suppose she gets around much now that her eyesight is failing. I should come and visit her, but there never seems to be enough time."

"She would like that. It must be a coincidence, but she mentioned you just the other day. Said she didn't see you around in the village much anymore." Maisie looked pleased at his comment, and Jack wondered if Violet stopped her from having many friends.

"I have to help Ma look after Abigail. It was a lot

THE RUNAWAY SISTER

for her to have another baby at her age, but we love her so much, I'm not complaining."

"I'll tell Granny you asked after her." Duke fidgeted in his harness, and Jack talked faster. "Where are you going with your ma today?" He needed to get on, but really, he wanted to stay and enjoy Maisie's company for longer. The tug of attraction in his chest caught him by surprise, and he busied himself with checking Duke's harness to squash his expectations. *Don't be daft, Jack. She'll never be interested in someone like you. Besides, Violet probably has aspirations for her to marry a clerk, not a lowly rag-and-bone man.*

Maisie held up the bunch of flowers in her hands. "It's the anniversary today."

"Anniversary?" Jack could have kicked himself. "Of course, it's a year since your pa's funeral, isn't it? No wonder your ma is feeling out of sorts. I should have remembered."

"We're putting these on Papa's grave, and then I'll be going down to the river to go mudlarking afterwards."

A sudden rustle behind him made Jack turn round, and he saw that Violet had walked back. "He was a good man, your husband, Mrs Griffin," he said politely. "I'm sure those hellebore flowers will look nice on his grave."

Violet's eyebrows twitched upwards in surprise. "How did you know they're hellebores? Most young men your age wouldn't have the first idea about such a thing. They were one of Robert's favourite plants."

"*Helleborus orientalis*," Jack said quietly. He shuffled his feet awkwardly as Violet looked even more startled that he knew the proper botanical name. "I hoped to become a gardener when I was younger. Mr Griffin gave me a book all about plants when I was a nipper. I still have it today, and he encouraged me to learn as much as I could. But then…well, things changed. I would have liked to work at the Manor for Lord Pickering, but Jeffrey Clatterbrook isn't in any hurry to put in a good word for me. He doesn't approve of my family, so I decided to buy Badger and set myself up in the rag-and-bone trade instead."

Violet's expression softened slightly, and she gave him a small smile. "That sounds exactly like the sort of thing Robert would do."

Another sharp gust of wind whistled through the village, and Violet shivered just as Abigail started to grizzle.

"Why don't you sit up in my cart, and I can take you to the churchyard? It's not really out of my way, and it looks like it might start raining in a minute. You won't want the little 'un to get any colder, I'm sure." He looked hopefully between Maisie and Violet, and Badger yapped excitedly and twirled, trying to grab the end of his tail.

"Thank you for offering, but we'll be fine," Violet

THE RUNAWAY SISTER

said crisply. Jack wondered why she seemed to rebuff any offers of help or friendship. His granny had told him that Violet was a proud woman, but she didn't look very well, and he had been brought up to help out whenever he could. Maisie stifled a sigh. Clearly, she was used to her mother cutting off her nose to spite her face.

"Honestly, it's no bother. Isn't that what friends and neighbours are for?" He caught Maisie's eye, and she gave him a grateful smile.

Violet dabbed a handkerchief at her nose, which had a bluish-purple tinge and shook her head. "Like you said, Jack, you have a living to make to keep your family fed. We won't keep you any longer." With that, Violet linked arms with Maisie and swept her away.

"I'll have to try harder next time, eh Duke?" Jack muttered under his breath. "Some folk don't know a kind deed when it's offered in plain English." He admired Maisie's patience and started to think how he might engineer another meeting so he could get to know her better.

Hopping up onto the wooden seat of his cart, he picked up the reins and clicked his tongue against his teeth to tell Duke to trot on. He'd been telling the truth when he told Florence that it was a difficult time of year. People didn't want to come to the door when there was an icy wind howling through the village, and December had been bad because of the snow. He glanced over his shoulder at the meagre pile of rags and oddments of other people's rubbish. He knew that Fred hadn't found much scavenging in the mud lately, either. It would be a lean month if he couldn't come up with a better idea soon.

He rounded the corner past the village square, and the majestic sight of Frampton Manor came into view. It was the country home of Lord and Lady Pickering, who divided their time between the West Country and London.

If only I'd had the chance to work there. We might have had a cottage in the grounds, and I wouldn't be chasing my tail for every shilling I can make. He sighed and pulled his cap lower against the wind. "I suppose there's no point wishing for things to be different," he mumbled to himself. Jack was not normally given to thoughts of regret, and he turned up his collar as an idea came into his head.

Usually, he didn't bother asking at the Manor house for rags because Lord Pickering didn't like tradesmen loitering outside, but he'd heard on good authority that his lordship was up in London at the moment. He grinned to himself. Perhaps he could make this a regular stop every time Lord Pickering was away. *They're bound to have some good quality bits and pieces I can sort through, and what he doesn't know won't harm him.*

He pulled lightly on the reins, and Duke turned

into the wide driveway that was flanked by two enormous stone gateposts next to the lodge house. If he was quick, he would be able to get around the back to the kitchens without anyone seeing him. He knew that Polly Partridge had started working there as a maid recently, and she was a good sort. His granny had made a herbal tonic for Polly's little brother last year when he'd eaten some poisonous mushrooms and gone into a delirium. When he got better, Polly said she would be happy to return the favour someday.

He sat back in his seat and gazed around at the rolling grassland dotted with mature oak trees. In the distance, he could see the lake, which he knew was well stocked with fish, and beyond it, a herd of roe deer grazed the winter pastures. Lord Pickering often hosted hunting and fishing parties with lavish entertainment laid on for the guests. Rumour had it there was once a performing bear and opera singers from Paris and so much food the servants were still eating the leftovers a week later. His stomach rumbled. It would be a long time until dinner, and he wondered if Polly might slip him a slice of cold pie.

What would it be like to work here? His thoughts drifted, and he imagined how proud he would be to tend the bountiful kitchen garden and grow exotic blooms in the new glasshouse, which he could see glinting in the grey light. Lady Pickering would lavish praise on him—

"Oi! What do you think you're doing?"

The angry shout dragged Jack out of his pleasant daydreams, and his heart sank as he saw Jeffrey Clatterbrook up ahead with his arms folded across his worn leather waistcoat.

"Just trying to earn a crust, Mr Clatterbrook." Jack gave him a deferential nod. "I'm sure the big house must have some rags and bits and bobs I can take away. I'll be doing them a favour. You won't even know I've been, I'll be so quick."

Clatterbrook was having none of it, and he stepped out into the middle of the driveway so that Jack had to bring Duke to a sharp stop. "We don't want the likes of you anywhere on the estate." He looked Jack up and down with a scowl. "Just typical that a Piper brat would try and sneak in when Lord Pickering isn't here. Be gone with you before I throw you out myself."

Jack felt his temper rising at the injustice. "What's wrong with me trying to earn a living? You're no grander than the rest of us villagers, so why are you looking down your nose at me?"

Jeffrey Clatterbrook stood his ground and jerked his head to indicate that Jack should turn around. "Elsie and I are nothing like your family," he snorted with disdain. "Your ma, a woman of the night in the

THE RUNAWAY SISTER

taverns of Gloucester docks...you and Fred with different fathers who you've never even met...and Ava sticking her nose into everybody's business when it doesn't concern her." His expression hardened. "I know you fancy working here in the gardens, but I ain't having someone with your background eyeing up my job. Lord Pickering only employs decent folk, so you'd better be on your way."

Jack squared his shoulders and carefully manoeuvred Duke and the cart around. "I can't deny that my ma fell into bad ways, but that doesn't give you the right to judge me and Fred. And, as for Granny, what sort of a man speaks ill of a harmless old lady like her?"

"There's nothing harmless about that old biddy." Jeffrey Clatterbrook shook his head with annoyance and stomped back to his wheelbarrow, picking up his spade again. "There's bad blood in your family, Jack Piper, and everyone knows it. You'll never come to anything. You stick to scratching around for old rags, and don't let me see you trying to come onto his lordship's property again, or I'll report you to the constable."

With Clatterbrook's parting threat ringing in his ears, Jack flicked the reins and set Duke into a brisk trot. "I'll show you I'm not the failure everyone thinks I am," he said through gritted teeth, more for his own benefit than anything.

It was true that his ma had turned to entertaining the men in the docks to try and feed the family, but it had taken its toll on her, leaving them motherless. *But that doesn't mean I'll turn out wrong.* Fred and his granny relied on him, and he was determined to make something of his life. He just didn't know how yet.

CHAPTER 4

*B*y the time Jack finished his rounds at the end of Frampton village and turned Duke to head for home, the glowering grey clouds had increased, rolling in from the west and almost making it feel like dusk. The weak winter sun had long since disappeared, and with sudden ferocity, the weather had changed for the worse. The cold rain quickly turned to hail and sleet, stinging his eyes as the wind scythed across the estuary, carrying the freezing cold flakes with it. He hunched his shoulders and pulled his cap down. Even Badger wasn't happy, quivering next to him on the seat of his cart.

Jack flicked the reins, urging Duke to trot faster. Fred would already be trudging home, and he ground his teeth with frustration at the thought of how sodden the rugs in the back of his cart would become. The oilskin blanket he had draped over the top was no match for the combination of wind and sleet, which he knew would find its way into every nook and cranny. It would take days of draping them in front of the fire to dry them because the rag merchant wouldn't buy them wet.

They rounded the corner at the end of Church End Road, and he was surprised to see Violet and Maisie up ahead. They must have taken longer than intended at the churchyard, but at least it gave him a chance to speak to Maisie again. "You'll have a lift now, won't you, Mrs Griffin?" The wind snatched his words away, unheard.

As the cart drew closer, Jack was shocked to see Violet weaving erratically in his pathway.

"Ma! Take my arm." Maisie leaned into the wind, her thin cloak flapping behind her, and hurried to Violet's side.

Before she had a chance to reach her mother, Violet suddenly clutched at her chest and staggered three steps before slowly collapsing, first onto her knees and then into a crumpled mound, face down on the cobbles.

"Ma! Get up. Help...somebody help us!" Maisie's shout was full of anguish. She balanced Abigail on her hip at the same time as trying to pull Violet up again, but she was like a dead weight.

"It's alright, Maisie. You're not alone; let me help

THE RUNAWAY SISTER

you." Jack leapt down and sprinted the last few yards, slithering on the icy cobbles as he came to a halt next to them.

"I kept telling her that we should get home and that it was too cold for her to be outside, but she wouldn't listen." Tears trembled on Maisie's eyelashes, and she dashed them away with the back of her hand. "It's my fault." Her teeth chattered from the shock and cold.

"You mustn't blame yourself. You weren't to know this hail and sleet would blow in so fast. We've all been caught out by it."

"I should have put my foot down. Pa is dead, and I know Ma wanted to mark the occasion, but what good does that do if she ends up dying as well?" She looked up at Jack beseechingly.

"You've had a shock, but let's not jump to conclusions." Jack glanced up and down the lane, but it was empty. Everyone was sheltering inside, waiting for the terrible weather to pass. "Your ma is probably stronger than you think. I'll get her into the cart, and we'll take her home."

Jack carefully rolled Violet over and lifted her into a sitting position. Although her cheeks had a strange grey tinge, her eyes fluttered open, and she looked around in confusion. "You had a fall, Mrs Griffin." He could feel the tremors of cold and illness in her frail shoulders. "We're going to take you home and sit you by the fire. You'll be better in no time."

"Robert?" Violet blinked slowly, and then her blank expression was transformed by a hesitant smile. "Robert, is it you? I feel so cold and tired... exhausted...but you're here to save me. Shouldn't you be at work? I don't want to take you away from your pupils."

Jack saw the worry and fear chasing across Maisie's face. "She thinks you're Papa," she whispered. "We have to get her into bed as quickly as possible. There's no warmth in her cloak, and she's already weak from being ill before Christmas."

Abigail's arms sprang free from the shawl, and she waved her fists, starting to hiccup with distress as the sleet swirled around them. Her cheeks reddened, and the hiccups turned into sobs that quickly escalated.

"Don't let the baby cry, Maisie," Violet said in alarm. "We mustn't interrupt Robert while he's working." Her eyes clouded with confusion as she looked between Maisie and Jack. "I hope you're going to stand by Maisie now that you've had a baby with her," she said, sounding more forceful. "It's not right having a child and then abandoning her."

Jack's heart squeezed with pity as the delirium took hold of Violet, and he rested his hand on Maisie's shoulder for a moment to reassure her. "This isn't my baby, Mrs Griffin. This is your little 'un,

Abigail. Try not to worry. She's only crying because she's cold...and hungry too, I shouldn't wonder. Maisie is taking great care of her for you. Now then, I'm going to lift you up and put you on a nice comfy pile of rags in the cart, and we'll take you home. You'll be back safe and sound and warm by the fire before you know it."

Violet blinked slowly and smiled again, this time with relief. "You're a good boy, Jack Piper. I always said to Ava that she had a good grandson in you." She seemed to have forgotten all about Robert, which was something of a blessing. It would be too harsh to tell her now that he had died over a year ago.

Jack and Maisie exchanged a glance, and she nodded for him to go ahead. "Ready then?" Jack scooped Mrs Griffin up into his arms. She felt scarcely heavier than a child in spite of her sodden cloak, and two unnaturally bright spots of pink had appeared on her cheeks. She would be in the grip of a bad fever before the day was out, he could already tell, so time was of the essence.

"SHE'S A BONNY BABY," Jack said once Violet was settled in the cart and he was sitting next to Maisie up front. He tickled Abigail under the chin and chuckled as she gave him a gummy smile. "You be a good girl for your big sister now, Abigail. No more tears otherwise, Uncle Jack will have to tickle you again."

Duke clopped in front of them, and they were back at the cottage within a few minutes.

"I'll go on ahead and stoke up the fire." Maisie sounded almost as weary as her ma, and Jack wondered how much the family had been struggling behind closed doors. Poverty was no stranger for many of the families in Frampton, but most folks weren't too proud to ask for help, unlike Violet.

Jack jumped down and hitched the reins before turning back to take Abigail from Maisie. "Let me take her and help you down. The cobbles are slippery, and you can't afford to hurt yourself." He glanced down at Abigail once she was in his arms. For a moment, he had a strange sense of contentment. He had often looked after Fred when he was a baby, but this felt different. As Maisie clambered down to stand next to him and the wind tugged at her hair, he had a glimpse of what it must feel like to be married with a child. *Don't go getting silly ideas, Jack. You haven't got time for heartache.* He pushed the thought away quickly. He didn't want to fall in love with someone who would likely never look twice at him. "You'd better get Abigail into the warm, and I'll carry your ma in now."

The cottage was larger than it looked from the outside, and Jack looked around curiously once they had settled Violet into the armchair in front of the fire. There was a tall bookcase crammed with books on one wall and an elegant dresser with a matching china tea set on it. He could see the influence of Mr Griffin still and that Violet had at one time strived to better the family. There were no such luxuries where he lived with his granny and Fred, he thought ruefully.

Maisie turned up the oil lamps, riddled the embers of the fire, and added a few lumps of coal. Against the dreary weather through the window, the soft light made the room feel cosy, and steam soon started to rise from the hem of Violet's gown.

"I still owe the coalman for the last delivery," Maisie said quietly, looking at the half-empty coal bucket. "He said we could have it on tick because of Ma being ill, but I don't know how much longer this lot will last."

Jack rushed to reassure her. "I chopped a load of wood last week, and there's plenty more where that came from."

"Not from the estate grounds, I hope?"

He shrugged and felt better when he saw a glint of amusement in her eyes. "I only take what comes down in the storms. It's not as if Lord Pickering does much else to help the villagers. Anyway, I have some dry, seasoned logs, and I'm sure my granny won't

DAISY CARTER

mind you having some. It's important to keep the cottage warm until your ma recovers."

"That's kind, thank you." Maisie leaned over Violet and rested her hand gently on her forehead. "You're burning up, Ma, even though your hands are freezing. I think we should send for Doctor Harding. It won't take me long to run to Peartree Villa and see if he's at home. I'll make you a cup of tea, as well."

Violet's eyes fluttered open again, and she plucked at her apron, looking distressed. "No...not the doctor, we can't afford it." Her voice was barely more than a rasping croak, but there was no mistaking the firmness of her tone.

The kettle whistled as it came to a boil, and Maisie didn't comment as she made a pot of tea and warmed some milk for Abigail.

"What can I do to help?" Jack took the bowl of bread and milk out of Maisie's hands. "I can feed Abigail if you want to help your ma drink her tea."

"I didn't have you down as the fatherly kind," Maisie murmured, sounding surprised.

"Who do you think looked after Fred when he was a nipper, and our ma was working at the docks of an evening?" He was sure the whole village probably knew about his mother's dubious activities as a woman of the night, but he had a feeling that Maisie would not judge them for it.

She smiled apologetically. "Well, Fred has certainly grown up to be a lively, thoughtful boy, so I would say you did a grand job raising him with your granny."

Jack felt a quiet glow of pride at her praise. Maisie wasn't like the other girls in the village who looked down their noses at the Piper family. It made him even more determined to help her and Violet. "Do you think we should put your ma to bed? Perhaps a good night's sleep is what she needs more than anything."

Maisie held the cup of tea to Violet's lips, which were still pale and bloodless. "Drink this, Ma, it will do you good."

Violet barely managed a couple of sips before turning her head away and pressing her lips together. "I think I'm not much longer for this earth," she mumbled, sounding resigned. "Perhaps it's time to be with Robert again."

"Of course you are," Maisie said stoutly. Jack could hear the slight waver in her voice, and his heart went out to her. "I'm going to run and fetch Doctor Harding. We can worry about how to pay him later, even if I have to work through the night doing more sewing for Mrs Wheeler."

"Don't, Maisie," Violet pleaded. "I don't want us indebted to anyone. If it's God's will for me to live, there's no point fetching the doctor. And if not..."

She left the sentence unfinished, and her head lolled forward as she dozed off again.

Jack scooped the last spoonful of milky bread into Abigail's mouth. "She'll be asleep in a minute," he said quietly to Maisie. He laid her in the wooden cot and tucked a blanket around her. "If you won't let us fetch the doctor, Mrs Griffin, why don't I go and get my granny? I expect she has a tonic which will help you."

Violet's head jerked up, and she eyed Jack suspiciously. "I don't want Ava coming here...she knows too much. She promised never to tell, but I don't know if I can trust her."

"Ma! Don't say that. You've known Ava all your life, and she's always been a good friend to you." Maisie paced back and forth, casting worried glances at her mother. "You're saying some strange things, Ma. You're not yourself, and that's why we must get the right help."

Violet tried to speak again, but the effort seemed to exhaust her even more. She waved her hand feebly and shook her head.

Jack buttoned up his coat, stepping towards the door, and Maisie hurried to show him out.

"I don't know what's got into her," she said apologetically. "I always remember my ma and your granny being good friends, but ever since my illness and Abigail being born, Ma seems suspicious of everyone for some reason." She looked back into the parlour and pursed her lips, coming to a decision. "The thing is, we can't really afford to ask Doctor Harding to come out. Do you think Ava might have something to help?"

Jack nodded. "I don't think your ma is in any fit state to know what's best for her, to be honest. I'll go and fetch Granny and tell her what's happened. She would want to help. You're right; they did use to be friends, and I don't know what has caused this falling out, but they'll just have to put it behind them."

He held Maisie's gaze momentarily as she wrestled with her worries. "I'm scared she might not survive, Jack. She barely even recognised Abigail when we were walking back from the church. I should never have let her go out in this weather."

"You mustn't blame yourself," Jack said firmly. "Your mother is a strong-minded woman, so all we can do now is work together to try and get her well again."

As he hurried back to the cart, he sent up a hasty prayer that they hadn't left it too late already. He knew only too well what it was like to have no parents, and he wouldn't want to wish that on Maisie and Abigail.

CHAPTER 5

Maisie pulled off her wool stockings and stuffed them into her boots before tucking them under an overhang on the river's edge. She had heard that the mudlarks in Gloucester had to tie their boots together and carry them slung around their necks as they worked, or they would be stolen, but that was one small mercy of living in the village. Everyone knew each other, and there would soon be a rumpus if anyone dared make off with someone else's belongings. She grabbed a sturdy stick and hopped nimbly from one tuft of grass to the next before stepping out onto the mudflats.

The weather was mild, and there was even a hint of spring sunshine in the air. Several months had passed since the terrifying day her ma had collapsed in the lane, but miraculously, she had survived.

Maisie paused to collect her thoughts, then glanced around her, looking for tell-tale dimples in the mud, which might indicate something was buried just below the surface.

"Don't just stand there, gawking, Maisie," Fred called from a few dozen yards away. He gave her a cheeky grin and resumed his digging. "Granny told me yer ma is on the mend. I'm pleased to hear it."

"It's taken a few months, but she's certainly better than she was. And I wasn't gawking, as you put it. Just reading the mud, if you must know." Maisie chuckled to herself as she watched him shaking his head in amusement.

Fred Piper reminded her of a scrappy, tenacious terrier, the way he scrabbled in the mud, and she marvelled at how the two brothers could look so different. Jack had never told her directly, but she had heard Elsie Clatterbrook's spiteful whispers that they had different fathers because Bessie Piper had the morals of an alley cat. Maisie had wanted to tell Elsie that at least the Piper family didn't gossip and spread malicious rumours, but she had bitten her tongue. The last thing she wanted to do was jeopardise any chance that Jeffrey Clatterbrook might find it in his heart to offer Jack a gardening job. But it was true that the brothers did look very different. Although they both had freckles and brown eyes, Jack was broad-shouldered with wavy, dark hair, whereas Fred was whippet-thin with ginger hair that stood up at all angles. But despite their differences, they were as close as any two brothers could be. She found it heartwarming how Jack looked out for Fred. She had seen time and again over the last couple of months since her ma's collapse that Fred was never far from Jack's mind. He worried about Jack getting stuck in the mud or swept away in the river and often extended that worry to Maisie as well.

She tried to think of Jack like a brother, but sometimes, the pitter-patter of her heart in his company made her daydream about something more. *What about Florence?* She pulled a face as she remembered that Elsie and Caroline had been gossiping outside church a few weeks ago, and she'd overheard them saying that Jack was sweet on Florence Porter, the housemaid at Mr Fisher's. Perhaps there was some truth in it this time because she'd seen with her own eyes the way Florence blushed and giggled when she handed over a bundle of rags. She sighed with disappointment. Jack was handsome and kind. What would he see in a girl like her, who crawled in the mud to make a living when he could choose any of the maids at the houses he called at? *He's just a caring sort of fellow. Don't get any notions of romance in your head, Maisie.*

"Get on with it then," Fred yelled, startling her.

She picked a spot and started digging. It was

repetitive work that allowed her mind to meander, which was no bad thing, as she felt responsible for keeping the family going, and there was always a list of jobs that needed seeing to. It had been touch and go with her ma after her collapse. For three long days and nights, Violet had hovered feverishly between delirium and moments of being semi-lucid. Ava had come hobbling up the lane every day with a freshly made tonic of her own secret herbal recipe.

"I takes a pinch o' this and a peck o' that from the herbs and flowers I dry during the summer," she told Maisie in her broad west country burr. Her milky blue eyes had twinkled with intrigue as she chuckled to herself. "Them busybodies in the village always want to know what's in my tonics and tinctures, but 'tis a secret handed down from my mother and her mother before her. The ancient wisdom of the women who would have been burned in the past for being witches," she said, lowering her voice. "You just trust that I'll help your ma as much as I can, and that's all you need to know."

Maisie had been grateful for Ava's help, and although the old woman made no promises, Violet gradually regained her strength, although she would never be as energetic as she had been. Even though Ava assured her that the illness had passed, the light had gone from Violet's eyes. It was as if she had given up. She tried to hide it from Maisie, but it was there in the way her fingers trailed over Robert's books when she stood by the bookcase and how she had taken to laying out his nightclothes on the pillow next to her every night as if it would make her closer to him again.

"I think she's heartsick," Ava murmured a week after Violet started coming back downstairs again. "I've seen it before when someone loses their true love. I thought it might happen when your pa first passed, but baby Abigail kept her spirits up." She tiptoed over to Violet, who was fast asleep by the fire and puffed her wrinkled cheeks out, looking perplexed. "I think the anniversary of his death hit her hard. Keep giving her the Motherwort tea, and we'll see how she goes."

A FLOCK of oystercatchers flew past, skimming low over the mud, pulling Maisie out of her thoughts. She straightened up, rubbing her hands on the small of her back to try and ease the aches and pains in her muscles. Her pockets were heavy from the usual finds: hairpins, a couple of coins, some china which should clean up well, two tortoiseshell hair combs with a couple of teeth missing, and an old hairbrush that she hoped might be silver-backed but was most likely not.

"I'm off now to go and check on Ma. Don't stay

too long," she called to Fred. It was their habit to let each other know when they were leaving, and she trudged back towards the riverbank. The tide had turned, and now that it was spring, she had to be even more careful. A high neap tide could come racing in faster than a horse could gallop, Jack had told her sternly when she'd had a close call one day. If she didn't pay attention, the water could silently fill the runnels, leaving her trapped with no way of getting back to the riverbank. And now that she was the only person bringing in any money, she couldn't risk being stuck out on the mudflats...or worse, drowning in the mighty river.

Maisie found a puddle to wash the rest of the mud off her feet and dried them on the corner of her apron, then pulled on her stockings and boots before setting off for home, hurrying across the marshes to the village. She was looking forward to a nice cup of tea and a sliver of fruit cake. It was a bit stale, but with a scrape of butter, it would keep her hunger at bay for a few hours.

"Miss Griffin! Not so fast." The strident shout carried on the breeze, and Maisie groaned inwardly. It was the last person she wanted to see.

"Good afternoon, Mr Drew," she said sweetly, turning around.

"I'm not so sure I would call it a good afternoon," Saul Drew grumbled. His ruddy jowls and drooping

THE RUNAWAY SISTER

eyes made him look like a mournful bloodhound, and he had a permanent air of being aggrieved, which didn't help to dispel the image. "Not when I have to loiter in the lanes having to chase after Lord Pickering's tenants who are trying to avoid paying their rent."

Maisie tried to keep the guilt off her face and gave him a sympathetic smile instead. "I can understand that would be rather wearing, but we're all trying to do our best." She thought about the meagre handful of coins in the tin her ma kept on top of the dresser. It was nowhere near enough to pay the rent, and she would need a few more days of good pickings from mudlarking to make up the difference that was needed.

Mr Drew pulled out a spotted handkerchief and blew his nose noisily before tucking it back into his pocket with an ostentatious flourish. He had grown up in one of the estate cottages, no better off than most, but since being made Lord Pickering's land agent and rent collector, he had taken to dressing like a dandy with a bright silk cravat and a garishly checked frock coat, which was at odds with his glum demeanour.

"I've called at the cottage several times, and I know your ma is home because I can hear the baby crying. I don't know why she thinks it's acceptable to hide from me." He shook his head. "You know what

DAISY CARTER

happens to people who don't pay their rent, don't you?"

Maisie ignored the ripple of fear that shivered down her spine. Mr Drew had made a big deal of generously allowing them to miss a month's rent straight after Pa had died. But she knew his patience was wearing thin with how often she asked for a few more days' grace. "I almost have enough money to pay," she said hastily. "The trouble is, Ma has been ill. You know she was sick before Christmas, and then she collapsed again in January—"

"Yes, yes," Mr Drew snapped impatiently. He took hold of his lapels and rocked on his heels, harrumphing as he looked her up and down, taking in the mud-spattered hem of her dress and the way her hair had tangled in the wind. "Trust me, Miss Griffin, I get a blow-by-blow account of all the ailments of the tenants who are falling behind on the rent. Your pitiful tale is no different from everyone else's. Being ill…falling on hard times…even being incapacitated from too much brandy…as if that was a valid reason. I hear all the excuses with tedious regularity, but that doesn't take away from the fact that Lord Pickering's rent needs to be paid."

"Have a heart, Mr Drew," she shot back. "It's not as if we're trying to deceive you, and we scrimp and save in every way we can. Poor Abigail barely has enough to eat, and we didn't even call Doctor

THE RUNAWAY SISTER

Harding when Ma fell ill to save those few extra shillings. I'll give you the money as soon as I have it, just like I always do."

His eyes narrowed, but then he heaved a sigh and relented slightly. "I did hear from Ava Piper that your ma had a nasty fever." He looked furtively over his shoulder as if he half expected Lord Pickering to be standing in the shadows and eavesdropping. "I can't let you off the rent again, Maisie, I'm sure you understand that I have a job to do as well."

"Of course, but—"

"My Beryl has our little 'un to look after, so she doesn't work in the manor kitchen anymore, and I have standards to maintain. Imagine if I were to lose my job because Lord Pickering got wind of me letting folks fall behind on their rent. It wouldn't be good for me...or you, for that matter. I'm just trying to stop you from ending up homeless." The corners of his mouth drooped, making him look even more mournful.

Maisie could sense him softening, and she seized the opportunity to buy herself a few more days. "I've got lots of sewing to do for Mrs Wheeler, so I'll work through the night and make sure you're paid before next week."

"You make sure of it," Mr Drew said gruffly. He pinched the bridge of his nose with a pained expression. "I ain't the hard-hearted man most of the villagers think I am, but keep this between us; otherwise, everyone will be asking for some leeway."

"Oh, thank you." Maisie bobbed a little curtsy and grinned at him. "Tell Beryl I'll sew something nice for baby Melissa from my scraps. And for no charge." Before Mr Drew could change his mind, she curtsied again, picked up her skirts and ran towards West Lane and home. It didn't solve all her problems, but if she could stay on Mr Drew's good side and, God willing, have a few successful days mudlarking on the river, she might be able to keep her promise and pay the rent in full for once.

CHAPTER 6

Maisie was surprised to see Ava Piper standing outside the cottage as she hurried down the lane. She cut an unusual-looking figure, but the more Maisie got to know her, the more she was convinced that was her intention. She was rarely without her moth-eaten burgundy velvet cloak, which billowed behind her in the breeze, and her black bonnet was old-fashioned, tied beneath her chin in a bow. Whereas the other ladies in the village adorned their bonnets with silk flowers, Ava preferred feathers she found on her slow walks through the woods, where she went to pick wild herbs and berries.

"I wear these to remind myself that we are part of nature, not superior to the creatures who live alongside us," she had explained when Maisie commented how unusual they looked. Today, the hat was adorned with a black-tipped russet feather from a pheasant's breast, a flash of iridescent blue from a jay, and one she was never without from a female barn owl, white and amber with four distinctive brown bars.

"How are you, my dear?" She leaned on her walking stick, which Jack had whittled from her favourite spinney of hazel trees at the edge of the manor's land.

"I'm all the better for seeing you, Ava," Maisie said. "I just had an encounter with Mr Drew, but I've persuaded him to give me a few more days until he calls for the rent. Come inside and have a cup of tea and some fruit cake. Ma will be pleased to have the company."

Just as she reached for the door, Ava stepped in front of her and touched her arm. "I wasn't expecting to come today, but I read the cards...they said you might need my help."

Maisie was getting used to Ava's strange ways now that she spent more time in her company. The likes of Elsie Clatterbrook and her sister Caroline rudely said that she dabbled in the dark arts, but Ava had told her differently that first evening she came with a tonic for her ma. She had been born with the gift of second sight, and she gave tarot card readings if people sought her out to get a glimpse of the future. "I don't go looking for business, but when someone needs my help, it would be mean to turn them away. I charge a few pennies for my trouble if I think they can afford it."

At first, Maisie thought it was a harmless deception that Ava practised to help feed the family. But the old woman had an uncanny way of knowing when to turn up with a word of encouragement or a pouch of herbs to help Violet. She had once explained it was nothing more than seeing the signs and listening to her intuition. "Anyone can do it if they still their minds for long enough to see what's all around us."

The old woman gave her a steady look as if there was more to what the cards had said. "You know I'll always help you, Maisie, don't you?"

"Yes...I...I'm glad you and Ma have put your differences aside." She felt a shiver of foreboding but ignored it. "I'm not sure we need your help, Ava, but it's nice to see you anyway." Perhaps Ava was lonely. Many of the other women in the village shunned her because of her premonitions, and she decided she would try and persuade her ma to visit the Pipers more often. It would do her good to get out and walk to Acorn Cottage, even if she did insist that she and Ava were not as friendly as they used to be, for a reason that Maisie still did not understand.

"The cards never lie, my dear," Ava said quietly. "They told me I needed to be here for you, so I came."

The sound of Abigail crying interrupted them, and Maisie lifted the latch and hurried inside. "I'm coming, Abigail. Look Ma, we have a visitor. Ava's here to see us."

The room felt unnaturally cold as she rushed past the armchair where her ma had dozed off to pick her sister up from the cot. She was red-faced, and her cheeks were damp with tears. "Hush now," she cooed. Abigail's cries softened to whimpers.

"Daddaa," she babbled, reaching to grab Masie's collar and wriggling in her arms. "Daddaa...Mammma."

"Why did you let the fire go out, Ma?" Maisie leaned over the fire and was relieved to see it hadn't gone out completely. "I hope you weren't scrimping on the coal again. We agreed that you must use as much as you need to stay warm."

There was no reply, and she gasped with shock as she turned to face the armchair. Her ma's face was chalky white, and her mouth sagged. She looked as though she'd aged ten years since the morning.

"Ma! What's wrong? Have you had a bad turn?" Abigail whimpered, and Maisie whirled around, looking at Ava for guidance. "What should we do? I must run and get Doctor Harding this time...never mind the cost of it."

"No," Violet croaked, "it's too late." She gave Maisie a beseeching look. "Stay with me. I don't want to be alone, and there's something I need to tell you."

"Let me take the baby," Ava said. She was surprisingly strong for her age, and she lifted Abigail gently out of Maisie's arms.

"It's not too late, Ma." Her voice sounded thick with emotion, and she shook her head, not wanting it to be true.

"Don't be sad when I'm gone, Maisie." Violet twitched her fingers so that Maisie would hold hands with her. Each breath rattled in her chest, and her lips were already starting to look faintly blue as death beckoned. "I will be with my darling Robert, so I'm not afraid. But I can't leave this earthly realm worrying about what will happen to you and Abigail."

"I'll work harder, Ma." Maisie blinked back her tears, wanting to stay strong for her. "I'll always make sure that Abigail and I have a home here in our cottage. Mr Drew will understand. I've already told him I'll do whatever it takes to pay the rent."

For a moment, the only sound in the cottage was the ticking of the clock and Violet's laboured breathing, but a moment later, she shook her head.

"Is there something else you should say to Maisie while you can?" Ava asked gently. She stood next to the armchair and rested her hand lightly on Violet's shoulder. It was a gesture that spoke of forgiveness and the connection of many years of friendship that transcended whatever they may have disagreed about recently.

Violet's eyes flickered up to look at Ava, and there seemed to be an unspoken agreement between them.

"No," she murmured. She reached up and brushed her frail hand against Abigail's cheek with a soft sigh before looking back at Maisie. "I don't want you working yourself into an early grave, trying to stay in this cottage. It's too hard for you to raise your sister alone." Her voice was getting weaker, and Maisie had to lean forward to catch what she was saying. "You must go and live with your aunt and uncle at the Inn. You'll be able to carry on with the dressmaking, but they will give you and Abigail a room...and I'll rest easy knowing you're with family."

"Go and live at the Jolly Sailor?" Maisie couldn't keep the surprise from her voice. Her ma rarely spoke of her brother, Josiah Snape, and his wife, Edith, and she barely knew them herself. "Are you sure, Ma? I thought you said there was a falling out when you married Pa? You said they disapproved of the wedding and that you were trying to marry above your station." She glanced up at Ava to see if her words held any truth, but the old woman's expression gave nothing away.

"That's all in the past." Violet's eyelids were practically translucent, and she was struggling to keep them open. "Please, Maisie. Promise me you will take Abigail and live with them. Josiah is a good man beneath his rough exterior, and Edith will be glad to have you there, I'm sure."

"Wel…if it makes you happy, then, yes, Ma, of course I will."

Maisie could see the relief flash across her mother's face.

"You're a good girl. Be happy, my love," Violet gave a long sigh, but this time, her chest did not rise again. She had shed the earthly tethers of pain and illness and would never experience the warm spring sun on her face again.

"Oh, Ma. I'm sorry I couldn't help you get better…" The tears she had been holding back finally rolled down Maisie's cheeks, and she bowed her head over their entwined hands. Violet had cheated death more than once during her illness in the winter, but the grief was sharp nonetheless. *How will we manage without you? What if I'm not up to the task of raising Abigail?* With her anguish came a new realisation that she had to be strong. She was an orphan, and her little sister depended on her now like never before.

THE SOUND of rumbling wheels outside reached Maisie, and she stood up and dried her tears.

"Hello, Granny…Maisie?" The door creaked open,

and Jack stood there, his brow furrowed with concern. "I saw Fred, and he told me that you were here. Is it what I think it is?" He stepped into the room and took Maisie's hands in his own, chafing some warmth back into them.

"Ma is gone," she said shakily. "She seemed alright this morning. I never should have left her."

Jack shook his head firmly, but his brown eyes were kind. "You're not to think like that again."

Ava nodded in agreement. "She told me that evening she collapsed in January that she was ready to join Robert, but she hung on a few weeks longer because she wanted to make sure that you would be taken care of."

"I'm not quite sure what you mean."

"Mamma." Abigail looked up at the feathers on Ava's bonnet, her eyes round with fascination, and the old woman rocked her slightly as she hobbled back and forth across the parlour.

"You'd better tell her, Jack."

"Tell me what?" Maisie felt the day was spinning even more out of her control. Why was everyone speaking in riddles?

"When your ma was well enough, she insisted that I should take her to the Jolly Sailor in my cart. She wanted to make sure that Josiah would take you and Abigail in if she got ill again."

"She did? But...she never said a word about it to me."

Jack looked apologetic. "Violet made us promise not to tell you. You know what your ma was like. She had a very set idea of how things should be, but her greatest worry was that you might be thrown out of the cottage because of not being able to pay the rent. She swallowed her pride and made up with her brother so you would be alright."

In spite of her heartache, Maisie managed a small smile. "You're right about Ma having her own idea of how she wanted things to be. Some people might have called it stubbornness, but I think it was determination. All she ever wanted was for us to have a good life." She closed her eyes briefly, wondering whether she could live up to her ma's expectations.

As if reading her mind, Ava patted her arm. "She was very proud of you. And I know that you will show the same courage and determination she had."

Without asking, Jack put the kettle on the range to boil. "I'm going to make you a cup of tea, and then I'll take the cart and fetch Doctor Harding so he can make the arrangements for the funeral with the vicar."

"I'll go with you," Ava said quickly. She gave Maisie a reassuring smile. "You've had a shock today, and you need one of my herbal teas to help you sleep. There will be a lot to arrange over the coming days, not to mention packing up your belongings and going to live with your uncle."

"Oh, I'll be alright. I'm not ill." She was grateful for their help but suddenly felt an overwhelming need to be alone in the cottage, just her and Abigail, to consider their future.

"Granny is never wrong when she suggests one of her herbal teas," Jack said, giving his grandmother a fond glance. "If she says it will help you, it's for the best. She gives them to Fred and me to ward off colds and all sorts. You must stay well now that you have the little 'un to look after." He poured some water into the teapot and brought it to the table with a mug from the dresser, adding two spoonfuls of sugar. "Sweet tea will help you until we get back. Drink it down, no ifs or buts, and we'll be back in no time."

The room felt eerily silent as Jack walked out, followed by Ava. She looked around the place she had only ever known as home, blinking back tears again as she caught sight of the unfinished knitting Violet had been working on the previous evening. Someone else would be sitting in front of the hearth in a few weeks. Another family would grow up here; perhaps new babies would be born, and a different husband and wife would grow old together. Her breath caught in her throat as she waited to be engulfed in grief again, but strangely, it was a softer sense of nostalgia which filled her. It was as though, on some level, she had subconsciously known this would happen and that her future did not lie within these four walls anymore.

She sank onto one of the kitchen chairs, slightly away from Violet, and wrapped her hands around the mug of hot, sweet tea, feeling grateful for Jack's thoughtfulness. *Where should I start?* She supposed a visit to her uncle would be first to tell him what had happened, although news of a death usually spread through the village like wildfire.

The tapping of Ava's walking stick interrupted her thoughts, and she looked up with surprise.

"I left my reticule when I put it down to hold Abigail," Ava explained as she hobbled back in again. "It has some dried chamomile in it, which I need to make your herbal tea."

"There's no hurry, Ava," Maisie said wearily. She put her tea down and stood up to hand the old woman her patchwork bag from where she'd left it on the dresser. "I don't mind being alone with my thoughts. I know my life will be a struggle, but I'm determined to do Ma proud."

A sea mist had rolled up the estuary, making it gloomy inside the cottage, and the light from the oil lamp flickered as a sudden gust of wind blew in through the open door, casting tall shadows on the wall.

"Give me your hand," Ava said softly.

Maisie did as she was asked and was surprised when Ava took hold of her hand and turned it over to look intently at her palm. The silence stretched between as Ava slowly traced her finger along the lines, still faintly ingrained with mud.

"What is it?

She looked up at Maisie, and her milky eyes seemed unfocused, as if she could see something known only to her. "Your fortunes will change, child." Ava's voice sounded different, almost sing-songy. She traced the lines again, muttering under her breath, and then nodded. "Your fortunes will change…after a secret is revealed."

Maisie shivered. "What do you mean?"

The oil lamp flame flickered again as another draught blew in, but Ava shook her head. "I can't say yet. The time is not right." She turned Maisie's hand over and patted the back, giving her a reassuring smile, suddenly business-like again. "Jack and I will be back soon. Don't worry, Maisie. We will always help you however we can." With that, she hobbled away again, her walking stick tapping on the flagstone floor on her way out.

CHAPTER 7

"That's the last bundle of books done." Jack gathered up the corners of the blanket he had stacked the books in and tied a rope around it. "Are you sure there's nothing else you would like us to keep at our cottage for you?"

Maisie stood in the middle of the parlour, looking around at what was left. An empty dresser, a few books on the bookshelf, and their two wingback chairs in front of the hearth. The place no longer felt like home, and she gave a rueful shrug. "Ava has already been more than generous agreeing to keep Pa's desk and Ma's dressing table for us until I have a home of my own." She picked up a couple more books and reluctantly put them down again. "I'd better not take anymore. Aunt Edith was very sniffy about not wanting the Jolly Sailor filled with ma's cast-offs, even in the room I'll be sharing with Abigail." Her tone was light, but Jack could sense the hurt behind it.

"Are you almost finished, Miss Griffin?" Saul Drew loomed in the doorway, blinking as his eyes adjusted from the brightness outside. "I told the new folks they could move in later today."

"So soon? Who is it?" Jack asked.

"It's the Freemans and their five children. They're so excited they've been loading their belongings in a handcart since before dawn, apparently."

Maisie smiled. " I'm glad Lord Pickering agreed they could have it. It will be good to know the cottage is full of laughter, and I know they were struggling in her old place with the damp."

"They'll be glad of those few pieces of furniture you've left behind as well." Mr Drew stepped into the parlour and looked around with a critical eye. "I know you've probably left the place in good repair, but I have to make sure and see for myself. I'll go upstairs in a minute."

"Maisie probably won't tell you herself, but she's scrubbed the place from top to bottom over the last couple of days."

Mr Drew had the grace to look slightly embarrassed at Jack's remark. "I appreciate that, Miss Griffin, especially as I know it was your ma's funeral just a few days ago." He hastily took his hat off as a mark

THE RUNAWAY SISTER

of respect and twisted it in his hands. "In that case, I won't go upstairs. I can see by how clean this room is that you've done a good job. You'd be surprised how some of the tenants leave their cottages. I've had rats' nests, birds up the chimney; you wouldn't believe it."

"Anything else I can take out to the cart?" Fred called cheerfully.

"Just these books."

Abigail started to babble excitedly when Fred came into the cottage, lifting her arms to be picked up.

"How's the little 'un coping?" Mr Drew asked. "I expect she misses her ma a great deal."

Maisie's expression clouded momentarily, and Jack pushed down the urge to put his arm around her shoulders to comfort her. It was not the time or place, and she might think he was being too forward. "In some ways, I think perhaps it's a blessing that she's still so young. I shall tell Abigail all about Ma, but I don't suppose she will remember her as she grows up, or this cottage."

Mr Drew nodded. "I'm inclined to agree with you. It's good that you're a sensible young woman. It's time for a new start, and although I'll be sorry to see your family gone from this cottage, times move on."

Maisie picked up Abigail and lifted her high, making her giggle. "We'll be alright, Abigail, won't we? Ma said that Uncle Josiah and Aunt Edith will look after us, and we'll have our friends as well." She smiled over Abigail's soft curls at Jack, and he thought again how brave she was.

"Right then, I'll take these books and help you up into the cart." Fred slung the bundle over his shoulder and waited for Maisie to go on ahead of him.

"So they're going to live at the Jolly Sailor with the Snapes, are they?" Mr Drew's eyebrows twitched upward in surprise as Jack took one last look around the room to make sure nothing had been left behind.

Jack wondered whether to ask something which had been on his mind and decided to risk it. "You must know Mr and Mrs Snape quite well," he said casually. "Lord Pickering owns the Jolly Sailor, doesn't he? So they are your tenants as well. Do you think it's a good place for Maisie and Abigail to live?" He thought about the rumours he had heard of smuggled rum being sold there and the rough men who frequented the place. What he really wanted to ask was whether he thought Maisie would be safe surrounded by drunken men, but with his ma's past, he couldn't exactly ask outright.

"It's funny you mention it," Saul Drew said, lowering his voice and glancing outside to make sure they wouldn't be overheard. "I must confess I was surprised when I heard that Violet wanted her daughters to live there, but I suppose blood is thicker than water, and Maisie couldn't have continued renting this cottage on her own."

"Why were you surprised? Do you mean because Violet wasn't close to her brother, Josiah Snape?" Jack frowned. "He's a hard-working man, isn't he? Maisie told me that Violet had agreed with them that she could carry on doing the dressmaking for Mrs Wheeler. If that goes well, she might even be able to set up a little dressmaking business of her own soon."

Mr Drew adjusted his cravat and puffed his cheeks out. "Hard-working? That's a matter of opinion," he muttered, glancing towards the door again. "Between you and me, Josiah is a bit too fond of sampling his own wares, if you get what I'm saying. He likes to pontificate with anyone who will listen about what an astute businessman he is, but...let's just say he's not always on time with his rent."

It was Jack's turn to be surprised. Now that he was eighteen, he occasionally called at the Jolly Sailor to enjoy a pint of ale with some of the farm labourers on the estate. He had often heard Josiah Snape loudly discussing how successful the inn was with him as the landlord. *Perhaps he's just putting on a good front? That might explain the rumours about smuggled rum, which he can get on the cheap.* He squirrelled the information away, hoping that Maisie was not going from one bad situation to another.

"I'll keep an eye on her," he said to Mr Drew. "And what you've told me will be just between us."

"To be honest, I'm not sure how much longer Josiah will be running the inn. Lord Pickering might sell the place in the future." Saul seemed to be warming to his subject, and Jack was surprised he was talking so freely. "I'm not sure I would want my daughters growing up in such a rough environment, but it's not for me to pass comment—"

Maisie appeared in the doorway, catching the end of the conversation. She squared her shoulders and smiled. "Don't worry about me, Mr Drew. I can stick up for myself."

"Of course, of course," he said hastily, turning red, "and I'm sure your ma had the best of intentions sending you there. It's best to stick with family."

"We'd better get going now," Jack said. He could see that Maisie looked worried by Saul's comment even though she was trying to hide it. "I expect your aunt Edith will be keen to get you both settled in. It's good that you won't be mudlarking at the river anymore. That's something. She's probably got a nice room out the back for you to do your dressmaking, and you'll be able to spend more time with little Abigail."

They all walked outside, and Mr Drew slammed the cottage door shut firmly behind them, heralding the end of an era for Maisie. He extended his arm

THE RUNAWAY SISTER ·

and shook hands with her. "Good luck in your new home, Miss Griffin. I'm sorry you're leaving under such sad circumstances, but I'm sure your mother will be happy to know that you haven't gone far."

"Thank you, Mr Drew." Her eyes twinkled mischievously. "You won't have to chase me through the village for the rent anymore now."

He put his hat back on and smiled. "I shouldn't say this, but you were far from the worst of some of the tenants." He twirled his cane and started to walk away but then remembered something. "Beryl said thank you for the charming little dress you made for baby Melissa. She's going to put in a good word about you with some of the other well-to-do ladies in the village and see if she can persuade them to use your dressmaking services."

* * *

MAISIE WAS quiet as Duke clopped through the village, taking her away from the only home she had ever known. Jack wished there was something he could say to ease her worries, but he felt unusually tongue-tied, concerned that he might make her more upset.

"I'll miss you when I'm mudlarking," Fred piped up cheerfully, oblivious to Maisie's change in mood. He was perched in the back of the cart, just behind them, on a pile of rags. He grinned happily, glad to enjoy a rare few hours off work because Jack had asked for his help.

"Maybe I'll come down to the river now and again for old times' sake." Maisie jiggled Abigail on her knee and looked happier now that they were on their way. The spring sunshine was warm on their shoulders, and the cherry trees were already bedecked with blossom. Jack was glad it wasn't raining like it had been on the day of Violet's funeral.

"I wish you would. Granny would probably say it was something to do with magic, but you were like a lucky charm." Fred scratched his head, not caring that his ginger hair was sticking up in tufts. "The last few times you were mudlarking with us, I found more on those days than I did in some whole months."

"Really? I'm glad for you, Fred, but I'm sure it was just a coincidence," Maisie chuckled. "I'll miss it in the summer, but I can't say I will in the winter. I'd rather be sewing for Mrs Wheeler."

Fred leaned forward between them and pulled a face, which made Abigail wriggle, and she tried to grab Jack's sleeve. "Lord, help us when she starts talking," he said, pulling another face to make her giggle. "She's a happy little soul, and she looks more like you every time I see her. There ain't no mistaking that she's your little sister, not like me and Jack."

THE RUNAWAY SISTER

Before Maisie could reply, Jack guided Duke around the final bend in the lane and reined him to a halt. The Jolly Sailor Inn was right before them, and he looked at it with fresh eyes now that it was going to be where Maisie lived.

The main building was built from the same honey-coloured stone as all the cottages in the village, but instead of a slate roof, it was thatched. Two beady-eyed seagulls perched on top watching them, and the thatch had seen better days and looked like it needed to be replaced in several spots. There was a cobbled courtyard in front of the inn, with stables off to one side and sheds on the other for storage. Because it was situated right at the edge of the village, it had a slightly desolate air, set apart from the hustle and bustle of the busier village lanes where cottages jostled with the shops. Beyond the inn, the land was dotted with sheep grazing on the wiry grass on the edge of the river. It would be easy enough for a boat to moor up and deliver smuggled goods under the cover of darkness. The sign above the door was held up by two rusty hooks, and it creaked slightly in the breeze. The paint was peeling off the window frames, and he shivered as he imagined what the place would be like in the depths of winter, with a thick sea fret sending tentacles of damp mist into every nook and cranny.

"This looks very quaint, doesn't it, Abigail?"

85

Maisie's cheerful voice didn't deceive Jack. He reached across and squeezed her hand, and a faint pink flush crept up her cheeks.

"I'm not one to drink much ale, but I'll come in whenever I can to make sure the regulars are treating you nicely." With the sun behind catching golden glints in her hair, Jack thought she looked even more beautiful than usual.

"Ava might not be too pleased to hear that. I don't want to be the cause of you spending money you haven't got on drink instead of food."

"Can I come too," Fred asked eagerly. "Granny told me you used to sneak up here when you were my age, Jack, so it ain't fair if you say no."

Maisie's musical laugh rang out, and Jack was relieved to see her relax. "You'll have to sort that out with Granny," he said, rolling his eyes at his younger brother in good humour.

Just as Jack was climbing out of the cart, the heavy wooden door at the front of the inn burst open, and Josiah Snape sauntered towards them, followed by Edith.

"Well...I never thought I would see this day... Violet's family coming to live in such a place of ill repute." He threw back his head and laughed loudly at his own joke before bowing to Maisie with a flourish of his hand. "Welcome to our humble abode."

"What's a place of ill repute?" Fred whispered.

"Your ma always thought she was too grand for a place like this with her high and mighty ideas of bettering herself, but I told her it's not so different from church." He paused, relishing the way they were all waiting for him to explain what he meant. "There's plenty of men who've discovered some sort of salvation at the bottom of a bottle of rum in my taproom." His rotund stomach jiggled as he started laughing again. "Don't tell the vicar, though," he chuckled, wiping away tears of mirth with a grubby handkerchief.

"Thank you again for taking us in. I'm very grateful." Maisie handed Abigail down to Jack and picked up her skirts to step down from the cart.

"I could hardly say no to my little sister, Violet, could I? Funny how she changed her mind about us, but there we are. I'll never be accused of not welcoming someone in need."

Jack wondered whether he was the only person who had noticed the tinge of resentment in Josiah's welcome. He looked at the man more closely, thinking about what Saul Drew had told him earlier. Even though Josiah had a jovial air about him, his ruddy cheeks and the fleshy pouches under his eyes revealed that he was fond of a drink.

"Where shall we take all this to, missus?" Fred had already started unloading the cart, and he grinned cheerfully at Edith Snape, ready to be shown inside.

DAISY CARTER

"Goodness me, Maisie, how much did you bring? I thought I told you that your room is small." Her narrow lips pinched together in disapproval, and she stood on tiptoes to peer into the cart, eyeing the contents with darting blue eyes that missed nothing. "I don't want a load of old rubbish from your ma and pa. What do you want with all them books, anyway?" She picked up one of Robert's natural history books that had escaped from its bundle and pulled a face. "This ain't the sort of place where you can lay about reading all day. We've no use for lollygagging here."

"I'm no layabout," Maisie said defensively. "They're just a few of my parents' belongings that I wanted to keep for sentimental value. I want to be able to give them to Abigail when she's older...so we have something to remember our parents by."

Edith folded her arms across her narrow chest with a stubborn glint in her eyes. "You can store them in that shed over yonder." She pointed towards a ramshackle building. "It ain't waterproof, but Abigail won't have any need for books. And as for things to remember your parents by, I don't hold with such mawkish emotions. Your parents are dead, and it's time to move on. Some of us don't have the luxury of wallowing in self-pity."

Josiah ambled over to his wife and smacked a kiss on her cheek, which made her blush and suddenly look coy. "I don't know where I'd be without Edith,"

THE RUNAWAY SISTER

he chuckled. "She keeps us all on the straight and narrow, and if she seems a bit brusque, it's only because she wants the best for you, Maisie."

Jack was half-tempted to tell Fred to load the cart up again. He didn't like Edith's manner one little bit.

"Are you sure you want to be here, Maisie?" he murmured quietly. "I could ask Granny if we could fit an extra truckle bed in her room at home. It will be a bit of a squash, but..." He glanced towards Edith, not needing to finish his sentence.

"I'm beginning to understand why Ma wasn't in touch with them, but my aunt can't be that bad," she whispered back.

"If you're sure."

Maisie hesitated for a beat but then lifted her chin with determination and gave Edith a beaming smile. "The shed will be fine for now, thank you, Aunt Edith. I'll pick a few books out to bring inside before winter, and I'm sure Abigail and I won't mind things being a bit of a squash in our bedroom. I know all of this was rather unexpected, but Ma always spoke very highly of you."

"Did she?" Edith looked suspicious for a moment but then nodded. "I can understand that. Your mother thought she was bettering herself by marrying Robert, but the truth is, I was the lucky one. Josiah's business sense is the envy of many a man in Frampton, and your poor ma wasn't to know that Robert would be such a pauper in spite of all his book learning." She was gracious in her superiority now that Violet had come begging for their help.

"We'd better get you inside then, hadn't we?" Josiah prodded Abigail with a pudgy finger and chuckled as Abigail shrank back to bury herself in Maisie's hair.

"She can be a little shy with new people."

"She'll have to get over that soon enough," Josiah said jovially. "And you too. There's no time for being shy or modest when you work in the Jolly Sailor, is there Edith."

"No," she agreed, "you must be polite and friendly at all times; it's what the customers expect. And I don't want to hear any crying from Abigail, either."

"Would you like us to help bring some things inside?" Jack picked up a pile of blankets and the colourful patchwork quilt that Maisie had brought with her to make their room more cheerful.

Edith gave him a long look and sniffed. "We'll be fine. I expect you need to get back to your grandmother, don't you? Before she meddles in someone else's business with those ridiculous notions of seeing into the future."

Jack ignored the jibe and jerked his head for Fred to get back in the cart. "I'll come by for a pint of ale soon, Maisie," he said quietly.

"Thank you for all your kindness these last few

weeks." Tears shimmered in her eyes, but she blinked them away before Edith could see them. "You're good friends. I'll visit Ava as soon as I can."

As Duke trotted on and the cart bumped over the cobbles, Jack felt a mixture of emotions. He was proud of Maisie for courageously stepping into this new life with her aunt and uncle, but his doubts and fears had not been eased by their welcome. He suspected they would be hard taskmasters and that they were none too pleased with having two more mouths to feed.

"Poor Maisie," Fred said, twisting in his seat to watch her going into the inn. "They're not the sort of people I would like to live with."

Jack wanted to agree, but he bit his tongue. Fred had a way of speaking his mind without thinking first, and he didn't want to cause trouble between Maisie and her family.

"You should start courting her." Fred nudged Jack and winked. "You could get a little house of your own with her then."

Jack snorted with amusement. "Don't be so ridiculous. Besides, you're too young to be talking about such things, and who I'm sweet on....not that I am...is none of your business. I'll go home via the river. You should be able to get a few hours of mudlarking in before the tide turns." Jack clicked his tongue to tell Duke to trot faster. If he got a move on, he would still have time to visit a few houses and pick up some rags. He needed the extra money if he was going to start visiting the Jolly Sailor more often to keep an eye on Maisie.

CHAPTER 8

Four Years Later

Maisie quietly pulled a white cotton blouse from her sewing basket and sat down in the small chair next to the window in the bedroom. She threaded her needle and sewed the first few stitches of the tuck she was making. The blouse belonged to Doctor Harding's wife, who had recently had her third child, and she wanted it taken in to fit again.

The sun was just rising over the village, and the stars slowly faded as the sky turned pearly pink. It was going to be another long, hot summer's day, and Maisie stifled a yawn. It only felt like a couple of hours since she had finished cleaning the kitchen from the evening before, but she had to make the most of the early morning daylight to get on with her sewing.

She paused for a moment to enjoy the view, watching a cat stealthily stalking two rabbits, which had hopped into the courtyard from the fields. A cockerel crowed at Downfield Farm next door, interrupting the moment, and Maisie started sewing again. If she was lucky, she might get an hour to herself before Abigail woke up and it was time to start the chores downstairs.

Her mind wandered as her neat stitches progressed. It was a little over four years since they had arrived at the Jolly Sailor, and she could hardly believe so much time had passed. In many ways, her life felt completely unrecognisable from when they had lived at the cottage in West Lane, but in other ways, she felt as though she was stuck in a monotonous rut, where one week bled into the next and her days were filled with work and little more.

She could still remember her shock and disappointment the day after they arrived when she asked Aunt Edith whether she might be able to use one of the six rooms upstairs to start her dressmaking business. Edith had chuckled with humourless laughter and shaken her head as though she'd never heard such a ridiculous idea.

"A dressmaking business? You're as la-de-da as yer ma. Is that what she said you'd be doing?"

Once Maisie had explained that her ma had told her Uncle Josiah was more than happy to support her

THE RUNAWAY SISTER

dreams of having her own little seamstress business, Edith had laughed again.

"Violet must have caught him on a day when he'd had a drink or two. Now that you're living here as part of our family, the inn takes priority. I've got more than enough work in the kitchen to keep you busy. There's all the food to prepare and the rooms upstairs to clean. We let travelling guests stay overnight, and it's a nice little earner. And Josiah will want you to help serve in the taproom. That last wench we had got herself in the family way and left to get married. Very inconvenient it was, too."

"But what about my sewing?" Maisie had asked.

Edith's eyes had lit up with a crafty gleam. "I suppose you have some sort of obligation to Mrs Wheeler. You can carry on taking in small dress-making projects, but you're to do it in your own time, and you'll have to give me a few coins from it for your keep. Your uncle and I ain't rolling in money, you know."

In that single conversation, Maisie's life had become fixed into a new routine. She rose at the crack of dawn to sew, and the rest of the morning was spent in a procession of chores, including cooking and cleaning. At lunchtime, she changed into her smart green gown. Edith had reluctantly taken some money from the wooden till behind the bar so she could buy the dress from the second-hand

95

clothes shop and allowed her a few hours to alter it to fit and add a new lace collar. Then, the rest of the day was spent serving food and drinks in the taproom and back parlour, doing her best to keep the customers happy as the ale flowed and the men became more raucous.

"Is it time to get up already?" Abigail's tousled head emerged from under the patchwork quilt, and she yawned loudly, rubbing her knuckles in her eyes. "I was having a lovely dream about eating a big roast dinner." She flopped back on the pillows and groaned. "There was beef and gravy, roast 'taters, and even a big slice of treacle tart for pudding. I wish it was true."

Maisie finished the last few stitches she was working on and tied the cotton off, snipping the loose ends with a small pair of dressmaker's scissors. "I can't offer you a roast dinner, but how about a nice boiled egg for breakfast? Mrs Bidwell called in with a basket of eggs from her chickens yesterday, and I kept a couple back."

"Will Aunt Edith let me?" Abigail didn't look hopeful. "You know she usually tells us a bit of bread and scrape is more than enough." She sighed and wrapped her arms around her knees.

"If we go down to the kitchen early, she won't need to know." Maisie smiled as Abigail's eyes lit up.

THE RUNAWAY SISTER

"Keep it a secret, just between us, you mean?" She clapped her hand over her mouth and giggled.

"Not a secret. More, just something that we don't need to draw her attention to." They shared a conspiratorial smile, and Abigail jumped out of bed. "Let me just finish mending this bottom hem." Maisie pulled a length of cotton from her bobbin and threaded her needle again. She had promised Mrs Harding she would take the blouse to her before the end of the week, and she didn't like to go back on her word.

"Budge up a bit, will you, Maisie? I'll sit quietly if you tell me a story." Abigail slipped out of her white nightgown and tugged her grey work dress over her head. She dragged a comb through her unruly brown curls, and her tongue poked out with concentration as she tried to tie it back with a ribbon.

Maisie let her do it but knew she would need to retie it later. Now that Abigail was almost five years old, she had become fiercely independent and wanted to do everything herself. Her little sister was high-spirited, and her green eyes often sparkled with mischief. *Too much mischief for Aunt Edith's liking.* Maisie worried about her because she knew that Aunt Edith thought her strong-willed and stubborn. She would want to crush that sense of independence and joy in the future, but for now, Maisie was able to rein in Abigail's mischievousness enough to stay on Edith's good side most of the time.

Abigail wriggled into the chair next to her and rested her head against her arm. "Tell me about when Ma and Pa first met," she mumbled, sticking her thumb in her mouth, still sleepy. "And then tell me about how Pa was so kind to the children he used to teach." Her eyelids started to droop again as Maisie began to speak. Abigail's favourite part of the day was when she curled up in bed at night, and Maisie was allowed a few minutes to settle her before going back to work serving the drinks. She loved to hear stories about their parents, and Maisie knew she would doze off again now within a matter of minutes, which would allow her to finish Mrs Harding's blouse.

"It was the village summer fair and a hot day, just like this one..."

"Maisie! Abigail! Get yourselves down here now!" Edith's screech shattered the morning peace, and Maisie hastily packed her sewing away and nudged her sister to wake her up.

"We're coming, Aunt Edith," she called back.

Edith was standing at the bottom of the stairs with her hands on her hips, tapping her foot impatiently. "Do you expect me to run this place single-handed while you two layabouts idle away the morning upstairs in bed?"

"The time got away from us," Maisie said. "I just had a bit more to do to finish that sewing job for Mrs Harding, and it's not even six o'clock yet." She glanced at the clock behind Edith, but her aunt was having none of it.

"An apology would have done, instead of a stream of excuses." A frown furrowed her brow as she watched them hurry down the stairs. "That reminds me. I saw that Mrs McLean came to collect her new summer gown yesterday. I hope you weren't going to forget to hand the money over, Maisie. You know what our agreement was."

"It ain't fair that you take the money for Maisie's sewing," Abigail said mutinously.

Edith gasped and grabbed Abigail's arm, giving her a shake. "Best you run along to the scullery and start washing up, you ungrateful child. Your uncle and I took you in out of the goodness of our hearts when that wretched mother of yours inconveniently died, and if you think I'll put up with your rudeness, you can think again."

Abigail yelped as Edith's fingers dug into her arm as she shoved her towards the kitchen. "I'm sorry, Auntie Edith. I didn't mean to be rude, but some-times it doesn't seem fair that Maisie and I work so hard, but all we have is the little room upstairs and a few of Ma's belongings." Her chin trembled, and tears pooled in her eyes. "When we were walking through the village the other day, I saw a beautiful doll in the window of the toy shop. I thought if Maisie could buy it for me, she could make pretty clothes for it and—"

"Waste money on a doll?" Edith's voice rose a notch. "What sort of stupid ideas have you been filling your sister's head with now?" she demanded, turning back to glare at Maisie.

Maisie opened her mouth to apologise again, but then a flicker of defiance unfurled in her chest. "It's not a stupid idea, Aunt Edith. I wanted to save up and buy something nice for Abigail for her birthday. Is that such a terrible thing to want to do? After being orphaned, she deserves one nice toy for her birthday, don't you think?"

The air crackled with tension between them, and an ugly flush of red stained Edith's thin cheeks. Her eyes narrowed, and she drew herself up to her full height. "For that insolence, I'll have all the money you earned from making Mrs McLean's gown. Perhaps it will remind you to show a bit of gratitude for everything your uncle and I have done for you, you ungrateful hussy." She spun around and pointed towards the kitchen. "Get in the scullery now, Abigail, and start washing those dishes." She waited in silence as Abigail slunk away. "As for you, Maisie," she said, turning back to her, "the taproom needs cleaning. You can scrub the floor on your hands and knees from one end to the other and give it a good airing."

"But what about preparing the food for tonight's guests?" Maisie knew that Edith was only demanding she should scrub the taproom out of spite. She had done it only a few days ago, and it was one of the jobs she least enjoyed, and her aunt knew it.

"Yes, the vegetables need to be peeled as well, so you'd better look lively. Perhaps if you spent a bit less time encouraging Jack Piper to flirt with you last night, you wouldn't be feeling so tired."

"He wasn't flirting!" Maisie cried indignantly. "He's my friend, that's all. You know how much he helped us when Ma died."

Edith gave her a triumphant smile. "Nothing escapes my attention, young lady. You might think Jack Piper is a good catch, but I won't let you throw yourself away on a lowly rag-and-bone man. Your uncle and I will decide who you're to marry."

"That's not fair." Maisie wished she could march out with a parting rebuttal over her shoulder, but it would only spur Edith on to new levels of spiteful-ness. She had discovered it was best to quietly agree, although there were many times she couldn't help but answer back.

"We're only doing what your ma would want,"

Edith said innocently. She knew how to bait Maisie and then back down at the last moment, making it look as though Maisie was the one at fault. "We have a few ideas in mind, and you can rest assured it will be a union that will benefit all of us. You owe us that, at least, for everything we've done for you and Abigail." There was a glint of jealousy in her eyes as she raked her gaze up and down Maisie's womanly curves. "Not that we want you to get married yet, mind you. I can't run this place alone, and it will take a few more years of hard work to pay your debt for us taking you in."

Maisie didn't dignify her aunt's outburst with a reply. She sidled past her instead to boil a kettle of water and fill the bucket. It would be a long day, and the quicker she got started, the quicker it would be over.

CHAPTER 9

As Maisie scrubbed the taproom floor on her hands and knees with the soapy water, she thought about what her aunt Edith had just said. It seemed so unfair that she should have to hand over all her dressmaking money, but Edith was stubborn. Usually, she took the lion's share but grudgingly let Maisie keep some of it. However, she knew this time Edith would be true to her word and keep all of it, just to prove her point.

She sat back on her heels and brushed a lock of hair off her forehead with the back of her hand. It was a tedious job, but the only thing keeping her going was the fact that Jack had promised he would visit again that night.

True to his word, Jack was a regular at the Jolly Sailor now. He would carefully make his pint of ale last all evening rather than spend too much, and somehow, Maisie always felt safer knowing that he was there on those evenings.

Now that she was in her twenties, with a womanly figure, she had noticed that it came with unwanted attention from many of the men who drank at the inn. Her aunt Edith pursed her lips resentfully as their bleary eyes looked straight through her to seek out Maisie. Yet sometimes, her aunt seemed to encourage the men by telling Maisie to serve their drinks instead of Josiah.

"It's so they stay drinking for longer," Jack had growled one evening after stepping in to stop a drunken sea merchant from grabbing her around the waist and trying to kiss her. "She's throwing you out like meat to the wolves to increase her profits."

Maisie had quickly got used to weaving between the tables, just out of reach, and being friendly enough with the customers to keep them buying but not too friendly that they might get the wrong idea. But it still rankled that Josiah had gone back on his word.

Will I ever have the business I dreamed of when I used to sit with Ma, helping her with the sewing? She dunked her scrubbing brush back in the water, dreaming of a day when she might not have to worry about being ogled by drunken men anymore. Falling asleep at night, she loved to imagine a

THE RUNAWAY SISTER

quaint dressmaker's shop in the village, with bow-fronted windows and colourful displays of lace and ribbons, which elegant ladies would stop and admire before availing themselves of her services to sew new gowns for them. It was just a foolish dream, but it helped on the nights when she thought she might be stuck at the Jolly Sailor forever.

By the time she finished scrubbing the floor, the warm summer air flowing through the open front door had already dried the floorboards. She emptied the suds outside and hurried across to the storeroom, where Josiah kept the sawdust they used on the floor to soak up spilt drinks. All she needed to do now was throw the sawdust down and polish the tables, and then she would be able to go and start work in the kitchen with Abigail. *Let's hope she hasn't got into any trouble while I've been busy.* She smiled inwardly at the thought. Even though Edith found Abigail a handful, Maisie couldn't help but admire her plucky spirit. She would need to be resilient to keep their aunt and uncle happy as she grew older and worked more. Edith had already started saying that going to school would be a waste of time for Abigail when she had a perfectly good day's work to be getting on with in the kitchens.

The sound of a horse trotting made her look up. "Mr Drew. How are you? But more importantly, how's your wife? I hope the little 'uns are behaving for her."

Saul Drew dismounted from his chestnut mare and tied the reins to the hitching post on the edge of the courtyard. "She's very well, thank you, Maisie. Melissa is old enough to be a great help with the two younger ones now. Much like your Abigail, I expect." He took his hat off and fastidiously brushed a speck of dust from the rim. "Is your uncle awake yet?"

Maisie glanced up at the window above the door and saw that the curtains were open. He might still be half asleep, but he was at least out of bed, which was something to be said these days. "Of course," she said brightly. "Follow me, and I'll fetch him for you."

Josiah was pouring his first tot of rum for the day as they went into the taproom. His face fell at the sight of the land agent, but then he hastily rearranged his features into a jovial smile. "Saul, fancy seeing you today. You'll join me for a nip of rum, won't you?" Without waiting for a reply, he splashed a generous amount into a glass and pushed it across the bar.

Mr Drew frowned and shook his head. "I don't mind accepting hospitality, Josiah, but I draw the line at drinking rum when the sun has barely been up for a couple of hours."

Maisie started scattering the sawdust, knowing what would come next.

THE RUNAWAY SISTER

"You said you would have the rent money for me today, I seem to recall."

Josiah feigned surprise. "Did I? I'm sure we agreed on next week, Saul. You're getting forgetful. It must be those little ones of yours keeping you awake during the night." He chuckled, exuding good humour and nudged the glass a bit closer towards him. "That's why you need to drink this. It will help you sleep better tonight."

Edith came bustling into the taproom and grimaced when she caught sight of him. "We ain't got the rent money for you today," she said matter-of-factly. "Times are hard since Lord Pickering let the Red Lion reopen at the other end of the village, and Miss La-de-da and her little sister are eating me out of house and home." She shot Maisie a sour look.

Mr Drew sighed and put his hat back on again. "I'll need all the rent money next week; otherwise, I'll have to start charging you extra. Lord Pickering expects his tenants to work hard. If you can't deal with a little bit of healthy competition from another pub, perhaps you shouldn't be running the Jolly Sailor after all."

Josiah shrugged but looked worried as Mr Drew stalked back outside. "He's another one who's got above himself," he grumbled. "I still remember when he was a snotty-nosed child, growing up in one of the estate cottages, but ever since he became Pickering's land agent, you'd think he was born with a silver spoon in his mouth."

Edith started polishing the glasses with such vigour that Maisie wondered whether she might break one. "I'm getting tired of having to dodge Mr Drew every month, Josiah." She glanced furtively out through the door to make sure he had gone. "Selling the smuggled rum isn't bringing in enough money. I'm working my fingers to the bone, and I've had enough of it."

Josiah ambled over to her and threw his arm around her shoulder, pinching her cheek until she smiled. "Don't worry, Edith. I'll come up with a good idea soon, and our fortunes will change, you'll see."

Edith rolled her eyes with affection and stepped aside to let the first few early customers through the door. "I hope so, Josiah. We need a bit of luck. In fact, we deserve it."

Walter Grant, the retired gamekeeper, shuffled to the bar and slapped some coins on the counter. "Mornin' all, 'tis another fine day out there." He took his greasy hat off and huffed as he lowered himself onto a bar stool.

"Your usual, Walter?" Maisie asked. She bustled behind the bar and reached for his tankard, filling it with foaming ale from one of the barrels.

Suddenly, there was a scream, and Abigail came running through from the kitchen. "There's a rat in

THE RUNAWAY SISTER

the flour sacks, Maisie! It's bigger than a cat, and I ain't staying in there washing up. It might run up my legs."

Walter watched with amusement. "Yer sister's turning into a pretty little thing, Maisie. And spirited with it."

"I bet there's a whole nest of rats." Abigail hopped from one foot to the other, shuddering as she shook the hem of her dress. "It had horrible black eyes and a tail this long." She held her hands wide apart, warming to her audience as Walter laughed.

"Don't be so impertinent talking about a rat in front of the customers," Edith snapped. "This is a clean and tidy establishment." She tried to grab Abigail, but the little girl ducked out of her reach and ran to Maisie, instead clinging onto her skirt. "I ain't going back in the kitchen with a rat there, Aunt Edith. You can't make me."

"Why...you little tinker..." Edith drew back her hand to strike Abigail, but Josiah burst out laughing.

"Leave her be, Edith. I'll fetch the tomcat and shut him in the store cupboard for a few minutes. He'll soon catch the beggar. Pour me another tot before I go, Maisie."

Josiah settled at the bar next to Walter, seemingly in no hurry, and Edith fumed as she started polishing the tables.

"You should 'ave her serving the customers. We'll

enjoy the entertainment," Walter said, still grinning as he watched Abigail darting from table to table to put the chairs in place. "Mind you, with her pretty looks, she'll soon turn into a proper looker like her big sister. And being a hard worker as well, she's a useful asset to you, Josiah."

Maisie didn't like the way they were discussing Abigail, and she took hold of her hand. "We'll go and fetch the cat, Uncle. Abigail didn't mean to cause any bother."

As they headed outside into the sunshine, calling for the big ginger tomcat who kept down the mice in the outbuildings, Josiah watched with a thoughtful expression. Old Walter had just given him an idea about how he might change their fortunes if he did but know it.

CHAPTER 10

The sound of Josiah's cheerful whistling drifted across the courtyard, making Maisie smile. He had somehow managed to scrape together enough money to pay the rent when Saul Drew called back a week later and had been more jovial than usual ever since. She wondered whether he would get despondent again in a couple of weeks when the rent was due again, but it was nice to hear him so cheerful in the meantime. His good mood meant that Edith was less likely to find fault with Abigail.

She picked up the last wet sheet from her washing basket and draped it over the line, pulling two wooden pegs from her apron pocket to secure it firmly in place. There was a brisk breeze, and she had a sense of satisfaction as the sheets billowed and flapped. They would be dry in no time and wouldn't take much ironing, which would save her a job.

"Maisie!" Abigail's excited cry from the Inn front door caught her attention, and she started heading back across the courtyard. "Look what I've got. Aunt Edith just gave it to me."

Abigail ran across the cobbles towards her, her curls bouncing. "Isn't it beautiful." She held her arms wide and did a twirl.

Maisie couldn't keep the surprise off her face at the sight of the new sprigged cotton gown her little sister was wearing. It had a scalloped lace collar, and the skirt fell in frilly tiers, ending just above her ankles. "Aunt Edith gave you this?" Her heart swelled with love at how Abigail's eyes were shining because of the rare treat, almost choking her with emotion. It felt like so long since something good had happened.

"Yes," Abigail exclaimed. She picked up her skirts and did a little jig, and then grabbed Maisie's hands so they could twirl around together. "She said it's an early birthday present. It's so pretty, I never want to take it off."

Maisie laughed at her sister's irrepressible enthusiasm. "You're the prettiest girl in Frampton, but you must save it for best, Abigail. It's a wonderful surprise, but we don't want to spoil it by getting it dirty in the kitchen."

Edith appeared in the doorway, and Maisie felt a surge of affection for her cantankerous, waspish aunt, which took her by surprise. *Perhaps I've misjudged her all this time.* "Thank you so much, Aunt Edith. What a wonderfully generous thing to do. I know times have been hard, and we haven't always seen eye to eye, but I don't know how to thank you for being so thoughtful for Abigail's birthday."

Edith waved her thanks away and rested her hand on Abigail's shoulder, smiling down at her. "I know I can be a bit short-tempered when we're short of money, but we can't let little Abigail's birthday go past without celebrating it a little bit. I thought a new gown was more sensible than a doll."

Maisie felt a pang of guilt. Even though she had tried to save what little money Edith let her keep from her dressmaking, it hadn't been enough to buy the doll from the toy shop that Abigail had longed for. Instead, she had been sewing a new nightgown for her in secret before she woke up every morning for the last few days with some new soft cotton fabric she had managed to buy, but it seemed rather meagre compared to Aunt Edith's extravagant gesture, which was so out of character.

"You've both been working very hard recently," Josiah chimed in as he ambled out from the bar. He exchanged a glance with Edith as though he wanted to confirm something with her, and she nodded. "You can have a couple of hours off if you like, Maisie. It will give you a chance to go and look around some of the shops in the village." He wiggled his eyebrows and cocked his head surreptitiously in Abigail's direction.

Maisie found herself surprised again. She hadn't thought that Josiah would remember Abigail's birthday was coming up soon with all his worries, let alone think to give her a couple of hours off away from the Jolly Sailor to go and buy some small gifts. She played along, smiling back. "That's perfect, Uncle Josiah. I finished Mrs Harding's new summer gown this morning, so I can take it to her earlier than she was expecting it."

"Can I come? We might see Jack on his rounds." Abigail started skipping across the courtyard, eager to show off her new dress to their friends in the village.

"Wait a minute." Maisie opened her arms, and Abigail ran back towards her, leaping up for a hug. "Not this time, poppet."

Abigail's face fell with disappointment, and she buried her head in Maisie's hair, making her feel guilty. They were barely ever apart, and perhaps it wouldn't harm. She could always run to the haberdashery shop another day, where she had spied some ribbons that she wanted to buy for her sister.

"What about when Walter comes in for his ale

shortly," Edith asked quickly. "Don't you want to show him your new gown, Abigail? I'll even let you sit on a stool behind the bar with your Uncle Josiah until Maisie gets back instead of working in the kitchen. How does that sound?"

Maisie loosened Abigail's arms from around her neck and gave her a small wink of encouragement. They were so used to Edith's bad tempers that this sudden change caught them both by surprise, but she didn't want Edith to be offended and think Abigail was ungrateful for what she had done. "I'll be back before you know it, Abigail. I wasn't going to let on, but I'm going to buy some chocolate from the grocers so we can make a chocolate cake next week for your birthday."

"Really? This is turning into the best day I've ever had," Abigail giggled. She twirled a lock of Maisie's hair around her fingers and pressed a kiss on her cheek, which made Maisie's heart melt as always. She was sad that Ma would never get to see what a delightful little girl Abigail was becoming, but it felt as though they had turned some sort of corner with Edith and Josiah, which went some way to making up for it. They would never feel like parents, but now it seemed as though they didn't resent taking in the two of them as much as she had feared when they first arrived.

"You can help me set up the glasses ready for

when the first customers come in," Josiah said with a twinkle in his eye. He held his hand out, and Abigail wriggled out of Maisie's arms to run back inside with him.

"Such a pretty little thing," Edith said. She smiled at Maisie again. "Take as long as you need, my dear. There's no need to rush back. She's better behaved now that she's older, and it's good for her to get used to being apart from you now and again."

THE PINK WILD mallow flowers and sprigs of green hazel foliage made a pretty splash of colour as Maisie laid them on Violet's grave. Now that she had the rare chance of a few hours away from the Jolly Sailor, she felt herself starting to relax. She adored Abigail and would always do her very best to raise her to the standard that she hoped would have pleased her ma, but it was also a responsibility because she wanted the best for Abigail. Her dream was still of owning her own dressmaking shop and perhaps of Abigail working alongside her when she was old enough, but it was just that…a dream.

"I know it's kind of Uncle Josiah and Aunt Edith to take us in, Ma, but I'm not sure serving drinks is really what you would have wanted for us." She stood in front of the plain headstone, surrounded by all the others. It was a stark reminder of life ticking by and, in many cases, ending too soon. They were lucky that Violet had a headstone instead of an unmarked pauper's grave, and she was grateful that she could come here and talk. It helped her straighten things out in her mind when there was nobody else to confide in. "I'm in a pickle, Ma, that's the problem. I'll never be able to save up enough money for my own dressmaking business while I have to give so much of what I earn to Aunt Edith. But living at the Jolly Sailor means I don't have to pay rent. I wish you and Papa were still here...you would have helped me figure out a way, I know you would."

The summer breeze pulled some tendrils of hair out of her bun, and she absentmindedly tucked them in again, thinking about what Mrs Harding had said to her not an hour before. She had been delighted with her new gown, even slipping her an extra shilling for finishing it so quickly.

"You should be doing more dressmaking instead of being stuck in that taproom, serving ale to the feckless men of the village," the doctor's wife commented. She disapproved of the men who drank to excess because it was her husband who invariably had to deal with the consequences of any brawls which broke out. "It can't understand why your aunt won't let you. I suppose it suits her to have you working as a barmaid, but it's a shame for your dressmaking skills always to be put last." She had shaken her head. "Edith Snape doesn't have the same aspirations your ma would have wanted for you. I'd say something myself, but Mr Harding tells me not to get involved. I don't want to get on the wrong side of Edith's short temper."

Although Maisie took heart from Mrs Harding's comments, they also left her feeling more frustrated. Even though Aunt Edith was being friendlier, there was no way she would agree to let Maisie step back from her duties in the kitchens and behind the bar...at least not until Abigail was old enough to replace her. "But that's not what I want for Abigail, Ma," she sighed. She bent down and pulled up some bindweed. Left unchecked, it would soon cover the headstone.

"Can I entice a fair maid to have a ride on my rag-and-bone cart?" Jack's shout was accompanied by a chuckle as he reined Duke to a halt at the churchyard gateway. He doffed his hat and gestured to the seat next to him where Badger was sitting. "The dog won't mind running alongside us for a while. It's the most comfortable cart in Frampton, and the rags aren't too smelly either, with this breeze."

Her spirits lifted, and she patted her hair, hoping she didn't look too untidy. "You make it sound almost irresistible, but I think I'd rather walk."

"I'm surprised to see you out and about at this

THE RUNAWAY SISTER

time of the day. Have you run away?" he joked. "I can't believe Josiah would willingly let you have time off when there are thirsty customers to serve."

Maisie slipped through the gate and patted Duke on his neck as he stood patiently. "I know. I was surprised when he let me out as well. Uncle Josiah has been in a good mood these last few weeks. He keeps talking about a change of fortune, but I have no idea what he actually means." She glanced up at Jack, admiring his tanned face and strong hands, before hastily reining in her errant thoughts. *I don't know why I have romance on my mind. It's the last thing Jack would be considering, I'm sure.*

"So you're enjoying some time to yourself? Or are you meeting someone?" He looked around with a frown.

"No!" It pleased her that he seemed slightly jealous. Perhaps he thought one of the village boys was hoping to walk out with her, but nothing could be further from the truth. "My uncle let me have a couple of hours off work to take some sewing to Mrs Harding, and so I could buy some ribbons for Abigail's birthday." She held up the brown parcel, feeling slightly flustered under Jack's gaze.

"He's talking about a change of fortune, you reckon?" Jack pushed his cap to the back of his head and grinned down at her. "I'd better come in for a pint of ale this evening and see if I can find out what he means. Someone is bound to know. Josiah is never shy about telling people how successful he is."

"How's your business doing? Is Mr Clatterbrook still doing his best to keep you off the estate?" Duke nuzzled Maisie's dress pocket, hoping for a treat, and she stepped back. "I'll give you a carrot next time I see you, boy." Badger barked from the cart seat, making Maisie laugh. "Yes, I haven't forgotten about you, Badger. I'll see if I can sneak a stale biscuit out for you next time your master comes calling for rags."

"I swear, Jeffrey Clatterbrook has a vendetta against me," Jack said, suddenly looking serious. "It's only because Elsie doesn't like to be proved wrong. Whenever she's full of doom and gloom about someone being ill, spreading rumours that they're at death's door, and then granny's tonics make them better, she takes it as a personal affront."

"That sounds about right. Elsie likes nothing more than causing upset and delighting in other people's misery. Whereas Ava is the complete opposite. I don't understand why the villagers can't see that she only wants to help."

"If there was a way of me being able to speak to Lord Pickering and ask him for a gardening job, I would, but Jeffrey seems to have eyes in the back of his head. Any time I try to go to the Manor house, he stops me."

"You're too good to work under Jeffrey Clatter-brook," Maisie said, jumping to his defence. "Perhaps you could look for work elsewhere?" She bit her lip, wishing she hadn't spoken so hastily. She didn't want to put ideas into Jack's head.

"Leave Frampton, you mean?" Jack's expression was hard to read. "I don't think I could do that, not leave everything we know."

"I mean...it would be good if you could fulfil your dream of gardening, but I don't think I could imagine not seeing you anymore." Maisie felt a blush creep up her cheeks. "You know how much Abigail looks forward to seeing you and Fred. And I would miss seeing Ava as well." She felt flustered as Jack's eyes glinted with amusement.

"For a minute, I thought you were going to say you might miss me."

"Well...perhaps I would...miss all of you, I mean." What she really wanted to say was that the long hours of drudgery at the Jolly Sailor would be unbearable without his visits, but that would be far too forward.

He shrugged and picked up the reins. "I'm happy enough with my little rag-and-bone business. Fred finds enough trinkets from the mudlarking for us to just about make ends meet. I don't think anything could persuade us to leave Frampton." Duke swished his tail as a fly buzzed around his legs. "If you're sure

DAISY CARTER

I can't give you a lift, I'd better be on my way. Florence promised she would keep some things back for me, so I need to get them before she changes her mind."

"Oh. Of course. See you later, perhaps." She felt foolish. Florence had turned into a buxom young woman, and Jack was bound to find her attractive. The church clock struck two, and Maisie hurried through the lanes to get back to the Jolly Sailor once Jack had left. She had spent longer than she intended at the churchyard, and she didn't want to risk her uncle's displeasure by being gone for too long.

She was surprised to see a brougham carriage in the courtyard when she turned the corner. It was far grander than anything which their usual customers drove. There was a liveried coachman on the box seat, and the gleaming pair of chestnut horses in the harness looked equally expensive to match. She paused in the shadow of the barn to make sure the parcel of ribbons for Abigail was hidden in the bottom of her basket, and a snatch of conversation drifted towards her.

"...good of you to come and visit us." Josiah sounded jovial.

Maisie's curiosity was piqued. It sounded as though he knew them, but he had never mentioned having toffs as customers before. Annoyingly, she couldn't get a clear view of the people inside the

THE RUNAWAY SISTER

carriage, but then something snagged at the edge of her mind. There was a gold and red heraldic crest painted on the door of the brougham that looked familiar. "Where have I seen that before?" she muttered to herself. The more she wracked her brain, the more elusive it was, like struggling to remember a dream upon waking. She walked closer, trying to get a better look, and noticed that Edith was standing near Josiah with Abigail on her hip.

"It's a pleasure dealing with you, and we can assure you, it's an excellent decision. You won't be disappointed."

Abigail fidgeted on Edith's hip, and Maisie waited for the usual flash of annoyance from her aunt, but instead, Edith smiled up at whoever was in the carriage. "Dear Abigail, she's such a delight," she cooed.

The coachman flicked his whip, and the horses leapt forward into a brisk trot, almost knocking Maisie over. The basket flew out of her hand. "Lookout!" she cried. She fell to her knees to save the ribbons before they were covered in dust.

"Out of our way," he said snootily.

By the time she had stood up again, all she could see was the back of the brougham, and she was none the wiser about who was inside.

"Maisie!" Abigail wriggled down from Edith and ran over. "Did you see them toffs? Look what the

123

man gave me." She held up a small china doll and then clutched it to her chest. "It's like the one we saw in the toyshop."

She looked between Abigail and her aunt, feeling confused. "Do you know those people? Who are they? Why did they give Abigail the doll?"

Edith rolled her eyes. "Goodness me, Maisie, so many questions."

"They'm just some rich folk enquiring about a room." Josiah stuck his thumbs in his waistcoat pockets and laughed. "We told them this wasn't their kind of establishment and sent them onward instead."

"They wanted to stay here?"

"It was just a mistake," Edith chimed in hastily. She shooed Abigail ahead of her back into the Inn. "Folks like them have more money than sense. They gave Abigail the doll to thank us for suggesting somewhere better for them to stay."

"You're not going to make me give it back, are you?" Abigail clutched the doll tighter, looking alarmed.

"No, my sweet. What a stroke of luck that they were so kind." Maisie supposed it didn't matter how Abigail had come by the doll. What mattered was that she would have a wonderful birthday next week. *Perhaps our fortunes really are changing*, she thought happily.

CHAPTER 11

"Surely you'll accept a ride home in my cart this time?"

Maisie was walking briskly through the village, and the familiar voice brought a smile to her face as she was pulled from her pleasant daydream about having her own dressmaking business.

Duke whinnied, and Jack reined his cart to a halt next to her. "There's room for one more."

"I suppose it would be rude to say no twice."

"Hop up," said Fred, shuffling along the seat. "I've got a thirst after a long day on the mud, and Jack's promised he'll buy me a pint of ale."

Maisie hitched up her skirts and climbed up next to them, glad of the offer this time. "Are you sure that's a good idea, Fred?" She looked between the two of them and burst out laughing. "I suppose you are

DAISY CARTER

fourteen, even though I still think of you as the nipper I first got to know at the river all those years ago. Abigail will be delighted that Jack has finally relented and agreed you can join him for a drink now and again."

Duke trotted on at a lively pace, and Badger stood in the back of the empty cart, wagging his tail every time they passed someone as though he owned the village.

"So what brings you into the village on a summer's evening, Maisie? And less than two weeks since the last time you were out." Jack tipped his hat to the vicar as they rumbled past him.

Maisie finally gave in to the excitement, which had been bubbling up inside her all day, now that she could share her news with her friends. "You remember I made a gown for Amelia Harding, the doctor's wife? Well, her sister is staying with them for a little while. Mrs Harding liked the last gown I made her so much that they asked me to make them two more gowns each. Uncle Josiah gave me the whole day off so I could go to Peartree Villa and do a dress fitting for them both."

"That sounds awful boring," Fred muttered. "I bet they were gossiping about women's things all day, like two sparrows."

"Mind your manners," Jack said, jabbing his elbow into Fred's side. "Sorry, Maisie. My brother has about as much business sense as a turnip. Two more dresses each sounds promising. Could this be the start of a proper business as a seamstress, do you think?"

"I really do hope so. If they tell a few more of their friends, and I get some more orders to make gowns, I'll be able to prove to Aunt Edith that there is a demand for my sewing work."

"So you'll be able to stop serving ale. And maybe get a little shop of your own." Fred shot Jack a triumphant smile as Maisie nodded eagerly. "See, I ain't such a turnip head, Jack Piper."

"Of course you aren't," Jack agreed good-naturedly. "I was just teasing to see if you were awake." He turned back to Maisie. "Our Fred has come across some good finds in the mud in the last few weeks. If I didn't know better, I would think it was a light-fingered thief getting rid of stolen goods before the constables put them in jail."

"Aye, plenty of thieves and dippers who'd rather chuck their haul in the river than get sent to the colonies for a lifetime of hard labour. I heard a rumour there were some burglaries up Nailsbridge way." Fred scratched his freckled nose and grinned widely. "I ain't complaining. I mean, I would never go thieving myself, but if I happen to find something valuable in the mud downriver, it's finders keepers, ain't it."

Maisie shrugged. It was a grey area, but if it meant that the Piper family had fewer money worries, she could only be glad. "What have you found?"

Fred pulled a coin from his pocket, and it glinted in the sun. Far from the usual thruppenny bits and occasional shillings, it was one guinea. "It's enough to keep Saul Drew happy with the rent for a little while. I found some earrings as well, a matching pair."

Jack's eyebrows shot up in surprise. "A pair? What are the odds of that? It sounds like it must definitely have been some sort of robbery."

"I pawned them already." Fred lifted his chin slightly defiantly. He wanted to be treated as an adult, not Jack's little brother. "Got a good price for 'em as well, although the pawnbroker did give me a funny look."

The muscles clenched in Jack's jaw. "I hope you put the money in the tin. And if you find more jewellery like that, for the love of all things common-sense, don't pawn them in Frampton again."

"Why not?" Fred frowned. "You should be pleased, not grumbling at me."

"We need to go further away in case the constable gets it into his head that it's us doing the thieving. You know there are plenty of folks looking for an opportunity to get us in trouble because they don't like Granny. And they think we're wrong 'uns because of what Ma did to earn a crust."

THE RUNAWAY SISTER

Maisie could sense an argument brewing, so she changed the subject. "Thank you for the wooden cot you made for Abigail's doll for her birthday. We have it in the corner of our bedroom." The brothers grinned at each other again, and good humour was restored. "She loves that doll as if it was a real baby. She sits it on the shelf in the kitchen when she's washing the dishes."

"That's alright. We enjoyed making it," Jack said easily.

The sound of loud laughter drifted towards them. "Looks like it's going to be a lively night at the Jolly Sailor," Fred tucked the coin inside his boot for safe-keeping as they turned the cart into the courtyard.

Just as they were getting down, Walter Grant hobbled out of the front door, and his face lit up when he caught sight of Maisie. "Your aunt and uncle are in fine fettle tonight," he called, slurring his words slightly. "It's surprising what a change of fortune can do for a fellow."

"...Free drinksshh on me tonight, everyone!" Josiah sounded exuberant and also very drunk.

"Crikey, Maisie, what's going on?" Jack frowned at the sound of smashing glass, followed by roars of laughter. "Do your aunt and uncle usually drink like this?"

"Not that I've ever seen." Maisie's heart sank. Even though it sounded as though her uncle had had some good luck, someone needed to step in and stop things getting out of hand. She had never known him to give out free ale in over four years, and he would regret it in the morning. "Will you help me if things get too lively?"

"Of course." Jack glowered at someone who barged past Maisie, and she instantly felt happier.

Maisie had never seen the taproom so full, and she could only assume it was because word had got out that Josiah Snape was in a generous mood. The noise was deafening as she pushed her way through the room. Farm labourers and men from the nearby docks at Frampton Basin were jostling to reach the bar, many of them already three sheets to the wind. Clearly, the carousing had been going on for some time, and she shook her head with a rueful smile as she caught sight of Fred's shocked expression. He might be regretting his decision to come in for a quiet ale with Jack now, she thought.

"What's going on?" She asked Arthur, one of the regulars.

"Your uncle's celebrating," he roared. He leaned closer, struggling to focus, and she was enveloped in a blast of beery breath as he chuckled. "Reckons he's come into some money and made his fortune. I've heard him saying it would 'appen many times over the years, but this time, it seems he was right. You'm all going to be well off now!"

"Fill that glass up with gin, will you, ducky," a toothless woman in a ragged skirt screeched. She linked arms with the man standing next to her, and they started a lively jig, humming an unrecognisable tune. Maisie had never seen them before, but the lure of a free drink must have brought folks rushing from far and wide.

Taking a deep breath, she wriggled between two burly dockers and managed to squeeze around the back of the bar. Edith was swaying with a glassy-eyed expression. It was the first time Maisie had ever seen her so drunk. Her aunt was fond of a tot or two of rum at the end of the night, claiming it helped her sleep, but it looked strange to see her with dishevelled hair and a vacant smile.

"Roll yer sleeves up and get to work, Maisie. I can't keep up with serving this lot." Josiah sloshed rum into a row of glasses, not caring that half of it had spilt onto the bar. He swiped a puddle away with his sleeve and hiccupped.

"What's this good fortune you've had?" She wondered if he'd won a game of cards or a bet on the horses, perhaps? "Have you had a lucky win?" She gathered up some dirty glasses into a tray.

Josiah's slack jowls quivered as he started laughing. "It's nothing to do with good luck, girl, just shrewd business sense." He tapped the side of his nose and winked at one of the drinkers, who nodded solemnly even though he could barely stand up.

"You always said you would own this place one day," another fellow yelled before banging his tankard down on the bar for a refill.

"I'll tell Mr Drew to shove his measly rent demands in his pipe and smoke them," Josiah roared, sending up fresh shouts of agreement from everyone at the bar. "Edith and I will buy this place outright and run it how we choose...with free rum for everyone, whenever we like!"

Another cheer went up, practically rattling the windows, and Maisie knew there was no point trying to get to the bottom of her uncle's sudden change in fortune for now. Even though his words were coherent, she could tell by the mottled hue of his cheeks and his bloodshot eyes that he had probably been drinking all day. She only hoped that Josiah and Edith would be able to stay awake long enough to see the evening shift through before collapsing into a stupor for the night.

"Want me to help you with those?" Jack appeared in front of her, with Fred behind, trying not to be crushed in the throng. He pointed at the glasses, but she shook her head and put the tray down again.

"Two pints coming up." She poured the frothing ale from the cask behind her and accepted a couple of coins, putting them in her apron pocket until she could get to the till under the counter. She knew neither of them would want to touch the eye-wateringly rough gin or the rum.

"I think I'm going to enjoy my first proper night," Fred said with a mischievous grin. He took a long gulp of the drink and wiped his mouth with the back of his hand.

"I'm going to take these glasses out to the kitchen and wash them up. If you could just make sure nobody starts fighting, that would be a great help."

"Where's Abigail?" Fred leaned sideways to peer down the hallway that led to the kitchen. "If she's got any sense, she'll stay well clear of this lot tonight."

"It's late. She's probably upstairs in bed already. I won't have time to read her a story tonight, but I'll run up and say goodnight and be back in a minute."

After the deafening din in the taproom and the fog of smoke from the men's clay pipes, the calm of the kitchen provided a welcome respite. Maisie was surprised to see a pile of dirty dishes in the middle of the kitchen table and no sign of any stew warming on top of the range. She supposed Edith had decided not to offer meals, which was probably a blessing in disguise. The bar was too crowded for people to sit at the tables to eat anyway, and there would be fewer spillages for her to have to clean up at closing time. She glanced up at the dresser, but the doll was not there, which told her that she was right; Abigail had already gone to bed.

She hastily washed the glasses and put them on the side to drain. Given how drunk everyone was, they probably wouldn't even notice what state the glasses were in, but she didn't want to let standards slip.

"Are you ready for bed?" Maisie called as she dried her hands on her apron and went upstairs. "I'm sorry about all the noise from the taproom, but I'm sure you'll be asleep in no time." She pushed the bedroom door open but stopped in the doorway as she saw the room was empty. "Abigail? Where are you?" Her voice sounded sharp, and she took a deep breath. "I don't have time to play hide and seek tonight, poppet. You need to come out from wherever you're hiding and get into bed. Uncle Josiah needs me back downstairs. It's never been so busy."

She expected to hear a giggle and see Abigail roll out from under the bed or reveal herself from inside the small wardrobe which held their gowns. "Abigail! Come on now, poppet. Let me tuck you into bed."

The silence in the room stretched out, and her stomach lurched. It was not like Abigail to hide from her. If anything, she would usually throw herself into Maisie's arms and demand to know how her day at Peartree Villa had gone.

Maisie darted around the bedroom, looking in

every corner and under the beds, before running along the upstairs landing and peering into every room. There were no guests staying that night, and by the time she reached the farthest room, an icy sense of dread gripped her. Abigail was nowhere to be seen and was not answering her increasingly frantic calls to come out if she was hiding. She picked up her skirts and ran down the stairs, bursting through the door into the taproom.

"Jack," she cried, "Abigail has gone. She's run away."

CHAPTER 12

Maisie spun around and grabbed her uncle's arm. "Did you send Abigail out to run an errand? I can't find her anywhere upstairs, and her doll is gone as well."

Josiah blinked, looking at her owlishly. He screwed up his face as though he was trying to remember but then shook his head. "I've been serving drinksshh for hours…no idea…" His words sounded more slurred than ever, and Maisie spotted an empty rum bottle behind him on the shelf. She sighed with frustration and peered through the drinkers at the bar, hoping that Edith might have sobered up. Her hopes were soon dashed as she saw her sprawled in the armchair next to the inglenook fireplace. Her mob cap had slipped to one side of her head, and her mouth gaped open as she snored, dead to the world.

"You won't get any sense out of those two," Jack pulled his cap out of his pocket and put it on, looking around at all the drunkards who were still carousing the evening away around them. "Fred and I will come with you. I'm sure she hasn't run away; she must have just wandered off for a little adventure." He had to shout to make himself heard, and Maisie nodded, grabbing her shawl from where she had hung it up behind the door.

A few minutes later, they stood outside in the cobbled courtyard. Fred had already sprinted around all the outbuildings, returning with a shake of his head. "She's not in any of the sheds. Where do you think she might have gone? Should we stick together or split up to look for her?"

Maisie's legs felt weak as fear coursed through her veins. "I don't know what to think. She's never done anything like this before...it's completely out of character. She knew I would be out all day, but I can't understand why she isn't upstairs tucked up in bed."

"Perhaps it was all the noise downstairs," Fred ventured. As if to underline his words, another roar of laughter split the air. The discordant sounds of someone attempting to play the piano, followed by an argument breaking out, made Maisie shudder. It was no place for her little sister, that was for sure.

Why are we still living here? I don't think I can stay with our aunt and uncle for much longer. Regret started to take hold, but she pushed it away. There was no time for that.

"We need to think logically," Jack said, keeping his voice steady. He looked at Maisie and came to a decision. "I'll stick with you. I know you must be worried, but I don't want you to take unnecessary risks and come to any harm. Fred will be fine going to look in a couple of places by himself, and then we can meet up again."

Maisie nodded, finding it hard to speak. "Thank you. Where should we start?" She clasped her hands together and took several deep breaths, trying to marshal her thoughts. "Perhaps she went to the churchyard to see Ma and Pa's graves. Or maybe she's gone into the village to the toy shop to look in the window. It's one of her favourite things to do." She glanced beyond the courtyard towards the marshland and river, almost too scared to voice her greatest fear.

Jack did it for her. "I think for our own peace of mind, we should check the riverbank first. Did you ever take her mudlarking?"

"Never," she exclaimed, shaking her head decisively. "I always told her to stay away from the mud and that it was too dangerous for a child as young as her."

Fred looked up at Jack, his face etched with worry. "She always used to ask what I'd found in the river," he said slightly apologetically. "I never encouraged her, but I could tell that she was interested. She used to say there was treasure in the mud, and I just laughed along...I never thought she would actually think it was real treasure."

Maisie's breath caught in her throat. "She was asking me about whether we might have a little dressmaking shop of our own one day recently." She blinked back the tears which pricked the back of her eyes. "I said the only chance of us setting up a place of our own would be if we found buried treasure." She clamped her hand to her mouth, desperately wishing she could take the words back. "What a fool I've been. Abigail knows how much I want to have my own business, perhaps she's gone looking in the mud."

Without waiting to discuss anything else, the three of them jumped up onto the cart seat, and Jack slapped the reins hard on Duke's back. He cantered out of the courtyard, and Maisie grabbed Jack's arm to steady herself as the cart rocked dangerously. Part of her wanted to get down and run, but she knew that Duke could get them down to the riverbank faster.

. . .

THE RUNAWAY SISTER

THE LIGHT WAS STARTING to fade as they came to the end of the track. Under any other circumstances, it would have been a beautiful evening. The sun was setting in a ball of fire over the water, painting the night sky with vivid streaks of mauve and orange, broken only by ripples of mackerel clouds high in the sky. The bubbling call of two curlews, which Maisie usually loved to hear, sounded mournful, and she was struck by how vast and dangerous the mudflats could be to an unsuspecting child.

"Abigail! Where are you? Can you hear us?" Her voice rang out, sending a flock of startled pigeons clattering up from the trees nearby. She cocked her head, desperate to hear Abigail's reply, but it didn't come, and Badger zig-zagged over the tussocky grass, nose to the ground.

They spent the next hour combing the marshland, shouting, but to no avail.

"I think we should try the other places you suggested before it gets too dark." Jack gave her a sympathetic smile. "We'll find her, Maisie. I can feel it in my bones."

Fred heard his remark and puffed his cheeks out. "Why didn't I think of it sooner? We should go and ask Granny to see if the cards are telling her anything."

"Let's go to the churchyard and the toy shop on the way. I don't want to disturb your granny only to

141

find out that Abigail was looking at the toys all along."

Sitting up in the cart again, Maisie did her best to look on the bright side. Abigail was a sensible little girl, and now that they had searched the mudflats, she felt more reassured that she hadn't got swept away in the river. There would have been some sort of clue if she had gone that way. She was sure of it.

Her tentative sense of optimism didn't last long. The churchyard was empty, and the lane outside the toy shop was deserted. The first stars were starting to twinkle in the sky, and people were going to bed.

"I can't spend the night not knowing where she's gone." She and Jack had scoured the lanes, and she wished they had brought a lantern with them to light their way.

Jack put his arm around her shoulders for a moment, and she rested her head against his chest, drawing comfort from his friendship. "I don't know what to say other than to tell you that we'll do whatever we can to help you, Maisie, you know that. We love Abigail as if she were family. We just have to hope it's some sort of misunderstanding, and she'll be back home safe and sound in no time."

"I'm going to go up and down every lane in the village, calling her name." Maisie squared her shoulders, needing to be doing something...anything.

"What about the old cottage where you used to live?"

Maisie smacked her head with her hand. "Of course! Why didn't I think to try there? She often talks about the new family who moved in, wondering what they're like. I said we would call in one day, but we're always so busy serving the customers that I haven't had time to take her. I bet they've taken her in, and she's sitting by their fire right now."

"It won't harm to call out for her on the way." Jack cupped his hands around his mouth. "Abigail! If you can hear us, shout back."

A shaft of light fell across the cobbled lane just ahead of them, and Maisie's spirits surged with hope. She ran towards it, just in time to see a shadowy figure step out into the lane. "Abigail?"

The figure held up a candle, and disappointment crashed through Maisie's chest as she realised it was just Elsie Clatterbrook.

"Some of us are trying to sleep," she said in a loud whisper. "What's all this shouting about? Haven't you got anything better to be doing at this time of night than waking up hard-working folk who are abed?" Her expression above her frilly white nightdress and shawl was indignant.

"We've lost Abigail." Maisie didn't care if the whole village was being kept from their beds if it meant she could find her little sister.

Elsie rolled her eyes. "That's what comes of being so high-spirited. Children her age should be seen and not heard, and she's far too rude for my liking. She accused me of gossiping when I saw the two of you outside the bakery last time." The candle flickered, and she glanced at the window above them. "I don't have time for this. Mr Clatterbrook has to be up early, and he won't like being disturbed for the sake of a naughty child."

"Well, I don't have time for your petty insults. Have you seen Abigail or not?"

Elsie's lips pinched together in outrage at Maisie's curt response.

"If you know anything about where Abigail has gone, Mrs Clatterbrook, we would be very grateful if you could tell us." Jack gave the older woman an earnest smile, trying to appeal to her better nature. "You can understand that Maisie is very worried, I'm sure."

His charm seemed to work, and Elsie Clatterbrook nodded, enjoying her moment of glory at being the person bearing news. "If you could have just asked me politely, Maisie, I would have told you straight away."

"Told me what?" Maisie resisted the urge to grab the woman's shoulders and shake the words out of her. "Please tell us what you know, Mrs Clatterbrook. I'd be most grateful, as Jack just said."

THE RUNAWAY SISTER

Elsie leaned slightly closer, lowering her voice as if she was about to impart something very important. "I saw your Abigail in a very smart carriage this afternoon. The coachman looked as snooty as you like and practically ran me down as I was minding my own business at the end of the lane. Very rude."

"Abigail was in a carriage?" Maisie frowned, not sure whether to believe her.

Elsie nodded vigorously, her grey curls bobbing in time with her nods. "Yes. Abigail was in a smart carriage. I ain't seen it before, but I'd recognise it if I saw it again. It had a red and gold crest painted on the door, and the man and woman inside the carriage looked like proper toffs, wearing clothes as fancy as Lord and Lady Pickering."

"Are you absolutely sure?" It made no sense, but Maisie suddenly remembered the brougham carriage she had seen outside the Jolly Sailor two weeks ago. *It must be the same one.* "Why was she with them?" Elsie's news only brought more questions.

"At least we know she's safe," Jack murmured.

Elsie shrugged. "How do you expect me to know why she was with them? I know you think I'm a busybody, but I'm just saying what I saw, that's all. The toffs inside the carriage looked far too posh for my liking, but your Abigail seemed happy enough. Chattering away to them as if it was all just a big adventure, and she even had the cheek to wave at me through the window as the carriage wheels practically went over my toes."

* * *

"THIS IS something to do with Uncle Josiah and his harebrained scheme to make money." Maisie was marching back to the cart, and Jack walked beside her with long strides.

"I don't see how it can be." Fred loped along behind them, sounding breathless. "I thought Josiah won at a game of cards?"

Maisie's mind whirled with a hundred unanswered questions until she landed with grim satisfaction on one fact she could grasp hold of. "I couldn't work out why he's been so jolly these last few weeks. He must have been hatching a plan, and from the way Elsie describes that carriage, it's the same one I saw in our courtyard a few weeks ago. It can't be a coincidence."

"Maybe they...I dunno." Jack scratched his head, drawing a blank. "The best thing we can do is ask them directly, although I doubt we'll get anything out of them tonight."

"Just you watch me." Anger bubbled up, giving Maisie the determination to defy Edith and Josiah. "Even if I have to throw a bucket of cold water over

THE RUNAWAY SISTER

them, I'm going to find out tonight, one way or another."

"At least it was toffs who have Abigail." Fred unhitched Duke's reins, and they all climbed back onto the cart. "Perhaps they'll be back for you in a few days as well," he added hopefully.

"We're not servants to be sent away. I promised Ma I would look after Abigail and Josiah has no right to do something without asking me first. Perhaps I should get the constable involved."

Jack squeezed her hand. "Let's not assume the worst. For all we know, they live just outside the village, and they thought Abigail was lost. In fact, maybe they've even taken her back to the Jolly Sailor while we've been out looking for her."

Maisie didn't hold out much hope, even though she knew Jack was doing his best to cheer her up. *At least she's not dead in the river.* The thought gave her a moment of relief, but the worry soon returned, gnawing away at her. She needed to know exactly who had taken Abigail and why.

As Duke clopped into the courtyard, the inn was dark apart from one oil lamp flickering in the taproom window. Maisie jumped down before Duke had even stopped and hitched up her skirts to run inside, throwing the door open and making it shudder on its hinges.

Josiah and Edith were both in front of the hearth, fast asleep in the two armchairs. The last of the revellers were slumped over tables, and the old woman Maisie had last seen dancing had curled up on a pile of coats in the corner of the room. Sodden sawdust clung to the hem of her dress, and the stench of stale alcohol filled her nostrils, making her grimace.

"Wake up, Uncle Josiah." She grabbed his shoulders and shook him, not caring if he would be in a bad mood. "And you, Aunt Edith." Maisie nudged her aunt's arm and leaned over her.

"Any luck?" Jack turned up two of the oil lamps.

"Shusshh...I'm trying to get some kip here.." The old woman rolled over and started snoring.

Maisie was just about to shake her head when Josiah's eyes slowly opened, and he looked at her blearily. "Wha— what time is it?" He tried to sit up straighter but then fell back into the chair with a groan, clutching his head. "Go away and come back in the morning, Maisie. Can't a man get some rest?"

Maisie put her hands on her hips and scowled down at him. "While you two have been asleep, Jack and Fred have been helping me look for Abigail. We've all been sick with worry, but you knew where she was all along, didn't you?"

A sly look flitted across her uncle's face, and he glanced towards Edith, who had just woken up as well.

THE RUNAWAY SISTER

"Oh, what are you making such a fuss about, Maisie?" Edith straightened her mob cap and stood up slowly, frowning with the effort. "We never promised your ma we would look after the two of you forever. You're useful behind the bar, but Abigail was nothing but a hungry mouth to feed." Her chin jutted out defiantly. "She was too clingy by half, always wanting to be with you. It was time for her to grow up instead of hanging onto your apron strings all the time."

"What do you mean?" Maisie wanted to howl with frustration. "She's only five." A new, chilling thought slid into her head. "You haven't sent her into service, have you?" Her heart sank at the idea of Abigail scrubbing dishes and sleeping on a wooden pallet under someone's kitchen table, torn away from her, without even knowing where she was going.

"What do you take us for?" Josiah lumbered to his feet, looking offended. "We've done our best for you both, but it's like Edith said. It's time for us to get something back for our efforts now."

"So where is she?" Maisie demanded. "Tell me now so I can go get her back."

"You can't do that." Edith folded her arms, and her eyes narrowed angrily. "Abigail will have the sort of life most people like us can only ever dream of, Maisie. The folks who have her now couldn't have children, and she's such a pretty little thing and so biddable. They liked her immediately, and now she'll grow up with them as her parents." Her voice rose into a shriek. "Instead of accusing us of being uncaring, you should be thanking us."

"Yes, indeed." Her uncle glared at Masie. "And you should remember a bit of gratitude that we've given her this chance wouldn't go amiss."

Now Uncle Josiah's change of fortune made sense to her. The money hadn't come from winning a game of cards or betting on the horses. "What are you saying?" She felt as though she had been punched in the stomach, the air squeezed from her lungs. "You let me believe she'd run away, but…but, you mean you've sent her away with those people in return for money…you've sold her?" she gasped.

"Well, I wouldn't put it quite like that," Josiah blustered. He looked at Edith, who just shrugged, and the last thing Maisie was aware of as she fainted was Jack's strong arms around her shoulders as her legs crumpled beneath her.

CHAPTER 13

"Is the eggs and bacon ready yet?" Edith bustled into the kitchen. "You know Josiah doesn't like to be kept waiting for his breakfast. Just because we haven't got any guests in today doesn't mean you can dawdle."

Maisie turned the bacon over in the frying pan, her mind miles away. It was two days since Abigail had gone, and she could hardly bear to be in the same room as her aunt and uncle, let alone carry on with everything as normal, which is what they seemed to expect of her.

"I'll let you know when it's done." She turned her back to Edith and tried to distract herself by making a pot of tea and cutting some slices of bread to go with the bacon and eggs. The irony was that they never normally ate this well, but since Josiah was feeling

DAISY CARTER

flush with money, he wanted only the best. Maisie felt sick to her stomach, and the thought of trying to eat breakfast while staring at the empty seat where Abigail should have been sitting was inconceivable. "I suppose letting me have a day away from the Jolly Sailor to make Mrs Harding's gowns was just a ruse to get me out of the way," she asked mutinously.

"You would only have spoilt our arrangement... you're not still sulking because of what's happened, are you?" Edith didn't bother to hide her irritation. "Nobody will want to drink here with your face as long as a fiddle."

Maisie whirled around to face her aunt. "All I'm asking is that you tell me where Abigail is so I can go and visit her. I can't bear to think that she'll be wondering why I didn't say goodbye. She might think I didn't care about her going, and nothing could be further from the truth."

Josiah loomed in the doorway, eyeing her warily. He didn't like arguing and usually left anything like that to Edith, but it was too late to back away, and he was hungry.

"Please, Uncle Josiah," Maisie begged. "For goodness sake, won't you tell me the names of the people who took Abigail? Let me go and visit her so that I can make sure she's going to be happy."

Edith tutted and rattled the plates unnecessarily

152

loudly as she fetched them from the dresser to put on the kitchen table. "That's a terrible idea, Maisie. Abigail needs to forget about her past, and you turning up unannounced will spoil everything. Don't you think she deserves a better life with the opportunity to be raised by a wealthy couple, where she will want for nothing?"

Maisie was choked with emotion. *What if Aunt Edith is right? Didn't I always say I wanted the best for Abigail?* Guilt, anger, and sorrow competed confusingly in her thoughts as Edith watched her like a hawk. "Of course I want the best for my sister, but not at the expense of cutting her off from her real family. Ma wanted us to stick together, and one way or another, I would have found a way to set up my own dressmaking business one day so Abigail would always be taken care of."

Josiah scratched his belly and sat down at the table with a grunt, looking expectantly at the frying pan. "Your aunt is right, Maisie. We're not going to tell you where she's gone because if you go gallivanting there, it will ruin her chances of a new, better life."

"What if she would rather live with me?" Maisie shot back stubbornly. She noticed a look of alarm in her uncle's eyes and knew that her comment had hit the mark. "All you're really worried about is that she will want to come home, and you'll have to give the money back. Isn't that right?"

Edith rushed to her side and gave her a sickly smile. "I don't know why you're thinking the worst of us all the time, dear. Haven't we always tried our hardest to give you both a good home?"

"Yes, but—"

"You and Abigail don't know how lucky you are," Edith said firmly, interrupting her. "When your ma died, you could have easily been split up, with you at the workhouse and her sent to the orphanage. We took you in and made you welcome...not that you've ever shown any gratitude." She shook her head and started buttering the bread with brisk efficiency.

Maisie brought the frying pan to the table and served the food, pushing the plate with the largest portion towards Josiah.

"It's not as if you won't hear from her again," he mumbled around his first mouthful. Bacon grease dribbled down his chin, and he wiped it away on the back of his hand. "'Tis just a storm in a teacup, all this."

Hope flared in Maisie's chest. "What do you mean? Can I visit her in the future? Are they going to bring her back here to see us again?"

"Well...not exactly." Josiah speared a crust of bread with his fork and dunked it in the runny yolk of his eggs before chewing it slowly. "The couple said they would send regular letters to let us know how Abigail is getting on. I thought it was very good of them, to be honest." He slurped his tea and smiled at her as if this would be the end of the matter.

"I still don't understand why you won't tell me their names." Maisie tried a different tack, hoping to glean some new morsel of information that she could use.

"They didn't tell us, that's why," Edith said defensively. Her cheeks turned a dull red.

"Why not?"

Josiah took another slurp of tea and shrugged as her fury grew at how nonchalant he was being about the whole thing.

"Haven't you ever heard the phrase 'don't look a gift horse in the mouth'?" He gestured vaguely at their surroundings. "For over twenty years, Edith and I have been scratching together the money to pay the rent on this place. This was my one and only chance to be able to buy it, and I know Lord Pickering and that snivelling Mr Drew had it in their minds that they didn't want me to stay on here. I had to accept the money to secure our future, and in return, Abigail will live a life of luxury."

Maisie saw her aunt and uncle exchange a glance across the table that was hard to read, but her gut was telling her there was more to this whole affair than they were letting on.

"It all happened so fast that we didn't want to press them for details of their names and where they live," Edith said airily. "The first time they came to the inn, they were perfectly charming, but I could tell they were sad that they couldn't have children of their own. I felt sorry for them, and when they gave Abigail the doll, and she warmed to them so easily, it was like a sign."

"The gentleman said he knew you from way back. He told us he was doing you a favour, and we're inclined to agree. It wasn't up to us to pry into the details of his name. Anyway, wealthy folk like them are as honest as the day is long, Maisie," Josiah added.

She frowned. "That's not what you say normally. What about when you accused Saul Drew that Lord Pickering was robbing you blind on the rent for this place? And that a wealthy toff like him should shove his money where—"

"That's different," Josiah said sharply, leaning back in his chair with a belligerent scowl.

"We'll have no more talk about this now, Maisie. We've done what we think is right for Abigail. The kindhearted family taking her in told us they would send a letter with the information you want, so you're making a fuss about nothing." Edith stood up abruptly, her chair scraping on the kitchen flag-

THE RUNAWAY SISTER

stones. "There's work to be done, and we don't want to hear another word about it. Is that clear?"

* * *

AN HOUR LATER, Maisie was on her hands and knees, scrubbing the taproom floor vigorously. She didn't care that her dress was wet or that her back ached. She had hardly slept a wink for the last two nights, and her mind raced with so many unanswered questions that she almost felt delirious.

"Good mornin' to you." Walter Grant hobbled in for his first pint of ale, carefully stepping over the wet suds to reach the bar. "You'll wear a hole in them floorboards if you're not careful, maid," he said with a chuckle. He perched on his usual barstool, happy to wait for Josiah to come out from the back to serve him.

"If I'm doing a job, I might as well do it properly," Maisie was not in the mood for conversation, and she scrubbed harder.

"You remind me of when my wife was about to have our first little 'un. I've never seen a woman scrubbing the floors like she did. The whole house was sparkling from top to bottom, and the day she finished was the day our Elijah was born." He grinned at Maisie and raised his eyebrows. "You ain't in the family way, are you? I've noticed that Jack Piper is sweet on you."

"No…of course not." The hairs on her arms stood up, and she shivered. Something about Walter's innocuous question made her thoughts shift uneasily as though she doubted herself. It felt like turning a kaleidoscope and seeing a familiar shape magically change into something completely different.

"Of course, I'm not in the family way," she muttered again under her breath. She picked up her brush and scrubbed the next section of the floor, but more slowly, as memories and images tumbled through her head. *The crest on the side of the carriage looked so familiar.* She cast her mind back to the people in the carriage. She hadn't seen them clearly, but she had glimpsed the man's silhouette against the sun as the coachman had driven past her. Did she know him? She wasn't sure, but the idea that perhaps she had met him in the past had taken root and refused to leave her. *Who are they?*

She sat back on her heels, feeling dazed, and closed her eyes. Immediately, new memories surfaced…

Pain ripping through her belly and the lusty cry of a newborn.

Seeing a baby in her arms looking up at her with a serious dark-eyed gaze and perfect rosebud lips.

Was it Abigail? She shook her head, and her eyes

snapped open again. "Nothing makes any sense." She scrambled to her feet and grabbed her shawl, throwing it over her shoulders.

"Oi!" Josiah roared as he came into the tap room and looked at the half-finished floor. "Where are you going? We'll be getting busy in a minute. Edith needs you to help in the kitchen."

"Not this time, Uncle Josiah," Maisie felt as though she might lose her mind if she didn't get answers, and she couldn't stay at the Jolly Sailor passively waiting for a letter to come. *A letter that will probably never come*, she finally admitted to herself. "I'm going out. I'm not sure how long I'll be." Her boots echoed on the floor as she strode towards the doorway, and she felt a grim sense of satisfaction at the way her uncle's mouth had gaped open in surprise at her defiance. She had been meek and biddable for too long. This was not what her ma would have wanted; she was sure of it.

CHAPTER 14

"This is a nice surprise." Ava Piper ushered her into Acorn Cottage, almost as though she had been expecting her. "Jack told me all about what's happened with Abigail. It must have come as a terrible shock."

Maisie felt the knot of tension in her chest loosen slightly, hearing the kindness and sympathy in Ava's voice. It was a welcome change from Edith's brusque dismissal of her feelings. "I feel as though I'm losing my mind. I haven't really slept since it happened, and I'm having very strange memories. Except they can't be memories because they make no sense. And they can't be dreams because they're happening when I'm awake." She smiled, hoping Jack's ma wouldn't be put off by her rambling explanation.

"Memories and dreams can seem strangely intertwined, but it's normal." Ava pulled out a chair at her kitchen table and gestured for Maisie to sit down. Without asking whether she wanted something to drink, she took down a jar from the shelf next to the small range and tipped a generous portion of the dried herbs and flowers it contained into a teapot. "We'll just let this steep for a few minutes, and then you must drink it. I'll give you some more to take home and drink this evening. It will soothe your worries and help you sleep."

The Pipers' tortoiseshell cat was stretched along the top of the wingback chair next to the fire, and it stood up and arched its back before jumping down and padding over to Maisie. She reached down and stroked its head and was rewarded by loud purring. There was something very comforting about the little cottage, and she always liked visiting Ava. The furniture was worn, but the well-thumbed books in the small bookcase reminded Maisie of when her pa was still alive and encouraged her to read. The dresser was crammed with all manner of curios from Ava's walks in the countryside. There was an old sheep's skull, bleached white from the sun, feathers from practically every bird she could think of, pinecones, pebbles, and more.

"I was hoping that you would call. Jack's worried about you." Ava poured the steeped tea into a cup and put it in front of Maisie. A fruity floral scent wafted up, making her feel more relaxed already.

"I can't get over how callous Aunt Edith and Uncle Josiah have been. To think that they've sent my sister away to live with strangers...for money. Ma always told me that she and Josiah didn't have much in common, but I never thought he would be so cruel. They know how close Abigail and I are."

"You are certainly very close," Ava agreed calmly. She looked out of the small cottage window to the fields beyond. "What are these memories that you've been having?"

The inside of the cottage was dark because the windows were small, and when Ava turned her milky gaze towards her, and the candles on the table flickered, Maisie had the strangest feeling that something momentous was about to happen in her life.

"I'm sure I recognised the crest on the side of the carriage. I expect Jack told you that it was outside the Jolly Sailor a few weeks ago. And Elsie Clatterbrook said it was the carriage she saw Abigail in." She leaned her elbows on the table and shook her head. "I've racked my brains to try and remember where I know it from, but it won't come to me."

"Is that everything?"

Maisie tapped the heel of her hand against her forehead and sighed, feeling frustrated at how elusive the memories were…if that's even what she could call them. "No. Walter asked me just before I came here whether I was in the family way. I wanted to tell him he was being ridiculous, but then I had a sudden thought…it's so silly, I can hardly bring myself to say it out loud…"

"But you must say it out loud," Ava said gently. She reached across the table to still Maisie's fretful hands. "Speak what's on your mind, child. You will feel better for it."

"I had a strong sense that I had a baby, but it can't be true. My mind is playing tricks on me just because I'm missing Abigail." Maisie waited for Ava to agree that it was a figment of her imagination, but the silence stretched between them. "It's not true, is it?"

Ava stood up and hobbled to the dresser, opening the top drawer. She rummaged through the contents and pulled out her deck of tarot cards, bringing them back to the table and sitting down again. "You're old enough to know the truth now, Maisie. Your ma swore me to secrecy, but she also put her trust in me to know when the time would be right to tell you."

"Tell me what?" Maisie's heart started to pound, and the blood roared in her ears.

"Before I explain, I want you to understand that your ma loved you very much. Everything she did was with the best intentions."

"I know," Maisie whispered. "I miss her terribly. She wouldn't have wanted Abigail to be sent away."

THE RUNAWAY SISTER

Ava patted Maisie's hand. "Abigail is not your sister, Maisie. She's your daughter."

"My...my...daughter?" Her voice cracked at the unfamiliar words on her tongue. "But...how?"

The cat wound itself sinuously around Maisie's ankles, and she stroked it absentmindedly, not wanting to take her eyes off Ava's face for a second.

"Not long before you became ill, a wealthy gentleman saw you down near the river. He befriended you...started courting you, I suppose, and he used to bring picnics for you to eat in his carriage. Your ma knew nothing of this at the time, but you gradually told her about it during your feverish bouts. This gentleman declared he was in love with you and promised marriage and a better life."

"Who is this...gentleman?" Maisie shivered as snatches of hazy memories started to come back to her.

"Your ma never found out. Either he didn't give you his name, or you forgot it." Ava sipped her tea, gathering her thoughts. "He took advantage of you, Maisie. By the time Violet realised you were in the family way, you were already unwell, and he had long since vanished. She helped you have the babies all by herself. But you had amnesia for many months from your fever. That's why you didn't remember anything about expecting or your confinement."

165

"Babies?" Maisie's thoughts were spinning out of control again. "Two?"

Ava gave a small nod. "You had twins. Sadly, only Abigail, the first baby, survived. Violet told me that by chance, the gravedigger was passing your cottage just as the second baby was born. He took it and must have given it a pauper's burial. Poor Violet was so worried she might lose you and Abigail as well that she trusted him to take care of it and never spoke of the other baby again."

Maisie blinked back tears. "How could I have forgotten all of this?" She glanced down at her stomach as though expecting to see some evidence that she was a mother, but her waist was slim and lithe. "I still don't understand. Why did Ma pretend that Abigail was hers?"

Ava cleared her throat, sounding slightly awkward for the first time in their conversation. "You know how proud your mother was and how much she cared about what people thought of her."

"Yes. She hated hearing gossip."

"She was worried that the villagers would be scandalised that a wealthy gentleman had taken advantage of you and then discarded you like a common woman of the night. It's not that she was ashamed of what happened. Your parents raised you to think the best of people, and you trusted that man to behave honourably. But you know what folk can

THE RUNAWAY SISTER

be like." She gave Maisie a kind smile. "I'm past caring about that sort of thing myself, but Violet didn't want the villagers whispering bad things about you. She kept thinking you would start to remember, but the fever seemed to have blocked your mind to everything that happened."

"It's so strange. I sometimes had dreams of seeing a man standing on the riverbank, but I always believed they were just that. Dreams."

"Your ma decided it was simpler to claim that Abigail was her daughter. She rarely left the cottage after Robert died, and you were bedbound with the fever, so nobody was any the wiser. She confided in me not long after Abigail was born, and the only other person who knows the truth of this is the gravedigger who took the other poor little 'un away to be buried."

Maisie's eyes blurred with tears again as she digested this news, and she wrapped her hands around the cup of herbal tea, drawing comfort from its warmth. Everything was starting to make more sense. It explained why she and Abigail were so close and why losing her to complete strangers felt like having her heart ripped out of her chest. "Do you...do you know where the other baby was buried? I would like to pay my respects and perhaps speak to Mr Garrett to thank him for taking care of the burial."

Ava shook her head. "Mr Garrett only came to Frampton when you were poorly if you remember?"

Maisie cast her mind back, but her thoughts were still confused.

"It would have been Bill Scott who buried the baby, but he and his wife moved away from the village not long after it happened. I never saw him to ask, I'm afraid. By the time Violet confided in me, they had already left."

Tears rolled down Maisie's cheek, and she dashed them away, taking a shaky breath. "I can't do anything about the baby I lost, but I can do something about Abigail. I won't let strangers have her, Ava. That...gentleman...might think he can claim Abigail for himself. If it is her papa who has taken her, why now? I meant nothing to him, so I want to get my daughter back."

Ava's wrinkled brown face split into a smile, and her eyes brightened. "That's it, Maisie. Use that fire in your belly to do what's right. Can you think of anything more about this man now that you know the truth?"

Maisie screwed her eyes shut, putting every ounce of energy into trying to claw back the memories which had slipped away from her while she had been ill. "I can't...it's all so muddled in my mind as if I don't know what's real and what's made up anymore." She jumped up, unable to sit still for a moment longer,

THE RUNAWAY SISTER

and the cat shot across the room in alarm as she started pacing back and forth. "I think he was tall with brown hair and well-spoken."

"That's a start. What else? Did he ever tell you where he lives?"

"I remember him talking about his papa." She stopped in the middle of the room and clasped her hands together, willing more details to come back to her. "There was...a mill. That's it! He spoke about his papa owning one of the mills in Nailsbridge, I'm sure of it. And he said he sometimes drank at a pub in Thruppley village." Excitement started to bubble up in her chest, even though the names meant very little to her.

"Nailsbridge and Thruppley?" Ava beamed at her. "Those villages aren't too far from here, Maisie. We'll send Jack up there for the day, and he can make some enquiries for you. We have to be discreet. A man as wealthy as him won't take kindly to you challenging his authority."

"I can't be completely sure it's the same man who took advantage of me, who has stolen Abigail. But if I can just find him...find him and Abigail, I'll be able to know for sure." She felt overwhelmed by the task ahead but determined to do something. "I'm just an impoverished young woman. What if he won't listen to me, even if I do discover where they are?"

"All you can do is try your best." Ava picked up

her tarot cards and took several long, slow breaths. "Will you let me read the cards for you, my dear? Choose three, and let me see what they reveal. We need to consult a higher wisdom from the ancients who came before us...the crones who knew that there is no bond greater than that of a mother and child." She spread them out on the table and nodded.

Time seemed to stand still as Maisie's fingers hovered over the cards. She touched three of them with the tip of her finger, and Ava pulled them towards her, nodding calmly. The old woman gazed at the cards intently, then closed her eyes, and her head drooped slightly.

"Fire...water...and light," she sighed. "I see flames...a fire against the night sky devouring everything in its way and starting a chain of events of great significance to people you will become close to... family of yours..."

The clock ticked quietly, and Maisie wondered if that was all Ava was going to say. "I don't have any other family—"

Ava's hand twitched, and she shook her head. "A tall ship... a dark-haired man is travelling across the ocean. He believes he is the master of his destiny, but forces will conspire to make him angry. He is a dangerous man...whoever he is." Her eyelids flickered as if she was dreaming, then she smiled. "And lastly, I see light. The sun is catching something that will set you on a different path. Hard choices await you, but when you trust yourself, you will do what's right."

Ava's eyes slowly opened again, and she gathered up the cards again, suddenly business-like. "Take of that what you will, Maisie. I cannot explain the meaning of what is shown to me, but you will understand it when you need to."

"Thank you." Maisie politely finished her tea as Ava hobbled back to the dresser. None of what Ava had just told her made much sense, but she felt calmer, and she wondered whether that was the aim of the readings. "I'm going to tell Aunt Edith that I want to find Abigail. I'll do whatever it takes to earn the money to get her back again, but I can't stay at the Jolly Sailor and accept what's happened. It's time for me to face up to my past."

"This is the only clue your ma had about the gentleman who is Abigail's pa." Ava brought something back from the dresser and put it on the table.

"A hip flask." Maisie picked up the slim silver flask and turned it over. "I remember this," she exclaimed when she saw the intricate etching of a horse on the back. "He told me the brandy was medicinal and would stop me feeling the cold when I was mudlarking." She shook it, but it was empty.

"You must have brought it back with you after one of your meetings. Your ma asked me to give it to you when we had this conversation. Also, I want you to have this." She pulled a smooth piece of wood, no bigger than a button, out of her pocket and pressed it into Maisie's hand. "It's carved with a celtic knot that symbolises love and unity, and t'will bring you luck."

Maisie stood up and put them in her apron pocket. "Thank you. There's no time to lose. I need to make a plan and think about how I'm going to make my way to Nailsbridge. I can't just leave it to Jack, Ava. I hope you understand. This is my mystery to solve."

"I thought you'd say that." Ava gave her usual wheezy chuckle and nodded. "You'm high-spirited, girl. Which you'll need to be if you're going to get Abigail back."

CHAPTER 15

"I could get used to being a rag-and-bone man if only there was enough work for both of us." Fred grinned at Jack as their cart rumbled over the cobbles into the courtyard of the Jolly Sailor. The sun was already hot even though it wasn't yet mid-morning, and he was helping Jack on his rounds because the tide had been too high to start mudlarking at daybreak. He cocked his head and winced as the sound of a woman shouting disturbed the tranquil morning. "Sounds like Edith Snape is in a right old tizzy."

"I reckon so." Jack felt a ripple of worry. Ava had told them all about Maisie's visit to the cottage the day before and how determined she was to go and find Abigail. He had wanted to rush straight around to the inn once Ava explained that Abigail was actually Maisie's daughter, but his granny had shaken her head.

"'Twas a lot for her to take in," she had said in her usual calm tone. "I said that you would help her try and find this gentleman who took advantage of her, but I think she needs an evening to herself to sort everything out in her mind."

"...get back into the kitchen...you...you ungrateful...dollymop." Edith's shout was laced with anger. Jack knew she had a hot temper and had seen it plenty of times when she dragged drunkards out by the ear and sent them sprawling onto the ground with help from a well-placed boot on their backsides, but this sounded different. More spiteful and desperate.

"Did she just call Maisie a street girl?" Fred looked shocked. "That's what Elsie and Caroline whispered about Ma working at the docks...but Maisie?"

"Stay here and look after Duke. I'm going in to make sure she's alright." He leapt from the cart, hoping he hadn't made a mistake by not coming the night before.

Before he could even get through the door, he was almost knocked over by Edith, who was backing out, brandishing a broom in front of her. "I won't let you leave the Jolly Sailor, Maisie," she shrieked. "I'll put this broom across the door to stop you if I have to. After everything we've done for you, I've never known such an ungrateful wretch. Your uncle needs you to serve drinks, and how do you expect me to manage everything in the kitchen on my own?"

"You can't stop her from leaving," Jack said firmly.

Edith wheeled around to face him, her cheeks quivering with outrage. "Jack Piper, I should have known you and your interfering grandmother would be behind this." Her lip curled with contempt. "Ava is as mad as a March Hare, the witchy old crone. Get out of my way and let me deal with my niece the way it should have been done from the start. I was too soft on her, and she's got above herself."

Badger barked and darted at the broom, making Edith angrier still.

"I'd call him off you, but he doesn't take kindly to people insulting our family," Jack said, shrugging.

"Get off me, you mangy creature." She swung the broom, and Badger bit the bristles, thinking it was an exciting game.

While Edith was chastising Jack, Maisie appeared in the doorway. She was carrying her carpet bag, and her eyes glinted with determination. "I don't belong to you, Edith. I'm old enough to make my own decisions now, and Abigail needs me. I promised Ma I would look after her, and I don't want to go back on my word."

"If you leave now, that's it," Edith snapped. "You won't be able to come crawling back here when you find out that Abigail is happy in her new life and better off without you. We won't take you back again, Maisie. If you walk away, you're on your own forever, and good riddance."

Maisie tossed her head and marched towards Fred and the cart. "If that's your wish, Aunt Edith, so be it. I'll make my own luck. Even if it takes me a week to walk to Nailsbridge, I'm going to find the man who took Abigail and give her the chance to live with me again. We'll stick together with or without your blessing."

For a moment, Jack wondered if Edith was going to run after Maisie and try and drag her back into the Jolly Sailor.

"Let her go," Josiah called from inside the taproom, sounding defeated. "My sister, Violet, could never be told what was best for her, and it seems that Maisie is just as foolish."

Edith glowered at Badger, who was sniffing some grass and slammed her broom on the ground in frustration before turning her back on them, muttering under her breath. "Don't think we're going to give back the money we were paid for Abigail," she said in one final parting shot over her shoulder. "We deserve every shilling and more. If you want her back, you'll have to find the money to give him, and it was a tidy sum, I'm warning you."

"That's not very nice, Mrs Snape." Jack's words

THE RUNAWAY SISTER

fell on deaf ears as the taproom door slammed shut in his face hard enough to make the windows rattle.

"Don't try and reason with her," Maisie said wearily. "I've been trying for most of the night, but there's no point." She shrugged and dropped her carpet bag at her feet. "I suppose Ava told you about the man who took advantage of me? Edith is convinced I'm a fallen woman and should count myself lucky that they will still let me carry on working like a skivvy for them."

Jack felt indignation coursing through his veins. "You're not a fallen woman, Maisie. And our ma wasn't either. It's easy enough for busybodies like Edith and Mrs Clatterbrook to pass judgement, but they haven't faced the sort of challenges you have. I won't let people slander your good name."

Fred jumped down from the cart and grabbed Maisie's carpet bag, swinging it into the back. "You're one of us now, Maisie. The villagers might think they can look down their noses at you, but we'll show them," he said stoutly. "We'll look after you, won't we, Jack."

Jack's heart went out to their friend as she sniffed, doing her best not to cry. "Of course we will," he agreed, giving her a warm smile. "I need to finish doing my rounds, and then I'm all yours, Maisie. We'll come up with a plan to try and find out more about this toff who's taken Abigail. You don't need to do this alone; we are your friends, remember, and friends stick together."

"Stop being so kind to me, or you'll make me cry properly," Maisie gave them both a watery smile and then blew her nose. "What are you both doing here, anyway? Shouldn't you be down at the river digging for buried treasures, Fred?"

He chuckled at the joke. "Seeing as you're going to be leaving Frampton soon, why don't you come mudlarking with me today, just for one last time."

"I haven't been on the mud since coming to the Jolly Sailor. And what about my gown? I'm not really dressed for it."

Fred clasped his hands together and adopted a wounded air. "Please," he wheedled. "How can you say no when I've asked so nicely? Tell her, Jack. You know she brings us good luck, and I ain't had a good find for ages."

"What about that guinea coin? And the earrings?" Maisie nudged him good-naturedly, and Jack could tell she had missed Fred's company being stuck behind the bar all the time. The colour was returning to her cheeks, and the breeze lifted the curls at the nape of her neck.

"Have you got any money to see you through your first couple of nights at Nailsbridge and Thruppley?" Jack climbed onto the cart seat after them, and Duke shook his mane and whinnied, eager to get going.

THE RUNAWAY SISTER

"Giddup," he called. Badger darted after them as Duke took up the strain in his harness, and the cart rolled forward.

"Not much," Maisie admitted. "Edith made me hand over most of what I earned from my dressmaking. I thought I would try and find work as soon as I arrived." She sounded doubtful all of a sudden.

"You have some spare time while I finish my round today."

"Go on, Maisie," Fred pleaded. "You'll enjoy it."

"Oh, alright, for old time's sake." Maisie shook her head and laughed. "You always could get round me, Fred Piper. And your brother, too." Her eyes sparkled with amusement, and Jack's heart lifted at the thought of helping her. He would enjoy the time with her, even though their quest might be fraught with all sorts of obstacles and dead ends.

* * *

THE SILKY MUD oozed up between Maisie's toes, and she turned her face to the sun, trying not to panic about her impulsive departure from the relative security of the Jolly Sailor. She had no idea whether she was leaving forever or if she would come back to Frampton. But more importantly, she had no idea whether it would be with Abigail. Even though she had a few crumbs of information to go on now, she knew the odds were stacked against her. Her pa had made sure she received a better education than many children in her situation, but she was no match for a wealthy man with money and influence.

"Don't just stand there, gawking," Fred shouted, snapping her out of her reverie.

"It's just like old times, hearing you say that," Maisie laughed. She tucked her skirts up and picked her way across the mud, doing it more to humour Fred than anything. Jack had told them he wouldn't be gone for long, and the chance of finding anything worth more than a few bob was slim.

"Put your back into it," Fred shouted again. He was digging like a terrier after a juicy bone, and Maisie put her worries out of her mind. Perhaps, just for once, luck would be on her side.

Two hours later, all she had for her efforts was a couple of buttons and an old saucer with a chip on one side. They would barely sell for enough to buy a loaf of bread, she thought, with a rueful smile. The sun was high in the sky, and even out on the mud flats, it felt too hot. Sweat prickled on her back, and worry was starting to gnaw at her again. *What if I don't find work? How will I survive?*

A plover scurried ahead of her in the mud, pausing every so often to peck at something, and she watched its progress. It would be strange moving away from the wide river that had provided the back-

THE RUNAWAY SISTER

drop of her entire life so far, but there was no point dwelling on the past. She had to look to the future and a new beginning, especially after Edith's angry tirade. Two more plovers flew down to join the one she was watching, and her eyes were drawn to the area where they were feeding. There was something in the mud which she hadn't noticed earlier. It was barely the size of a small pebble, but it was worth further investigation. She hurried over, mindful of the fact that Jack would be back any minute.

"Found anything good yet?" Fred's voice drifted towards her. "I'm going to search for a bit longer, but it ain't looking promising."

Maisie lifted her hand to wave at him. "Nothing much, though I have just spotted something." She plucked the item from its muddy resting place, took it to the nearest pool of brackish water, and swished it around to clean it, not holding out much hope.

Straightening up again, her heart skipped a beat as she stared at the small brooch in her palm. The sun glinted on the stones, making her breath catch in her throat. It looked like a cluster of rubies and diamonds, and she started to tremble. "Is this it," she muttered, "something valuable at last?" It was impossible to tell whether it was real or just costume jewellery, but either way, it was by far the best thing she had ever found in all her years of mudlarking. She tucked it safely inside her dress, suddenly terri-

DAISY CARTER

fied that she might drop it and it would be sucked back into the mud and lost forever.

"Fred! You won't believe it!" She slithered back across the mud as fast as she could, but Fred hadn't heard her. He was on his knees, looking intently at something in his hand.

Before she had a chance to reach him, Duke came trotting along the riverbank with the cart, and Jack waved his cap at them. "I finished earlier than I thought. Florence had a good haul of rags for me, so I've got enough for the day."

Maisie ignored the tiny pang of jealousy she felt, hearing that he had been to Mr Fisher's house. As far as she knew, Mr Fisher's housemaid still wasn't courting anybody, but if Jack was sweet on Florence, she would just have to accept it. *And get over my secret hope that one day, he might see me as more than just a friend.* She huffed with annoyance at herself, determined not to let matters of the heart spoil her exciting find.

"I told you, Maisie brought me luck, didn't I?" Fred squawked. "Wait 'til you see what I just found, Jack." He squelched through the mud, beaming at them both.

"You found something, too?" Maisie asked.

"What have you got, Fred?" Jack hopped down and strolled along the rutted track while Duke took the chance to graze on some tasty tufts of grass.

THE RUNAWAY SISTER

"It looks like some pearl earrings and a gold bracelet." He grinned as he opened his hands to reveal them like a magician

Jack gave a low whistle. "Our lucky day indeed!" He slapped Fred's shoulder. "Well spotted."

"And look at this," Maisie cried. She turned away slightly as she retrieved the brooch from inside her bodice and then held it out for them both to see. It sparkled in her hand, and Fred's mouth gaped open in comical surprise.

"Diamonds and rubies...well, I'll be jiggered—" He was practically lost for words.

"I don't want to get my hopes up. It might just be costume jewellery, but it must still be worth a few guineas, surely?" Maisie held the brooch up against the sun, and the stones had a depth of colour that she had never seen before.

Jack raked a hand through his hair before glancing over his shoulder to make sure that nobody was watching them. "Do you know what, I think these might be the real thing. We can't risk taking them to the pawnbroker in Frampton because they must have been stolen."

Maisie's excitement evaporated. "I suppose we should take them to the constable and hand them back."

"I ain't doing that! Finder's keepers, Maisie, you know how mudlarking works." Fred sounded indignant. "What about taking them to Nailsbridge or Thruppley?" He bit the gold bracelet and nodded. "I reckon this is the real thing, Jack. And the earrings look like proper pearls. You should get a good price for them."

Jack looked torn. "I suppose they could have been stolen years ago." He sighed. "Lord Pickering is putting the rent up, and we really need the money."

"In that case, Fred's right. Finder's keepers." Maisie needed money as well, but she was terrified of being accused of theft.

"Fred is right, Maisie. We must take these somewhere better than just our little pawnbroker in Frampton. I was thinking as well, that there is a new rag merchant in Nailsbridge. I've been meaning to take my rags up there to see if I can get a better price than the local fellow who is always trying to underpay me. Why don't we go this afternoon?"

Maisie nodded eagerly. "As long as Ava won't mind you being away for a little while? I've been worried about not knowing anyone while I'm looking for Abigail, but perhaps the rag merchant could suggest a boarding house which is suitable for single ladies." She turned the brooch over in her palm and then tucked it back into her bodice. "Are you sure I should take this to the pawnbroker? Perhaps I should hang onto it for a little while. I don't know

THE RUNAWAY SISTER

how much money I might need to try and pay off the man who took Abigail."

Jack rubbed his hand over his jaw, thinking. "It wouldn't harm to find out its value, and then you could decide what to do after that."

"I don't suppose I can come with you?" Fred asked hopefully.

"You need to stay here and look after Granny." Jack threw his arm over Fred's shoulder and gave him an affectionate thump. "Don't worry, little brother. If anyone asks, I'll make sure they know it was you who changed the Piper family fortunes."

Fred grinned. "Are you sure you want to spend the next few days in Jack's company?" he asked Maisie with a chuckle. "He can be very annoying, but I suppose you already know that."

As Maisie settled herself in the cart with Jack on one side and Fred on the other, she felt more hopeful than she had for days. Finding the brooch had changed everything. If she could get a decent sum of money for it, she wouldn't have to beg the man to give up Abigail out of the kindness of his heart. *What am I thinking? I already know there's no kindness in his heart.*

God willing, the brooch would be real, and she would have enough money to give him in exchange for her daughter. The thought that he might not want to give Abigail up flitted through her mind, but she quickly pushed it away. She couldn't allow herself to think that Abigail might be lost to her forever. She had to find a way to get her daughter back, and she would do whatever it took.

A sudden thought came to her. "Ava read my cards yesterday. She said she saw the sun and something bright...that it would set me on a new path."

"The cards are never wrong," Jack said softly. "It must have been the brooch."

His brown eyes crinkled at the edge when he smiled at her, and Maisie wished they could be together always, not just for the next few days.

CHAPTER 16

"Yer fancy man is at the door," Mrs Venn called up the stairs. "We don't usually get men calling at this time of the morning unless they're delivering something."

Maisie blushed as she emerged from her room onto the top landing, pulling a face as two other ladies smirked. "He's not my fancy man," she said hastily. "He's a good friend, that's all."

Vera Venn, proprietor of The Lilacs guesthouse in Thruppley, gave a good-natured chuckle as she waited for Maisie to come downstairs. "Call him what you will, Miss Griffin, as long as there's no funny business. I don't run that kind of establishment, as I told you on the first night you arrived." She laughed again and patted Maisie's shoulder. "I'm just larking around with you, ducky. I can tell you're not

DAISY CARTER

a woman of loose morals, otherwise, I wouldn't have let you rent a room here. And your fellow is waiting very politely outside, although I'm not so sure about that hairy ol' horse of his. The drayman will complain if he blocks the lane."

Maisie checked herself in the mirror hanging next to the hat stand and patted her hair, tucking a strand back in place. She didn't like to think what Mrs Venn might say if she knew the truth. Jack had suggested she should claim to be looking for a long-lost family friend with a young child if anyone asked. She wasn't sure whether they would believe that a woman of her low social standing might know anyone so grand, but it was the best excuse they could come up with.

"Is your room comfortable?" Mrs Venn asked. "I'm sorry it's on the small side, but you did ask for the cheapest one. Are you sure you don't want some breakfast?"

"The room is perfect, thank you." Maisie had spent three nights at The Lilacs already and wondered how much longer she would be able to afford to stay if she didn't find work soon. The smell of fresh bread and bacon wafted from the kitchen, and her mouth watered. But as hungry as she was, she would have to resist. "No breakfast for me, thank you. I'm not really hungry." She could see Jack's shadow through the front door and quickly put her shawl on.

188

"Going for another stroll around the village, are you?" Vera and Maisie stepped aside as a plump, matronly woman squeezed past them on her way out of the modest dining room. The guesthouse was clean and comfortable, several steps up from common lodgings, as Jack had insisted he didn't want Maisie staying anywhere rough. She hoped she might befriend some of the other women staying there, but not while her mind was still full of worries about Abigail. Her heart ached more for her daughter with each day that passed.

"I'm hoping that my friend, Mr Piper, has brought good news about the pawnbroker," Maisie said. "And I'll be looking for work as well in the next few days. If you know of anything suitable, I'd be very grateful if you could tell me."

Vera pulled an old rag out of her apron pocket and started applying beeswax polish to the mahogany sideboard in a methodical fashion. She prided herself on not letting a speck of dust escape her and was quick to tell new guests that she had never once had bedbugs in her establishment in the twenty years she had run it.

"I'll have a think, dear. I'd offer you work myself, but I only recently took on Judy in the kitchen to help me out...although Lord knows, she's a clumsy girl. Dropped two teacups already, and then we had floods of tears for the rest of the day." She lifted up a candlestick and buffed underneath it vigorously. "It's not her fault though, poor mite. They were quick to find fault at the orphanage, and she's still terrified I'll boot her out onto the street if she makes a mistake. As if I'd do such a thing."

Maisie's heart warmed to her landlady. Even though she had a brusque way with words, she was kind to those less fortunate. "If only everyone treated their workers so well." She grimaced as Aunt Edith's spiteful words came back to her. "Anyway, I expect Jack might have news of the pawnbroker. His younger brother is a mudlark, and he has a few things to sell."

"Don't hold yer breath. Henry Nelson is a terrible malingerer. I swear that man has more ailments than anyone in the whole village." She shook her head, and her mob cap wobbled precariously above her wispy grey bun. "When Mr Venn was still alive, he said it was because Henry made so much money in his pawnbroker's shop that he didn't need to work seven days a week like most of us."

"Hopefully, his cold is getting better."

"Cold…my foot! More like too much ale at The Black Lion on Friday evening." She tutted and then grinned. "Tell him Mrs Venn says he needs to get his scrawny backside back behind the counter and start serving the villagers again. Where else are the poor folk supposed to raise a penny or two for food when times are hard?"

Maisie was struck by the realisation that she wouldn't want to get on the wrong side of Vera, but she might be a good ally to help her get to know more people in the village. She and Jack had been disappointed to see the pawnbroker's shop dark, with no sign of life inside, when they arrived in Thruppley three days earlier. A snotty-nosed urchin sitting on the doorstep had told them forlornly that Mr Nelson was sick in bed with a stinking cold and wouldn't come down even if they were desperate. "Well, I'd better be on my way," Maisie said. Vera could talk the hind leg off a donkey once she got started, and she didn't want to keep Jack waiting.

"Alright, my dear. You'll be joining us for dinner tonight, will you?"

"Yes, please." She had budgeted for one hot dinner a day and tried not to think about how long it would be until the evening meal. "I'm already looking forward to it."

"Perhaps you could run an errand for me, and I can knock the price of your dinner off this week's rent." Vera gave her a kind smile, knowing full well that Maisie didn't have much money. "It's market day today, and I need apples, carrots, and potatoes. If you go to William Bagley's stall and tell him it's for me, he'll probably give you some roses to bring back as well." Her plump cheeks flushed slightly, and her eyes twinkled. "He's sweet on me. I'm not in any hurry to get married again, but we have an understanding." She sighed wistfully. "He's a kindhearted man, though, and good company."

Now, it was Maisie's turn to chuckle. "A fancy man, you mean?" She raised her eyebrows and took the wicker basket her landlady was handing her.

"Get away with you." Vera shooed her away with her duster. "You'll set tongues wagging if you call him that."

"BAD NEWS, I'M AFRAID," Jack said as Maisie joined him outside. "The pawnbroker's shop is still closed. I tried knocking him up, but it's like trying to raise the dead."

"I know, Vera was just telling me that it happens quite often."

They went to stand next to Duke, and Maisie patted his neck, feeling a surge of affection for the scruffy horse, who was so loyal to Jack. His whiskery muzzle tickled her palm as she slipped him some apple peelings, which Judy had saved for her.

Jack sighed and looked up and down the lane. "The thing is, Maisie, I'm sorry, but I don't know how much longer—"

Maisie rested her hand on Jack's arm to stop him.

THE RUNAWAY SISTER

"You don't need to apologise. You've done more than enough bringing me here to Thruppley and sleeping in your cart these last three nights to help me try and search for this wretched man."

"I hoped we would have made more progress by now."

She smiled up at him, wishing she didn't have to say the next words because she would miss him. "You need to get back to Frampton, Jack. I know Fred is a sensible lad, but your granny needs you, especially if Lord Pickering is putting your rent up for Acorn Cottage. You have to get back to work otherwise, people might give their rags to someone else." She kept her voice light even though she wished he could stay. "I have to stand on my own two feet if I'm going to keep the promise I made to myself to find Abigail."

"I don't like to leave you here alone. Are you sure you're going to be alright?"

His brown eyes were serious as he held her gaze, and Maisie's heart pitter-pattered in her chest. She had a sudden longing to be swept into his arms...to rest her head on his shoulder, and know that everything would work out...

"Of course." She cleared her throat, hoping that her face hadn't given away her innermost thoughts. "Thruppley's not so far from Frampton. Who knows, perhaps I'll get some money for the brooch, find Abigail in the next couple of days, and everything

DAISY CARTER

will be resolved." She lifted her chin, determined not to cry.

"I really do hope so. If anyone can do this, it's you. Abigail is lucky to have you as a ma." Duke swished his tail and fidgeted in the harness. "I've decided I'll go back to Frampton for a few days, and as soon as I have enough rags to make it worthwhile, I'll come back again. The merchant here gave me a better price, and hopefully, by then, Mr Nelson's shop will be open, and we can find out what your brooch is worth, and I can sell those pieces that Fred found."

"Thank you again for everything, Jack. Don't feel that you have to rush back if it's too difficult. Ava needs you, and your life is in Frampton."

"You're right, although…" Jack's words petered out, and his expression was difficult to read.

Maisie found herself wondering what it would be like to be kissed by him.

"Oi! Are you dawdling in this lane all day?" A shout interrupted her daydreams.

"How am I supposed to take my plough to be mended at yon forge with you blocking the way? Our Buttercup will need to be milked 'afore long. I don't 'ave all day." A ruddy-cheeked farmer with a rickety cart glared impatiently at them, and Jack shot him an apologetic smile.

"Sorry, mister. I'm going now." He hopped up on the wooden seat and took up the reins. "Don't do anything dangerous, Maisie. Remember, I'll be back in less than a week, I expect, so just find out what you can, but don't take any risks. This gentleman we're looking for would make a powerful enemy."

"Give Ava my love." Maisie fluttered her handkerchief and waved goodbye, feeling a pang of loneliness as she watched Duke trot away. Jack was her last connection with Frampton, and now she was all alone.

"Don't worry, maid," the farmer called cheerfully as he followed along behind Jack. "Your sweetheart will be back 'afore you know it."

"He's not my—" Maisie shook her head and chuckled. Everyone seemed determined to think that she and Jack were courting. *Perhaps it would be simpler just to let them believe it.* She allowed herself one delicious moment to imagine that it was true before smiling to herself at the absurdity of it. "He's just my friend," she called to the farmer's retreating back.

"Arr, per'aps." He winked over his shoulder. "Although you do make an 'andsome couple," he said in a thick country burr.

She blushed, glad that Jack hadn't overheard their exchange. It would have been too embarrassing if he'd felt the need to proclaim there and then that his heart lay with Florence Porter.

CHAPTER 17

Her spirits lifted as she wandered through the lanes that wound between the honey-coloured cottages of Thruppley. It was a perfect summer's day. Not too hot, and there was a pleasant breeze that rustled the leaves and set the flowers nodding in the cottage gardens she passed. She was already starting to recognise a few of the maids who bustled through the streets going about their errands, as well as several of the costermongers, pushing their handcarts from house to house, selling their wares.

Thruppley was a larger village than Frampton, with a river that meandered through one part before winding through the water meadows nearby. In the distance, the mill chimneys belched out smoke, and she occasionally heard the shouts and loud laughter of the folk who lived on their narrowboats on the nearby canal. The western edge of the village was flanked by rolling hills and common land, grazed by sheep and cattle that roamed freely, with steep hidden valleys in between. Even though Maisie was more used to the wide open skies over the marshland of the river Severn, there was something comforting about the way that Thruppley was cradled by the hills. She could imagine smoke curling up from the cottage chimneys in the winter and crunching through the snow in the narrow lanes with children throwing snowballs. Her heart suddenly contracted with a fierce pang of longing for Abigail, and tears pricked the back of her eyes.

No...I won't think like that. Thruppley is a nice place for Abigail and me to make a new home She'll love it, and we'll have a good life. She sniffed and walked faster. She couldn't give in to despair.

She decided to go straight to the market and buy the vegetables Vera needed before making any more enquiries about Abigail or the mysterious gentleman.

Just as Vera had predicted, William Bagley was generous with his portions when he knew that Maisie was shopping on Vera's behalf. "Tell her to try these pears," he said, popping a handful on top of the potatoes and carrots. "They're fresh from the orchards down Eastcombe way. Perfect for a fruit tart or crumble with them apples I've just given you."

THE RUNAWAY SISTER

Maisie nodded her thanks. "Perhaps I should suggest you might like to try whatever Vera makes with them," she said mischievously. His eyes lit up. "It seems only right if you're giving me the extra fruit, don't you think?"

"Well, I wouldn't say no." His hands were lined with soil from digging up potatoes, and he brushed them down the front of his old smock and straightened his spotted neckerchief. "I do scrub up quite well, even though Vera tells me she ain't interested in walking out with anyone again."

"Don't give up, Mr Bagley." Maisie picked up her basket. "Love might flourish when you least expect it, and I have a feeling she has a soft spot for you."

"Really?" He lifted his cap and smoothed a hand over his hair, which was threaded with grey, looking suddenly hopeful. "I've been asking her to walk out with me these last five years, so perhaps there's hope for us yet." He shook his head in astonishment.

"I'll make sure to tell her you gave her the best pears on your stall."

"Oh, and don't forget these." Mr Bagley quickly plucked some flower stems from a wooden bucket and wrapped a ribbon around them. "I always save the best for Vera," he added bashfully.

She laid them in her basket, taking care not to bruise the fragrant roses and lavender. Glancing around to make sure nobody was waiting to be

DAISY CARTER

served, she decided to risk a few questions. Mr Bagley seemed like the sort who would know if someone new had come to the village. "I don't suppose you've seen a well-to-do gentleman in these parts with a little girl? She's five years old and looks...similar to me. He's an old family friend who I'm trying to find for my late ma."

One of Mr Bagley's eyebrows twitched up with curiosity. "Don't you know his name?"

Maisie shrugged and hoped her blush wouldn't give the lie away. "That's the thing. Ma died before she could tell me. All I know is that he's well off, and his father owns one of the mills at Nailsbridge."

The old man's face brightened for a moment but then clouded with confusion. "I thought you were talking about Horace Smallwood then. His pa used to own one of the mills and lots of other places around here, too. But it can't be Master Horace because he doesn't have children." He scratched his head. "He got wed to Miss Shaw from the big house not long ago. I'm sure they don't have a little girl in the family."

Maisie swallowed her disappointment. For a second, she had thought she was onto something, but Jack was right. It wasn't going to be straightforward, no matter how much she might wish it was. Whoever she asked seemed to know nothing, and she was no closer to discovering where Abigail was. "Not to

THE RUNAWAY SISTER

worry," she said, hitching the basket into the crook of her elbow.

"I'll keep a lookout, miss. We get plenty of folks coming and going through Thruppley because of the canal. Perhaps you should ask at some of the taverns, but mind you go in the mornings before the men have had too much ale. Vera will give me a proper telling-off if you get into trouble on my say-so."

She handed over the money Vera had given her and went on her way. *Perhaps I'm looking in the wrong place altogether? Just because I remembered him mentioning Thruppley doesn't mean he's here anymore.* She sighed as the worries crowded into her mind once again.

The breeze rippled the surface of the river, and Maisie paused on her way back to the guesthouse to watch the swans gracefully gliding through the water from under the arches of the bridge. She tried not to think about the fact that the only person she could confide in would be halfway back to Frampton by now. Jack had promised he would be back soon, and she didn't doubt his word.

Several elegant couples from the Rodborough Hotel on the outskirts of the village strolled past her, and she wondered what it would be like to not have a care in the world like them. She didn't mind hard work, but part of her felt a germ of resentment that the scoundrel who had taken advantage of her innocence hadn't even bothered to make sure she had some degree of financial security. He had used her for his own pleasure and cast her aside, like so many poor women across the ages. She shivered in spite of the warmth of the sun. If it hadn't been for her ma's compassion, she could easily have ended up in the workhouse. She had that to be thankful for, and she squared her shoulders and carried on walking over the bridge to head back to The Lilacs. She would make the best of her situation. She would not let one man's selfishness ruin her life, she told herself.

Just ahead of her, another wealthy couple had stopped to look in one of the shop windows. It was a jewellery shop, and Maisie thought about the brooch she had hidden under the loose floorboard in the corner of her room for safekeeping. An idea came to her. Perhaps she could sell it outright to the jewellers instead of pawning it. Her pulse quickened as she got closer to the shop and saw an array of beautiful necklaces displayed on plump velvet cushions. The brooch would sit perfectly alongside such exquisite pieces. If she could persuade the jeweller to buy it, she would have more than enough money to exchange for Abigail, surely?

"...I like the necklace at the back best. The colour would go well with my new gown."

The couple's conversation drifted in her direction, and she listened curiously as she realised the woman had an accent. Maisie remembered the sailors who used to come into the inn occasionally, with their fast-talking twang and phrases she had never heard before. They had told her they were from New York, working on the ships which crossed the mighty ocean between their two great nations. The woman in front of her wore a sumptuous red silk gown and carried a matching parasol to keep the sun off her face. Her accent sounded more refined than the sailors', but there was no mistaking she was from America.

"Why, this village is absolutely charming, my darling. So quaint but far too parochial for my tastes. I declare I half expect to see a scarecrow walking down the street." The woman's voice was musical with amusement, and her gaze rested briefly on Maisie before she turned back to the man at her side, who was looking intently into the window of the jewellery shop.

"I'm not sure any of these baubles are good enough for you, Genevieve," the man said. He had his back to Maisie, but there was something familiar about his clipped tone, and she edged slightly closer. Should she ask them whether they knew who she was looking for? So far, she had only dared to ask the working-class people in the village. Perhaps that's where she had been going wrong, and she needed to ask the toffs who would be more likely to know the well-educated man who had snatched Abigail with such a sense of entitlement.

The woman gave a tinkling laugh and fluttered her eyelashes at him. "You are naughty, Dominic. I suppose you'll want to treat me to something much nicer when we get to Paris? I declare I can scarcely wait until we start our new life there. The high society folks will find us mighty intriguing, I'm sure of it. A wealthy Boston heiress and an upper-crust gentleman with a shady past." She laughed again, adjusting the beautiful choker at her throat, which winked in the sun as the jewels caught the light.

"It can't come soon enough," the man said. "I'm tired of all the stuffy traditions and expectations of this narrow-minded place. I would go to London, but it's not far enough. Paris will give us the new start we need, and we'll soon have them eating out of our hands. The French love nothing more than people with character...not like my boring family."

"Will you visit your papa and brother while we are here?" Genevieve pouted prettily, making several passers-by turn and stare appreciatively. She patted her glossy ringlets. "I'm not sure they'll approve of me being the new Mrs Smallwood, no matter how much money I have. I hear you aristocratic types can be sniffy about new money, even though my pa pulled himself up by his bootstraps to make his fortune."

THE RUNAWAY SISTER

The hairs on Maisie's arms stood up, and she stifled a gasp. *Did she just say Mrs Smallwood? The same Smallwoods who owned the mill in Nailsbridge?* Her heart started to thump, and she looked more closely at the man. His brown hair was swept back, and his elegant frock coat, cut in a style that she hadn't seen before, was probably worth more than she earned in a year.

"No, I don't see why I should bother. They turned their backs on me. I hoped that pompous solicitor, Mr Eckleton, might have been open to persuasion to pay off my debts, but it seems he is as dull-witted as the rest of my family, and I wasted my time visiting him." The man brushed an imaginary speck of dust off his shoulder and tucked Genevieve's hand into the crook of his arm. "It's time for us to go to Paris for a new start, my dear."

"Yes, mon chéri," Genevieve said, laughing. "Do you think they will call me Madame in Paris...Madame Dominic Smallwood?"

They turned round abruptly, and Maisie staggered backwards as she had her first clear look at the gentleman in front of her. The blood rang in her ears, and she felt giddy as she looked up into his familiar face with his hooded blue eyes and aquiline features.

"It's you," she gasped, "the man who promised me marriage and then left me in the family way."

The blood drained from Dominic's face, but he

205

DAISY CARTER

recovered in an instant. "I don't know what you're talking about," he said icily. His nose wrinkled up as though a vile odour was offending him, and he glanced at Genevieve, who was watching with curious fascination.

"You can't keep up this lie, Dominic. It's all coming back to me now." Maisie moved sideways to block their path.

"Don't tell me you had a dalliance with this serving girl," Genevieve drawled. "Really, Dominic, the sooner I get you away from this poky little place, the better. Lord knows who else will be making a false claim just to earn a few dollars...I mean... shillings." She laughed gaily, eyeing Maisie with careless disregard. "Can't you see my husband is a wealthy man? What would he see in a tramp like you?" she added, her American accent becoming more pronounced.

"I don't want money from you," Maisie cried. "I just want to know where Abigail is...our daughter." Tears filled her eyes, but she dashed them away. "It must be you who took her. Aunt Edith should never have agreed. Where are you hiding her?" She looked wildly around, not caring that people were starting to stare and whisper.

"Stop hurling accusations around, you little hussy." Genevieve's careless languor was replaced by outrage. "My husband is a powerful man, and you're a nobody."

Dominic stepped out into the cobbled street and waved his arm frantically. The coachman who had been waiting for them hastily whipped the horses into a prancing canter, and the gleaming carriage with the crest on the door that Maisie recognised from before pulled up alongside them. "Get in, Genevieve," Dominic urged. "Let me take care of this guttersnipe and her vile accusations." He bundled his wife into the carriage and spun round to face Maisie again.

"I can prove you're Abigail's pa." She lifted her chin defiantly, pleased to see a flicker of alarm in his eyes. "I have a silver hip flask which belonged to you—"

"And I shall just say you stole it," Dominic shot back. His dark eyes glittered with anger like shards of granite. "Who do you think people would believe?"

"Why did you steal Abigail from me?" Maisie threw him off kilter by changing track. "You never cared when I told you I was in the family way. All those promises of marriage meant nothing, did they."

Dominic strode forward and took hold of her arm, his powerful grip making her wince in pain. He pushed her back into the shadows and thrust his face closer. She could hardly believe that she had once found him handsome. Now, he just looked cruel and domineering. "I don't have the snivelling child anymore," he snarled. "Lord knows, Genevieve had the patience of a saint putting up with her whining for the two days she was with us."

"So...you did take her." Maisie's head started to spin. "Why? Why did you take my darling girl if you didn't want her."

"To pay off a debt, of course." Dominic shook his head as though she was a simpleton. "Did you honestly think my dear wife would want to bring up your brat when we have a charming life in France awaiting us?"

"I don't understand..." The words came out in a hoarse whisper.

"Shall we leave now, sir?" The coachman cast a scornful look in Maisie's direction as the highly-strung horses pranced on the spot.

Dominic's grip tightened on her arm. "Understand this, Maisie Griffin. You were nothing more than a pleasant diversion to me. And your wretched daughter has been given to a childless couple who will doubtless look after her far better than you ever could, to settle a debt I owed from the card tables." He sighed impatiently. "This infernal country and its insistence on doing the honourable thing."

"I have to know who you gave her to," she pleaded.

"Certainly not. You'll ruin everything. I shouldn't

even be here in Nailsbridge." He glanced over his shoulder, nodding curtly to the coachman, who took up the slack on the reins. "You'll never see her again, Maisie. I've done you a favour. You're free to live your life without a child holding you back."

"She's my daughter...I love her." Maisie glared at him. "I'll tell the constable...I'll tell everyone what you've done."

"Don't bother, my dear. Otherwise, I'll make sure it's you who's thrown in jail." Dominic's smile was cruelly cold. "Nobody cares about you, and I'll be long gone by the time anyone might listen to your delusional ramblings. Now I must go, and I suggest you don't bother trying to follow...or you'll regret it." With that, he suddenly released her arm, sending her staggering backwards.

The basket fell on the floor, and Dominic kicked the apples and pears out of the way as he jumped up into the carriage.

"Onward, driver!" He rapped on the roof, and the horses sprang forward, leaving Maisie flat on her back, watching dizzily in despair.

"Wait...wait!" she croaked. A wave of desolation engulfed her as her hopes of finding Abigail vanished with the callous man who held the information she craved.

CHAPTER 18

Maisie stared at the meagre pile of coins in her hand. She didn't have enough to pay for another night at The Lilacs guesthouse, and she hadn't managed to secure a new job. As for finding out where Abigail was, it felt as though she was on a wild goose chase. It was two days since her sickening encounter with Dominic, and although she had plucked up the courage to ask a few more people if they knew of a couple who had just adopted a little girl, nobody knew anything. She put her bonnet on and clattered down the stairs. She wasn't going to give up that easily. "Just one more try," she mumbled under her breath as she tied her shawl over her shoulders. "Please let my luck change today."

"Thruppence more by this evening if you want to stay longer, my dear." Mrs Venn's voice drifted out

DAISY CARTER

from the dining room where the other ladies were enjoying a hearty breakfast. "I had a couple of enquiries from new women looking for lodgings, but you're welcome to keep the room if you want."

Maisie poked her head through the door. "I'm hoping to find work today, so I'll pay you later if that's alright."

Her stomach rumbled as she started retracing her steps through Thruppley. So far, she had avoided looking for work in any of the inns and taverns, but perhaps she was being too choosy. She needed to find a way to earn money, but she couldn't afford to take a job as a live-in maid because otherwise, she wouldn't have the freedom to follow up any clues on wherever Abigail might be. She was in a bind, that was for sure.

The smell of warm meat pies and crusty bread fresh from the oven wafted out from the door of the bakery, and her stomach clenched with hunger again. She stopped by the window to gaze in longingly. It was too early in the day for the baker to be selling stale bread, so she would just have to wait until lunchtime and hope that there would be something then that she could afford.

Two women were chattering loudly as they walked along the cobbles towards her. The older one was short and walked with a limp as though troubled by arthritis. Her hair was grey, and her lined face above a peacock blue shawl was kind. The younger

THE RUNAWAY SISTER

woman had hair the colour of shiny conkers and was carrying a little boy in her arms. His brown curls reminded her of Abigail, and she tried not to stare.

"Come along, Dolly," the older woman said, "I knew we shouldn't have had that extra cup of tea visiting our Amy at the forge this morning. We'll be late; you know how tetchy Gloria gets if someone is late for a dress fitting."

Maisie stepped aside to let the two women pass, nodding her head in a polite good morning. She hadn't seen them before during her enquiries, and she threw caution to the wind. "Excuse me, I hope you don't mind me interrupting, but I'm asking everyone I meet. Would you happen to have seen a little girl who's newly arrived in Thruppley? She's five years old with green eyes like mine and light brown hair—"

The two women stopped. "Well, knock me down with a feather!" The older one blinked rapidly as she looked at Maisie, her mouth open in a circle of surprise. "It can't be, can it?" She stepped forward and took hold of Maisie's chin, turning her head one way and then the other. "Am I seeing things?"

"Verity! What are you doing?" The second woman shot Maisie an apologetic smile, and the little boy in her arms giggled at the unexpected conversation.

"If you ain't Violet's daughter, I must be seeing a ghost," Verity exclaimed. She stepped back and looked Maisie up and down before rushing forward and throwing her arms around her, pulling her into a motherly embrace. "You are, aren't you? I ain't seen Violet for over twenty years since she moved down Frampton way, but you look the spitting image of her. I'm never wrong about a face, am I, our Dolly?" She turned to the younger woman, who shook her head and laughed.

"No, Aunt Verity. Although perhaps we should give this poor young lady a chance to tell us herself who she is before she runs away in alarm."

"Well, go on then, dear," Verity urged. "You are Violet's daughter, aren't you? You must be. You look exactly like she did the last time I saw her." She peered over Maisie's shoulder, clearly expecting to see someone else. "Where's your ma? Have you come to live in Thruppley? Wait until I tell Bert. He'll be tickled pink."

Maisie managed to compose herself as Verity continued to stare at her. "Yes," she said hesitantly. "I'm Maisie Griffin, Violet Griffin's daughter. How did you know her?"

"Lawks, if you ain't just made my day, maid!" Verity jabbed Dolly with her elbow. "Remember I was only talking about Violet the other day, Dolly? The two of us were as thick as thieves when we were nippers, getting into all sorts of scrapes." She chuckled, her jowls wobbling merrily. "We'll have a fine old

THE RUNAWAY SISTER

time catching up. Is she in the bakery?" She peered over Maisie's shoulder again.

"No...I'm sorry to bring bad news, but my ma is dead now, and I'm all alone, so I've come to Thruppley to...find someone."

"Oh no, hark at me rabbiting on with as much tact as a bull in a china shop. Bert always says I speak before I think." Verity pulled her into another embrace and sniffed loudly as her eyes filled with tears before stepping back and seizing Maisie's hands. "You're not alone anymore," she declared. "We're your family now, ducky. Violet was my second cousin...possibly even my second cousin once removed, but she moved away. I often wondered what became of her, so you must come with us and tell us everything."

"I never knew you had other family, Aunt Verity." Dolly gave Maisie a warm smile. "How wonderful to discover that there are more of us. Will you come and have a cup of tea? Where are you staying?"

Maisie felt her cheeks turn pink. As delighted as she was to discover her new family, she didn't want them to think she was scrounging for help. "I've been staying at the Lilacs guesthouse for a week or so. Actually, that's why I'm out and about now. I'm looking for work so that I can carry on staying there. Mrs Venn has offered me a good rate, but I need to pay my way."

Verity took hold of Maisie's arm and swept her along the lane. "Goodness me, we can't have long-lost family staying in a guesthouse when we have a perfectly good cottage on the canal, can we, Dolly?"

"Certainly not," Dolly agreed. "Why don't you take Maisie to the cottage now, Verity? I'll pop in and speak to Gloria and catch you up. We can introduce you to the rest of the family, Maisie." She chuckled. "There are rather a lot of us, and things can get a bit noisy. I hope you don't mind."

"No, I like it." Any lingering shyness melted away in the face of their hospitality. A memory popped into her thoughts. "Do you know, a very wise old lady told me recently that something would happen for me to cross paths with more family members. I didn't believe her, but it seems she must have been right." A wave of relief swept through her. "I thought I was all alone, so this is a marvellous coincidence." She was already warming to the pair of them, who had treated her so kindly. Perhaps her luck was finally changing.

"You certainly ain't alone anymore," Verity said stoutly. "Now then, my dear. I don't suppose you've ever been to the canal, have you? Living down Frampton way, you must be more used to the big river instead?"

"Yes, living by the River Severn is all I ever knew."

"Well, let me tell you about the canal, ducky. My

husband Bert and I used to be what some folk call 'river rats'." Verity chuckled, walking surprisingly briskly for someone of her age along the cobbled streets. "What that means is we lived and worked on our narrowboat, *The River Maid*. 'Twas a very different way of life from what most folks are used to, but we loved it. We used to cart coal and grain up and down to Nailsbridge and Frampton Basin, stopping where we liked along the way. It was like having a dozen different homes! A new view every week and a proper community of people just like us. We worked hard to earn a crust, mind you."

"What about now? Have you given up?"

"Now there's a tale." Verity opened the gate onto the towpath, and a heron gave them a beady stare before flapping slowly away. "When Dolly and her brother and two sisters were just nippers, they were orphaned. The four of them came to live with me and Bert on *The River Maid,* and we made a fair do of it. Dolly took to it like a duck to water after Bert had his accident. She worked with Jester, the horse who pulled our boat."

Maisie was full of admiration. It sounded like they hadn't had things easy, much like her.

"Everything changed when there was a fire, and we thought that would be the end of us. But we had a bit of good fortune, and we've been living at the lock keeper's cottage for the last couple of years." She

DAISY CARTER

wheezed with laughter again. "It's a good thing, too, now that Dolly and Jack are married and have baby Albert. It would have been a tight squeeze for all of us to live on the narrowboat, but we would've managed. That's what our sort of folk do, isn't it?"

CHAPTER 19

An hour later, Maisie was sitting in the cosy kitchen of the lock keeper's cottage, and she started to feel more relaxed in the homely atmosphere. It reminded her a little of the cottage she had grown up in, with its stone windowsills and shirts hanging on the drying rack over the range.

"I suppose I should explain a bit better who we all are," Dolly said. She had already put a steaming mug of tea and a thick wedge of fruitcake in front of Maisie, telling her to eat up and that there was plenty more if she was hungry.

"I still can't believe your cousin Violet's daughter is sitting here with us," Bert said. His expression softened with affection every time he spoke to Verity. "There were so many times you felt sad that you'd lost touch with Violet for all these years. And then this wonderful coincidence happened out of the blue, bumping into Maisie today."

"I'd have recognised her anywhere." Verity smacked a kiss on Bert's cheek, completely unabashed. "We couldn't have children ourselves," she explained to Maisie, "and Bert is so kindhearted. That's why our door is always open to family."

Dolly settled Albert on a blanket in the corner of the kitchen, with some wooden bricks to play with, and Bob, their old terrier, snored in front of the range, twitching every now and again as he dreamt. Just at that moment, the door burst open, and two men walked in. "Perfect timing," Dolly said. "Maisie, this scruffy-looking fellow is my younger brother, Jonty." She gave him an affectionate nudge with her elbow as he hastily tried to tame his unruly hair and straightened his jacket. "And this is my husband, Joe."

Maisie nodded shyly, but Jonty and Joe both came forward to shake her hand.

"Maisie's ma, Violet, was Aunt Verity's second cousin," Dolly explained quickly. "We happened to bump into Maisie in the village today, and Verity knew immediately who she was because she looks so much like her late ma. Isn't it wonderful that we found each other?"

Jonty pulled up a chair and poured himself a mug of tea, giving Maisie a friendly smile once he'd had a

THE RUNAWAY SISTER

gulp of it. "What brings you to Thruppley, Maisie?" he asked.

Dolly swatted him good-naturedly with a tea towel. "Let the poor girl eat her cake in peace, Jonty." She rolled her eyes and took Joe's jacket off him to hang it up on the hooks behind the kitchen door. "Joe and Jonty converted our narrowboats to be leisure boats, and they do day trips on the canal for the high society ladies and gentlemen who come and stay at the hotel. You'd think mingling with the toffs would make Jonty better mannered, but it seems not."

"Hark at you, Dolly," Jonty shot back. "I heard you yelling like a fishwife at them youngsters who were jumping in the canal for a swim t'other day."

"She was just minding they were safe," Joe said. He slipped his arm around Dolly's slim waist, and they shared a smile.

The good-natured joshing between the family suddenly made Maisie feel a stab of sadness for everything that she had lost. She didn't think she could ever return to the Jolly Sailor, and the thought of not finding Abigail was unbearable.

"You look a bit upset, ducky," Verity said softly. She reached across and squeezed Maisie's hand. "You don't have to tell us what's wrong or even why you're here in Thruppley. Jonty's just being his usual nosey self."

Maisie hesitated for a moment, but as she glanced

DAISY CARTER

around, she saw only kindness in everyone's faces. It would be a relief to share the burden of everything that had happened, and she clung to the hope that perhaps they might know where Abigail could be.

"It's a bit of a story that led to me leaving Frampton. I hope you won't think badly of me for it."

Bert cleared his throat. "All of us have trials and tribulations, my dear. You don't get to be my grand old age without learning that sharing your problems generally helps, and there won't be any judgment from us, I can assure you."

A ripple of relief ran through Maisie, and she took a deep breath and began. "A well-to-do gentleman started courting me when I was not quite sixteen years old. He said we should keep it a secret and promised me marriage...but then he took advantage of my naivety. I got sick and lost my memory of everything at that time. When I got well again, Ma had another baby, my little sister Abigail. It was not long after Papa died."

"So where's your sister now—" Jonty blurted out. He turned red as Dolly shot a warning look at him across the table.

"After Ma died, Abigail and I went to live with my Aunt Edith and Uncle Josiah, working at the Jolly Sailor Inn." Maisie's voice wavered slightly as she got to the next part. "They were fooled by a toff. The man told them they were childless, so they agreed

THE RUNAWAY SISTER

that he could have my sister in exchange for money because Uncle Josiah wanted to buy the pub from Lord Pickering." Her eyes misted with tears, and she blinked them away. "They told me Abigail would have a better life with them."

Verity tutted loudly and squeezed Maisie's hand again. "Shocking…I'm sorry, ducky, they might be your relations, but who would do such a dreadful thing?"

"I thought she'd run away because they didn't tell me immediately. Jack, my friend, and his brother Fred helped me look for her, but we couldn't find her. I was terrified she'd gone mudlarking and got swept away in the river. When Aunt Edith told me the truth, I demanded to know who it was who took her. She said he didn't give his name, but I think they just didn't bother to ask."

Dolly poured another cup of tea out for Maisie. "You've been through so much." Her brown eyes were full of compassion.

"Jack's granny, Ava, is a wise woman. Some folks think she has second sight, and she reads tarot cards. I went to her cottage, and she told me the truth about Abigail. Ma confided in her but made her swear not to tell me until she thought the time was right. "

"The truth?" Verity and Bert both gave her an encouraging nod.

"The truth is that Abigail isn't my sister. She's my

daughter. When Ava told me that, the memories started to come flooding back to me. I caught a glimpse of the people who took Abigail in their carriage, you see, and the crest on the side of it looked familiar. I realised it was the same as the carriage belonging to the man who said he would marry me." She frowned, pushing down the regret that her memories hadn't come back soon enough to save Abigail. "I remembered that he told me that his father owned a mill in Nailsbridge, and he used to drink in Thruppley. I couldn't stay in Frampton and do nothing. I had to come here to look for Abigail."

"Owned a mill in Nailsbridge, you say?" Joe and Dolly exchanged a worried glance.

"The thing is, I saw him in Thruppley a couple of days ago." Maisie paused to take a sip of tea until she realised that everyone was hanging on her every word, waiting for her to go on. "Abigail's father...the man who promised to marry me is Dominic Smallwood."

"Dominic?" Dolly gasped. "You saw him in Thruppley?"

"That can't be possible," Joe said. "Last we heard, he was in America, getting married to a wealthy heiress."

"It was definitely him," Maisie said firmly.

"I can't believe that scoundrel dares show his face again in the village," Bert harrumphed. "He's brazen.

THE RUNAWAY SISTER

Only a man as arrogant as him would be so bold and think himself above the law."

"All the lost memories have come back to me now. And he admitted it, anyway. He left me in the family way, and you're quite right, he is married to a wealthy American woman. She was with him. I overheard parts of their conversation, and it sounds like he came back to Thruppley to try and persuade the family solicitor to help him out."

"Up to his old ways," Joe growled.

"But he didn't have any luck," Maisie said hastily. "I don't know how many debts Dominic has, but he told me straight to my face that he gave Aunt Edith a modest amount of money in exchange for Abigail. But he never wanted her for himself. He's given Abigail...his own daughter...to a childless couple. He lost at a game of cards, and this was how he solved it."

Jonty jumped up, practically knocking his chair over. "We must go and tell Constable Redfern that he's back. He shouldn't be allowed to get away with all his crimes."

"It's too late." Maisie felt bad as Jonty scowled with frustration. "I overheard Dominic and his wife, Genevieve, talking about starting a new life in Paris. I expect they're long gone. Dominic said that if I told anyone or tried to follow him, he would have the constable throw *me* in jail."

DAISY CARTER

"If anyone should be thrown in jail, it's Dominic Smallwood," Joe said through gritted teeth.

"What…what other crimes has he committed?" Maisie hardly dared to ask. Clearly, he was far more powerful and ruthless than she thought.

"He conspired with Arthur McKenzie, a criminal from London, to burn down his pa's mill at Nailsbridge for the insurance money," Dolly said.

"And when that didn't work, he was part of a string of burglaries on some of the wealthiest families in the area," Joe said, picking up the story. "He even forced Dolly to act as a go-between and take the jewels to Mr Ferguson, the yard manager at Frampton Basin. Not that she knew what was in the parcels he forced her to take to Ferguson. He was in on it, and they intended to send the jewels by ship to Europe so they could be sold."

"That's not the worst of it," Verity said indignantly. "When our Dolly and Joe got the better of him, he got his henchman, McKenzie, to set fire to *The River Maid*. We thought Dolly's little sister, Amy, had perished in the fire, but thankfully, she was walking on the towpath with Joe's brother, Billy."

"They're married now and live in a nice little cottage next to the Forge in Thruppley," Bert added helpfully.

Maisie's head was spinning with all this new information. "That must be the fire that Ava told me

THE RUNAWAY SISTER

about when she read my cards. I can't believe I was taken in by him."

"You weren't to know, ducky," Verity said quickly. "Dominic Smallwood is a wolf in sheep's clothing. He managed to escape to live in America and wriggle out of everything. McKenzie's in jail…and they caught Mr Ferguson too, eventually."

"It only confirms how dangerous he is," Maisie said slowly. "I want to find Abigail, but he warned me not to. Even if he's in Paris, he might still find out if I carry on searching."

Dolly gave her a kind smile. "We'll think of a way to outwit him, don't you worry. Dominic Smallwood is nothing more than a bully, and he delights in people being afraid of him so that he can get his own way."

"I think I just need to keep asking people," Maisie said quietly. "But first, I need to find work."

"We won't hear of you paying a penny more to stay in the guesthouse." Verity glanced at Bert, and he nodded in agreement. "You'm family, remember. You can stay here at the cottage with us."

As tempting as it sounded, Maisie didn't want to be a burden to anyone. "It's very kind of you, but Ma brought me up to stand on my own feet. If you know of anywhere I could work, that would be more than enough to help me."

"I can understand that. What do you do?"

"Mudlarking...working at the Jolly Sailor serving ale." Maisie ticked them off on her fingers and let out a sigh. It didn't sound very promising.

"Oh." Verity sounded disappointed. "I'm not sure that's suitable for you, ducky. We'll have to think of something else."

"I took over Ma's dressmaking job when she got too ill to do it herself."

Dolly's eyes lit up. "Dressmaking? That's perfect. My other sister, Gloria, has taken over the dressmaking shop in Thruppley since Betty's arthritis got too bad for her to carry on. She's so busy making wedding gowns she's rushed off her feet."

"And there's enough room for you to live over the shop." Verity beamed. "It will do Gloria good to have some company in the evenings. I keep saying she should be married by now, but there's no telling her."

"That would be like a dream come true." Maisie couldn't believe that she had gone from the depths of despair to feeling more hopeful about the future in such a short time.

"It's like it was meant to be," Jonty announced. "Now, can we have some more cake, our Dolly? I'm starving."

"He's always starving," Dolly chuckled. "You'll soon get used to it, Maisie. Welcome to the family."

CHAPTER 20

"What a godsend it is having you here," Gloria Hinton said for the third time in as many hours. She looked up from the white silk gown she was sewing tiny beads onto and watched Maisie's sewing for a moment. "Your ma taught you well."

Maisie flushed with pleasure at the compliment. "Everyone told Ma how good she was, and I always dreamt of working in a dressmaking shop like this." She looked round the cosy interior of Betty Jones's Gowns And Dressmaking with a happy sigh. She and Gloria were sitting by the bow-fronted windows, which looked out onto the lane and village square beyond. It was the best place for sewing, as it gave them the most amount of light, not to mention a view of all the comings and goings on the street, while Gloria kept up a running commentary on a who's who of Thruppley. There was a tall haberdasher's dresser at one side of the room, with dozens of tiny drawers full of beads, buttons, and lace. Colourful bolts of silks, velvets, and muslins were stacked on shelves on the other side of the shop, and there was a fitting room behind a velvet curtain. Narrow stairs led up from the back room into comfortable living quarters upstairs, and Gloria had happily helped Maisie settle into her new bedroom under the eaves.

"I was the same," Gloria said. "I loved life on *The River Maid*, but there wouldn't have been room for all of us to carry on living on it. Betty gave me a chance to work for her, and now that she's gone to stay with her daughter since her arthritis got bad, she's just happy that I agreed to carry on with the place. All the old regulars have continued coming here, but since I started offering wedding gowns as well, it was too much for me to do on my own."

"Abigail would love it here," Maisie said with a wistful sigh. It was hard to believe she had been at the shop for almost a week already. With so many introductions to customers and Gloria pointing out folks through the window, it felt as though she had been in Thruppley for months, not weeks. Although Gloria was more high-spirited and opinionated than Dolly, she had the same kindheartedness that the whole Hinton family had. When Dolly explained her situation, Gloria had agreed immediately that if Maisie needed time off to follow up on new snippets of information about Abigail, she only had to ask.

"Do you really think Dominic gave Abigail away to settle a gambling debt?" Gloria reached for her pin cushion and made a neat tuck in the piece of fabric on her table. "It barely makes sense when his family are so well-off, and he married a wealthy heiress."

"I've been wondering the same myself, but the more I've learned about Dominic from you and your family, the more I am inclined to agree with Jonty and Bert. Dominic has a cruel streak, I can see that now. And a sense of entitlement. It sounds as though he got away with so much before that he just assumes nothing bad will happen to him and that there won't be any consequences for what he's done." She shivered, gazing out of the window unseeing. "It was probably just a sport to him. If he owed money, he could have found it elsewhere, I'm sure. But it probably amused him to do this."

Gloria pulled a face. "He almost ruined all our lives, that's for sure. Poor Dolly was in a terrible state. He threatened that we would lose our contract for the mill unless she delivered the packages to Mr Fergeruson for him, which turned out to be the stolen jewellery. We would have been penniless without that work. Luckily, when everything came to light, Dominic's father, Edward, and his brother, Horace, disowned him."

"I suppose that's why he ran off to America with his tail between his legs." Maisie felt sick to the stomach at what a horrible man he was. "That and avoiding jail."

Gloria gave her a shrewd look. "You mustn't think that just because he's Abigail's pa, she might somehow turn out to be like him. The rest of his family are nothing like him." She sniffed disapprovingly. "But Dominic...he's a spiteful bully. I still can't believe he would use his own daughter in such a way."

"My aunt said he was charming," Maisie said drily. "But she never much liked having Abigail at the inn, especially if it took my attention from working day and night."

"She sounds dreadful, and you're better off away from there. Besides, I'm sure you've given her the best upbringing you can, and that will continue once we find her. You'll have all our support as well."

They continued sewing in companionable silence for a few minutes. Maisie wished she could share Gloria's confident optimism that they would find Abigail and bring her home again to her real family. With every day that passed, she feared that she might never see her again, but she took courage from her new rambunctious family and their warm-hearted

THE RUNAWAY SISTER

loudness. They had outwitted Dominic in the past, so perhaps it could happen again. She had to carry on hoping because the alternative was too awful to contemplate.

The bell on the door tinkled, and Maisie's heart lifted as Jack came into the shop, whipping his cap off and smoothing down his hair. "I hope I'm not disturbing you?"

"Jack! This is a lovely surprise. I have so much to tell you...I met Abigail's pa...Dominic Smallwood. But he's gone to Paris now." The news tumbled from her lips.

The corners of Gloria's mouth lifted in a smile, and she gave Maisie a wink. "So you're Jack Piper? I've heard an awful lot about you from cousin Maisie."

Jack grinned and raised his eyebrows. "All good, I hope?" He came further into the room and peered at the sprigged cotton blouse Maisie was altering. "I've only been away a short time, and it sounds like you've had all sorts of adventures and surprises. I've just come from The Lilacs. Mrs Venn told me all about your new family. Granny will be cock-a-hoop. She told me the cards showed you would meet them."

"Your granny reads cards?" Gloria's eyes rounded. "Her and Aunt Verity would get on like a house on fire. She always gets the travelling gypsies to read her palm when they come for the Midsummer Fair."

233

"Maybe I'll persuade Granny to come to Thrupley with me one day. My younger brother, Fred, can't wait to visit. He says he misses you, Maisie."

"Have you brought another load of rags to sell?" The church chimed noon, and Maisie stood up and stretched. They usually stopped for an hour to have some lunch, so she hoped Gloria might excuse her.

Jack's usual good cheer faltered slightly. "Yes. I'm sorry it took me a few days longer than I thought it would to collect enough rags to make it worth the journey of coming up here again."

"Is everything alright? Ava's not sickening for something, is she?" Maisie knew him well enough to sense that something was troubling him.

"I have someone coming in for a dress fitting soon." Gloria shook out the piece she had been working on and carefully put it back on the shelf behind her. "Why don't you two have a stroll by the river? It's a beautiful day, and I'm sure you have plenty to talk about. You can tell him all about meeting Dominic...horrible man that he is."

"That would give us a chance to see if the pawnbroker is finally open again." Maisie looked between them both as Jack's eyebrows raised. "Don't worry. I've told Gloria and her family...*my* family, everything. And now I need to tell you what's happened since you left. You won't believe it."

THE RUNAWAY SISTER

* * *

JACK WAS, by turns, shocked and horrified as Maisie told him all about her encounter with Dominic and Genevieve Smallwood.

"I feel terrible. I wish I'd been able to stay in Thruppley longer that day. How dare he treat you like that. I would have given him what for."

Maisie shrugged but was secretly rather touched by his protectiveness. "He's rich and powerful, with no morals. I suppose it was only to be expected."

"At least, if we can pawn the jewellery today, you'll have some money to help your search."

Her hand went unconsciously to her gown pocket, where she could feel the brooch nestled safely deep in the folds of material. "Do you have the earrings and gold bracelet?"

"I certainly do. Let's just hope that he offers us a decent price."

As they turned the corner, the three golden balls hanging over the pawnbroker's window glinted in the sun, and the scruffy urchin they had seen before was just leaving, his grubby hands clutching the few pennies he'd just been loaned. "It's open. About time." Jack glanced furtively up and down the lane and then ushered Maisie inside.

"Good morning." Henry Nelson, the pawnbroker, stood up slowly behind the counter, rubbing his

DAISY CARTER

hands together. He was tall and gaunt, with cadaverous cheeks and the tell-tale mottled complexion of a man who was too fond of going to the pub. "I ain't seen you two before. Are you buying or selling?" His bloodshot eyes looked slightly unfocused, and Maisie covered her mouth and coughed politely as the smell of stale beer wafted over them. "Or perhaps you want a loan?"

"We're selling," Maisie said firmly.

"She certainly knows her mind, doesn't she," Henry chuckled. "Let me guess, you're bringing a couple of trinkets from an elderly relation?" He eyed the darned patches on the elbows of Jack's coat. "Perhaps I'm being too generous. You don't look as though you have much to yer name, but I provide an important service for even the poorest people in the village." He swayed slightly and nodded in a self-satisfied fashion. "Although they plague me with silly requests, always trying to get a better price out of me." Even though it was warm, he had a moth-eaten scarf tied around his neck, and he straightened it and tugged his cuffs. "Henry Nelson at yer service. Never one to turn a needy person away."

"Perhaps you shouldn't judge people by how they look." Jack pulled a spotted handkerchief from the inside pocket of his jacket and laid it on the counter, carefully unfolding it to reveal the pearl earrings and gold bracelet. "We considered taking them straight to the jewellers, but we thought we would give you first refusal." He made it sound as though he was doing the man a special favour, and Maisie coughed again to cover the urge to laugh.

Henry Nelson's eyes narrowed slightly as he gave Jack a long stare, weighing him up.

"Mrs Venn said you're partial to a few drinks," Maisie said crisply, following Jack's lead. "Perhaps we should come back later when you've sobered up. I have a piece of jewellery as well, but I'm not sure you should see it in this state."

The pawnbroker's bony hand snaked out faster than expected, and he slapped it over Jack's offering. "I might have had a few drinks, but don't you worry, it ain't never affected my ability to do business before, and it won't today either." He gave Maisie an ingratiating grin and raised his bushy grey eyebrows. "How about you show me what you've got, miss? These two items from yer fellow have tickled my interest."

Maisie glanced discreetly at Jack, and he gave her a tiny nod. They both knew they needed to make the sale today while Mr Nelson was here, especially with his reputation for shutting up shop at the slightest excuse. It would be too risky trying to pawn the items back in Frampton, where so many busybodies were eager to prove the Piper family name untrustworthy and wanted to see their downfall.

"I should tell you before I show you what it is that I used to be a mudlark. I found this item fair and square, and I expect a good price for it." Even though Maisie's heart was hammering in her chest, she lifted her chin and gave Henry Nelson a defiant look. She was sick of being treated badly, and she wasn't afraid to tell him.

"Go on then, I'm intrigued now." Mr Nelson's tongue ran across his bottom lip, and his eyes brightened with a hungry gleam.

"It's a brooch. I've seen a few costume jewellery pieces during my mudlarking days, but I'm fairly certain this has proper stones in it." Maisie pulled the brooch out of her pocket and held it in her palm, not quite ready to hand it over to him.

"Hmmm, a pretty little bauble," Nelson said noncommittally. He reached for his magnifying jeweller's eyeglass and plucked the brooch out of Maisie's palm. "Let me see if you're right."

The silence stretched between them, punctuated only by Nelson's loud breathing. He brought the brooch closer to his face, examining it from every angle and holding it up to the light. "Yes...yes, I think so," he mumbled under his breath. His glance drifted towards the window, and his expression flickered with something that was difficult to read. It was more than plain greed, more like a smirk. For a moment, Maisie thought he was going to

THE RUNAWAY SISTER

pocket the brooch, but much to her surprise, he placed it back in her palm in a brisk, business-like fashion.

"I can give you a good price, the best you'll get around these parts, Miss..?"

"Miss Griffin, Maisie Griffin," she said quickly. "And my friend, Jack Piper."

"Indeed. I like to know who I'm buying from. I'm sure you understand." Nelson's smile widened, and then he lowered his voice and mentioned a sum of money which was almost treble what Maisie had hoped for.

She felt excitement bubbling up. "That sounds fair. And you'd be happy to purchase them today?" she asked eagerly.

"Yes, of course. You're absolutely certain that these items belong to you?"

"Yes. We found them in the mud by the river. Like I said, I'm a mudlark. At least, I used to be."

Henry Nelson nodded understandingly. "In that case, it will be a pleasure doing business with you, Miss Griffin and Mr Piper." He paused for a moment, his gaze suddenly distracted by something outside. He held up a bony finger and smiled again. "If you don't mind waiting here for a moment, I've just seen someone outside who I need to speak to. Don't go anywhere."

He hurried out from behind the counter and

DAISY CARTER

rushed through the door, pulling it firmly closed behind him.

"What do you think, Jack? He is rather eccentric, but at least he's agreed to the sale." Maisie grabbed his hands, barely able to contain her excitement. "It's far more than I was expecting. This should be enough to get Abigail back and to help you out with the increased rent on your cottage."

"Our fortunes are finally changing, and not before time!"

"I shall have to treat Fred to a visit to the tea shop for a slap-up meal. If he hadn't persuaded me to go mudlarking that one last time, we might never have found these."

The door creaked open behind them again, and Maisie hastily pulled her hands back from Jack's, blushing. Henry Nelson had returned, and another man was following him.

"This is them," Nelson declared to his companion.

The other man stepped forward, and Maisie gasped as she took in his blue high-collared tailcoat and white trousers. "I'm Constable Redfern. I'm arresting you for the theft of three items of jewellery stolen from Dudbridge Manor."

"What? We didn't steal the jewellery. We found it mudlarking, miles away from here."

Constable Redfern scowled. "Save your protestations, Miss Griffin. You're both coming with me to

THE RUNAWAY SISTER

the police station, and I shall be looking after these stolen items until we can return them to their rightful owner." He shook his head, almost looking sorrowful. "Poor, Lord Shaw. This isn't the first time he's had bad news about being robbed. You won't get away lightly with this."

"You've got it all wrong," Jack cried.

"Try telling that to my superiors in Gloucester." Redfern slapped a pair of handcuffs on their wrists, joining them together, and dragged them outside onto the cobbled street.

Before they had even gone five yards, an indignant shout split the air. "Harold Redfern! What on earth do you think you're doing?" Verity stomped towards them. Her cheeks were flushed with two red spots of colour, and her summer cloak billowed out behind her, making her look like a ship in full sail.

"I'm upholding the law, Mrs Webster."

"Don't 'Mrs Webster' me, Harold." She swatted him with her reticule. "Weren't you sitting at my kitchen table, enjoying a slice of poppyseed cake only yesterday?"

Constable Redfern shuffled his feet awkwardly and nodded. "Yes, but I'm working now," he muttered. "It was a very nice piece of cake, Verity. Thank you."

"Are you going to explain why you have my cousin's daughter and her friend in handcuffs,

Harold?" Verity placed her hands on her broad hips and glared at him again. "Don't you think my family has been through quite enough already these last few years without all this nonsense?"

"They have items in their possession which cannot possibly belong to them," he said, trying to be quiet so that people wouldn't overhear. "They're very valuable. They must have stolen them."

"I tried to explain, Verity," Maisie said hastily. "I told Mr Nelson we found the jewellery mudlarking down Frampton way. Finders keepers is the mudlarking rule, and we didn't know who they belonged to."

Henry Nelson loitered in the doorway, watching with interest. "I ain't mistaken, Constable Redfern. I saw Miss Shaw wearing that brooch a couple of years ago with my very own eyes. It was when she came with her pa, Lord Shaw, for the grand opening of the new village hall. I notice such things because of my profession."

"Lord Shaw?" Maisie felt a growing sense of terror at the mention of the name. How had her life become so complicated and entangled with such wealthy men when all she wanted to do was work and look after her daughter? "I promise we found them when we were mudlarking. We're not thieves."

"Surely you don't believe they could have stolen these items from Lillian Shaw, Harold?" Verity said

THE RUNAWAY SISTER

impatiently. "They're just two hard-working people trying to go about their business and earn a crust."

He drew himself up to his full height and glared at everyone. "You must call me Constable Redfern when I'm working, Verity," he said firmly. "I can tell that Henry Nelson is under the influence of too much ale, so I intend to keep Miss Griffin and Mr Piper in the police cells for a few hours while I investigate and give Mr Nelson a chance to sober up."

"He's not so innocent himself," Jack said, jerking his head towards the pawnbroker who was lounging against the door jamb as if he didn't have a care in the world. "He was just about to pay us a significant sum of money for the jewellery. He's probably only getting you involved because he thinks there might be some sort of reward from Lord Shaw."

"Enough!" Constable Redfern held up a hand to stop everyone talking. "I'm taking you to the cells now. And I won't be releasing you until I've got to the bottom of things."

Verity's face fell, but then she hobbled over to Maisie and threw her arms around her shoulders. "Don't worry, ducky. I believe you, and we'll soon get this mess sorted out. Constable Redfern should know better, but I suppose he has to be seen to be doing the right thing." She bestowed a regal smile on the flustered policeman. "I expect you're just taking Maisie and Jack away to keep your superiors at Gloucester

243

happy, but we both know they'm not criminals. I won't hold it against you next time you're down the canal, and you come in for tea and cake." She started hobbling off, holding her bonnet firmly in place. "I'll be back with help shortly, Maisie," she called over her shoulder. "Nobody gets the better of our family, you'll see."

CHAPTER 21

At first glance, it looked like there was a mound of rags in the corner of the police cell, and Maisie was startled when it moved, and a toothless old crone sat up and gave her a bleary smile. "Well, ain't this nice, a bit of company for me. How delightful of Constable Redfern to be so thoughtful." A wheezing chuckle came from deep in the woman's chest before it turned into a rasping cough.

"I shouldn't be in here; it's all a mistake," Maisie said. She frowned as the woman's cough got worse. "That doesn't sound too good."

"'Tis me lungs, dear. All them years of working in the woollen mill on the weaving looms, with so much dust it looked like snow. That was 'afore the laws changed of course, but the damage was done by then."

Maisie strode to the door of the cell and gripped the bars, trying to peer through them to see further along the corridor. She and Jack had been split up, with him going to the men's cell and her to the women's. "Constable Redfern," she called. "This lady…"

"Iris Buttercup," the old woman interjected, "like the flower."

"This lady, Mrs Buttercup, isn't feeling very well. She's troubled by a bad chest. Could you possibly find it in your heart to make her a cup of tea?"

"Can't a man get some peace? I'm trying to sleep here, and Iris should know that." The slurred complaint came from the men's cell. "All I want is a nice snooze."

"That's Mr Buttercup," the old woman muttered.

"You're both in jail?" Maisie felt as though she had stepped into a strange world where nothing made sense.

"He gets a bit handy with his fists when he's had too much to drink, so I clobbered him back this time with a loaf of bread." A wheezing laugh erupted from her again. "The only thing is, it was a loaf of bread I just liberated from the baker's stall at the market 'cos I didn't have nothin' at home for supper, and my daft husband spent our last few coins on beer." She balled

THE RUNAWAY SISTER

up her shawl and tucked it under her head again, making herself comfortable. "Mr Buttercup and I quite like a night in the cells, to be honest. It's not as damp as our little cottage, you see, and sometimes the constable brings us a bowl of soup."

The sound of approaching footsteps from the corridor announced Constable Redfern's return. He was carrying a tray with four tin mugs. "Don't think I'm going soft in the head doing this," he said. "It's a quiet afternoon, with only the four of you in cells, that's all."

"Bless you." Mrs Buttercup jumped up and came hurrying to the bars with surprising agility, and gave a little curtsy. Her dress was dirty and darned so much it was hard to tell the original colour, and a faint whiff of mothballs surrounded her. She coughed again and then gratefully took the tea as he passed it through the bars. "Thank you, Harold. You do make a good cup of tea, I'll give you that, even if you won't turn a blind eye to me helping myself to the odd crust of bread from the market."

Redfern rolled his eyes. "What is it with all the old women of this village that they think I should let crime go unpunished?" he muttered.

Maisie took a gulp of the hot, sweet tea and then put the mug down on the wooden bench at the back of the cell before hurrying back to the bars. "I can explain everything, Constable Redfern." She craned

DAISY CARTER

her neck, trying to look down the hallway to where he was standing outside the men's cell. A sudden fear gripped her that if he vanished back to his office at the front of the jailhouse, she might not get another chance to talk to him and try and make him see reason. "I found the brooch mudlarking on the banks of the River Severn down Frampton way. My daughter has been sold to a wealthy couple by her papa...a powerful man. I didn't agree to any of it, and I desperately needed the money from the brooch to try and find her and get her back."

"Oh, the poor lamb," Mrs Buttercup said mournfully. Two tears tracked down her lined cheeks, and she blew her nose loudly on the corner of her apron. "It ain't right, that sort of thing, Constable, and you know it." She pressed her face to the bars as well, determined to be heard. "A little girl should be with her ma, not with strangers," she yelled. "What's the world coming to?"

Emboldened by her unexpected new ally, Maisie decided to throw caution to the wind. "I'm not a dishonest woman, Constable. I had to go mudlarking to support my own ma before she died, and I want to do the right thing by Abigail, my little girl. But if the brooch truly does belong to the Shaw family, then I will do the right thing and give it back to them. Even though I came by it by fair means, not theft."

"You see, Constable." Iris Buttercup was enjoying

THE RUNAWAY SISTER

herself now, and her voice echoed along the hallway, "This young woman is trying to do the right thing. She shouldn't be in cells. You need to admit you've made a mistake and let her out so she can go and find her daughter."

A shadow fell across them as the constable appeared in front of the cell again. A muscle twitched in his jaw as though he was trying to keep a check on his temper. "I don't make the rules, Mrs Buttercup, as you know. And as for you, Miss Griffin, I told you I needed to look into this more. Imagine if someone had stolen something belonging to your family. I'm sure you would want a constable to do the right thing in that instance, wouldn't you?"

She sighed and nodded reluctantly. "Yes, Constable," she said quietly. "I'm just trying to say that I'm innocent. Thank you for the cup of tea, and I hope that one day I can return the favour to you at the lockkeeper's cottage with my family."

Constable Redfern gave her a curt nod. "I hope so, too, Miss Griffin. It gives me no pleasure accusing you of theft. However, it would be remiss of me not to do my job properly, especially if the item does turn out to belong to Lord Shaw's family."

With that, he turned on his heel and strode away, slamming his office door behind him to make it clear that the conversation was over.

DAISY CARTER

"You tried your best," Jack called. "We just have to hope that Verity manages to come with help soon."

"We'll be fine," Maisie called back. She sank onto the hard wooden bench and sipped her tea while Mrs Buttercup lay back down again.

"Get some sleep, ducky. T'will be a long night, and it ain't so bad once you get comfy."

How did it come to this? What if Vertiy and Dolly can't save me? She stifled a sigh and tried not to think about the fact that so often, her future seemed to lie in other people's hands...and not always those who wanted the best for her.

A movement in the shadowy corners of the cell caught her eye, and she grimaced as she saw it was a rat.

"Don't worry," Mrs Buttercup mumbled. "They'm quite friendly. I do give 'em a few crumbs out of my pocket because it's nice to have a bit of company. But we've got each other today."

Maisie leaned her head back against the cold stone wall behind her and let her eyes drift shut. Iris Buttercup's wheezy breaths became deeper and slower as she fell asleep, and the deep rumble of snoring from down the hallway told her that Mr Buttercup was doing the same. She only wished her own whirling, terrified thoughts would stop for long enough for her to drift off, but somehow, she doubted they would. *Where are you, Abigail? I pray that*

250

they're taking care of you, my darling girl. Her throat constricted with emotion as she imagined Abigail growing older and forgetting all about Frampton and her true family.

The finger of sunlight from the small window high in the wall behind them slowly crept across the floor as the minutes ticked by, turning into hours.

* * *

MAISIE WOKE WITH A START, staring around in confusion at the dreary cell and the slumbering old woman next to her. It took her a couple of seconds to remember where she was, and her heart sank as everything came flooding back.

Suddenly, she realised it was the sound of voices which had woken her. Footsteps approached again, and Constable Redfern produced a large key from his pocket and opened the cell door. "You can come out now, and I'll get Mr Piper too. There's somebody here to see you." He jerked his head towards the office as he hastily locked the door again, even though Iris was still fast asleep, snoring gently.

"Thank goodness Verity's plan worked," she whispered as Jack hurried to catch up with her. She was glad to have Jack by her side again as they entered Constable Redfern's office. She wasn't sure what to expect and was surprised to see a tall, distinguished-looking gentleman standing at the window with his arms crossed. An elegant woman with blonde ringlets, wearing a shot silk gown, was talking to him in a well-educated voice. Maisie had expected Verity or perhaps Dolly and Joe, not two toffs, and she glanced nervously at Jack as they awaited their fate.

The man at the window turned around, and his blue eyes brightened as he smiled at her. "Miss Griffin? And Mr Piper?" He reached out and shook hands with both of them. "I'm Horace Smallwood, and this is my wife, Lillian," he explained by way of introduction. "We've come to get you out of here."

"Now, just a minute," Constable Redfern said, marching in behind them. His cheeks were red, and he looked flustered. "I only said you could speak to them, Mr Smallwood."

"And that's what we're doing."

"Miss Griffin has been rambling on with some dubious tale of needing money to save her daughter. That's why she was trying to sell your brooch, Mrs Smallwood. Henry Nelson recognised it as yours because he said he saw you wearing it when Lord Shaw opened the new village hall." A frown creased his forehead. "I didn't say they could leave jail."

Horace opened his hand to look at the brooch, and Lillian nodded. "It is indeed my brooch. It belonged to my mama, which is why I was so upset

THE RUNAWAY SISTER

when it was stolen during that dreadful burglary a while ago."

Constable Redfern edged past Maisie and went to stand behind his desk, his shoes squeaking slightly on the red-tiled floor. He straightened his coat and rocked forward on his toes, determined to maintain an element of control in his own police station. "We only have their word for it that they weren't involved in the burglary," he said stiffly. Tension crackled in the air, and he took a deep breath. "I know this is a difficult topic to discuss, Mr Smallwood, because of the rumours that someone close to you was behind the burglaries." He sniffed as he eyed Maisie. "I've seen some funny things in my time, but it seems a fantastical notion that these two might somehow have miraculously dug up your lost jewellery out of the mud, don't you think?"

"Surely that is the very nature of mudlarking, Constable," Lillian Smallwood said calmly.

"Well, yes." He harrumphed and twirled the ends of his moustache. "If you put it like that, there might be some credence to their tale."

"Do you suppose that if the items were returned to their rightful owner, and said rightful owner didn't want to press any charges, one might forget the matter?" Lillian gave the constable a warm smile and arched one eyebrow.

"One might...? Said rightful owner...?" The

DAISY CARTER

Constable stumbled over the words and shook his head in irritation. "I mean, if what you're trying to say is that you don't want to bring them before the judge, I wouldn't be able to do anything more. I would have to let them go, but it's not something I would like to encourage." He picked up a sheaf of papers on his desk and officiously tapped them into a tidier pile to remind everyone how hard he worked to keep the criminal fraternity properly in hand. "This whole thing is highly irregular, Mrs Smallwood."

She nodded her head respectfully. "I understand, Constable Redfern. Indeed, I can see that you're a very busy person, which is why my husband and I have decided that this should be the end of the matter."

"The jewellery wasn't stolen by these two unfortunate people," Horace said firmly. "I think we should all be very grateful that it's only thanks to their hard work mudlarking the brooch and the other items came to light at all." He smiled round at everyone and picked up his hat. "That's it then. Shall we go?"

"I think that's for me to decide, Mr Smallwood," Constable Redfern said hastily. He rubbed his tired eyes and glared at Maisie and Jack, reminding her of a belligerent hound. "I'm sure you must have realised the items had been stolen at one point. The

THE RUNAWAY SISTER

honourable thing to do would have been to bring them to the police station."

"The mudlarking rule is finders keepers," Maisie replied, equally as firmly. "When your belly is rumbling because you haven't had anything to eat all day, and selling something that you found to the pawnbroker is the difference between going to bed hungry or not, doing the right thing isn't always quite so straightforward."

"Don't forget, Maisie did say earlier that she would give the brooch back to its rightful owner, Constable." Jack rested his hand protectively on her shoulder for a beat. "I heard her, and so did Mr and Mrs Buttercup. Maisie has been trying to do the right thing all along, but everyone is conspiring against her. She just wants to get her daughter back."

"I'm sure we can all sort this out amicably." Lillian Smallwood stepped forward and hitched her beaded reticule higher on her arm. "How is the new roof on the police station, Constable?" she asked brightly. "You said the place used to leak like a sieve every time we had rain until my papa, Lord Shaw, generously paid for all the repairs."

"Oh…yes, it's much better."

Everyone looked up at the ceiling for a moment, and Maisie stifled a giggle as she caught Jack's eye.

Lillian reached across the desk and patted the constable's arm approvingly. "Papa thinks it's very

255

DAISY CARTER

important to support local causes, especially for someone as important as you." She gave him a dazzling smile, and the tips of his ears turned pink. "You do such good work in our community, Constable. Catching the *real* criminals." Her meaning behind the emphasis on the word 'real' was perfectly clear, and Constable Redfern's officious demeanour reduced slightly as he basked in the compliment.

"Yes, please pass my thanks to Lord Shaw again," he replied. "Now, if you'll excuse me, I have some paperwork to do before I need to take a wander past the taverns to make sure everyone is behaving themselves."

"Marvellous," Horace said. He put his hat back on and gestured towards the door. "After you, Miss Griffin. I do believe your presence here is no longer required, and we won't need to talk about this matter again, will we, Constable."

"I suppose you'll want my help finding your daughter now?" he said wearily.

"No...thank you, Constable."

"No, we'll help her; no need for you to trouble yourself."

Horace and Maisie spoke over each other, and the constable showed them all out, looking very relieved he could get back to his paperwork.

CHAPTER 22

Never had Maisie been so grateful to feel the late afternoon sun on her face as when they left the police station.

"We would like to hear a little bit more about your side of things," Horace said. "My wife and I came as soon as Verity and Dolly told us what had happened. Dolly and her family have been good friends of mine for many years, so of course, we believed them when they said you didn't steal the jewellery."

Maisie shivered slightly, and Jack patted her arm to reassure her. It was only just starting to sink in now that, without the help of so many kind people, she could have been convicted of burglary and might never have had the chance to look for Abigail again.

"I meant what I said about returning the brooch

DAISY CARTER

to the rightful owner. I'm not a greedy person, and I know what it feels like to be wronged." She smiled at Lillian, feeling shy. "I'm very glad you have the brooch again, especially as it was a present from your ma. I lost my ma a few years ago, and I treasure the few things she left to me."

"Let's walk this way together, and you can tell us everything." Horace and Lillian linked arms as they strolled towards the river. "I own the Rodborough Hotel at the edge of the village. I need to get back there to do some more work if you would care to walk with us. We're less likely to be overheard as well."

"My relations, Jonty and Joe, take the leisure boats on the canal for the toffs to stay at your hotel," Maisie blurted out. She blushed and corrected herself. "I mean...the well-to-do ladies and gentlemen who come and visit from London."

Horace chuckled. "Between you and me, some of them are what I would call toffs. My papa, Edward Smallwood, wasn't born wealthy. He worked hard all his life, setting up Nailsbridge Mill, amongst other businesses. And my wife's father, Lord Shaw, has worked tirelessly for many years in parliament to try and improve working conditions." He grinned, and Maisie realised they might seem grand to her, but they were kind and caring beneath their wealthy trappings. "What I'm trying to say is that we

THE RUNAWAY SISTER

appreciate your honesty and hard work, Miss Griffin."

"What was Constable Redfern saying about you trying to find your daughter?" Lillian gave them both a sympathetic smile. "Are you Abigail's papa, Mr Piper?"

Jack shook his head hastily, looking embarrassed. "Oh, no, Maisie and I are just friends. We both grew up in Frampton village, and our families go back a few years. It's nothing more than that, although Fred and I are very fond of Abigail. She's like the little sister we never had."

"I don't know if you're going to like what I'm going to tell you," Maisie said hesitantly. "You're a grand family, and I know you wouldn't want any sort of scandal brought to your door."

Horace's expression became more serious. "Why don't you just tell us, Miss Griffin? I'm sure if you ask Dolly, she will tell you that I always do my best to keep an open mind. Papa and I helped Verity and Bert, and Dolly's family family in the past when they were taken advantage of. Certain relations of mine don't have an unblemished history; let me just say that."

Maisie puffed out her cheeks, wanting to choose her words carefully. Even though Gloria and Dolly had assured her that Dominic's brother and father were decent people, nothing like him, she had always

259

been brought up to form her own opinions before blindly trusting people. *I trusted Dominic, and look where that got me.*

"Go on, my dear. I promise we will listen without judgement, and perhaps we will be able to help you." Lillian ran her fingers through some lavender blossom and plucked one of the flowers to smell.

"Alright." Now that it was time, her nerves fluttered with anxiety. How would they receive the news she was about to share?

"Go on, Maisie," Jack murmured. He squeezed her hand. "How can they help if they don't know? Remember, you weren't to blame."

"Abigail's papa is your brother, Dominic Smallwood." Maisie plunged in, deciding it was best to be direct with them. "It's rather complicated. I was ill, and I lost my memory, and for a while, I believed Abigail was my little sister, as that is what my ma wanted me to think. I only recently discovered from Jack's granny that Abigail is my daughter. Also, I only recently remembered that it was Dominic who courted me and said we would be married." She gave them both a rueful smile. "Of course, I can see now that it was foolish of me to believe his sweet words, but I was young and flattered by his attention, I suppose."

Horace's expression hardened. "Dominic, I should have known," he snapped. "My brother always was

THE RUNAWAY SISTER

the black sheep of the family. I expect Dolly may have told you that he was the mastermind behind the robberies, including the one at Dudbridge Manor, where Lillian grew up. The fact that she fell in love with me and agreed to become my wife, even knowing what Dominic had done, is a miracle."

"That's because you're nothing like your brother," Lillian said, giving him a fond smile. "Never have two brothers been more different, and you, my dear, are by far the better person."

"We don't want Dominic's wrongdoings to be common knowledge," Horace continued. "Nearly everything was returned to the people he stole from, and I was worried a scandal would be the death of Papa. We thought that when Dominic escaped to go to America and marry a wealthy heiress, we had heard the last of him."

"Is it true that he's back?" Lillian asked. "Dolly told us you saw him the other day."

"Not for long," Jack replied quickly. "Maisie came across him by pure coincidence. They only spoke for a few minutes, just long enough for him to tell her nobody would believe her…and threaten her to leave well alone." He squeezed Maisie's hand again. "They were on their way to Paris. If anything, seeing Maisie probably made them flee faster."

"Our solicitor, Mr Eckleton, told me Dominic approached him, but I didn't want to believe it was

DAISY CARTER

true. That he would be bold enough...or foolish enough to waltz back to Thruppley and try and get more money from Papa's business investments."

"Do you believe me when I say that Dominic is Abigail's pa?" Maisie had to know before she could carry on telling them the rest.

"Yes, my dear. What reason would you have to lie?"

"Dominic wasn't all bad," Maisie said. "I caught a terrible chill one day, and he gave me a drink to warm me up. It was from a silver hip flask with an etching of a horse on the back. I still have it. He gave it to me as a gift, and I thought it would be something to give to Abigail one day. I can show you if you need to see it to believe me."

Horace shook his head. "I know exactly what you're describing. I have one as well. Our papa gave us identical hip flasks on our eighteenth birthdays, so I know you're telling the truth, Miss Griffin."

"Tell them the rest," Jack urged. "You need all the help you can get to try and find Abigail, and it's only right that they should know what Dominic did."

"He bought Abigail from my aunt and uncle without me knowing," Maisie said flatly. "Then he gave her to another couple to settle some sort of debt he had with them."

Lillian gasped, and her hands flew to her mouth in shock. "Oh, you poor thing, no wonder you said

THE RUNAWAY SISTER

you were desperate to find your daughter. That's awful, even by Dominic's standards."

Horace sighed heavily but didn't look shocked. If anything, his face was etched with weariness and disappointment. "I owe you an apology on his behalf, Miss Griffin. We will help you in any way we can. I'm usually at the hotel most days, so you can come and find me any time. You only have to ask."

"Thank you." She almost felt sorry for Horace. It seemed as though Dominic didn't care for his brother and father at all. "You're not to blame for Dominic's behaviour."

"Maisie might need money to offer to the couple who have Abigail." Jack sounded as though he expected to be rebuffed, but Horace only nodded.

"Of course. And we're happy to provide it."

"But I have to find her first," Maisie said. She felt buoyed up by the fact that Horace and Lillian believed her about Abigail. "I don't want you to get dragged into this, Mr Smallwood. If they find out you're making enquiries, they might take her away." She considered her options. "Perhaps it's better if I carry on looking for her alone for now. Nobody would suspect a commoner like me asking questions."

"You're a plucky young woman, not a commoner," Horace shot back.

263

Maisie shrugged. "I don't call myself that, thinking it's a bad thing. It's just how it is."

"Well, as I said, you only have to ask if you need my support. I want to try and do what I can to make up for Dominic's appalling behaviour."

Jack bent over and picked some flowers from the verge, handing some to Maisie and some to Lillian. "You've been very understanding, Mrs Smallwood. We haven't got much between us, me and Maisie, but it would please me for you to have these flowers."

"St John's Wort. How delightful." Lillian sniffed them and smiled at Jack.

"*Hypericum*, Mrs Smallwood." Jack grinned. "It symbolises courage and hope for those who believe in such things, which I do, thanks to Granny's wisdom. She's rarely wrong."

Horace looked surprised, which made Maisie chuckle. "Jack isn't just a lowly rag-and-bone man, Mr Smallwood. He has dreams of becoming a gardener one day, and if I can ever help him achieve it, I will. It will be a small way of thanking him for all his support. I'm not sure I would have survived the last few years without Jack's friendship."

"Indeed." Horace nodded politely with a thoughtful expression as they parted ways. "A good friend is something to be treasured."

CHAPTER 23

"Maisie! Thank goodness you're home again. I was beginning to give up hope that you'd get out today." Gloria threw her arms around Maisie's shoulders after opening the door of the shop to her. "Dolly and Verity came here earlier to tell me about you and Jack being arrested. I've never heard anything so ridiculous in all my life."

"If Verity hadn't spotted us when she was running errands in the village, we would probably still be in the cells now," Jack said. He chuckled. "Your aunt reminds me of my granny. Not a woman to be crossed."

"She doesn't take kindly to anyone in her family being treated badly," Gloria agreed. "That's why we were so lucky that Verity and Bert took care of us when we were orphaned. People underestimate her

DAISY CARTER

because of being one of the narrowboat folk, but they do so at their peril."

Maisie started to laugh, partly from relief and partly as the shock of everything caught up with her. "I don't think I've ever seen a constable look so flustered as when she hit him with her reticule, and I expect Henry Nelson will be avoiding her for a few days as well."

"Oh yes, Aunt Verity had plenty to say to that scoundrel. Fancy him getting you both arrested in the hope of pocketing a reward for that brooch. The cheek of it! He'll have some grovelling to do to get back into Verity's good books."

The oil lamp flickering in the shop window cast a cosy glow over the room, and the heady fragrance of the honeysuckle growing up the front of the shop wafted in the night air, a welcome reprieve from Mrs Buttercup's malodourous mothball-ridden clothes.

"What will happen now?" Gloria asked. "If you want to stay in Thruppley for a few days, Jack, Dolly has agreed that you're very welcome to stay at the lockkeeper's cottage."

"Oh, there's no need for that, I'm happy enough sleeping under my cart. I left Duke grazing on the common and paid a lad sixpence to look after the cart. I'd better get back there now before he wonders where I got to and leaves."

"Nonsense," Gloria said firmly. "Maisie is family,

so any friend of Maisie's is like family too. There's plenty of room for Duke to graze in the field behind the lockkeeper's cottage, and Dolly will be offended if you don't go down there."

A wave of weariness suddenly engulfed Maisie, and she thought longingly of a cup of hot chocolate and a good night's sleep, ready to start afresh with everything in the morning. "You said you wanted to have a couple of days collecting rags in and around Thruppley, and staying at the lockkeeper's cottage will be better than being on the common." Maisie shot Jack a grateful smile. "You already lost a day's work, thanks to Henry Nelson. I bet Joe and Dolly will be able to recommend some houses to get rags from as well."

Jack nodded slowly. "You're right. Before I got sidetracked with Constable Redfern and everything that happened today, I was wondering whether I could find a cheaper cottage in Thruppley to rent for me and Granny and Fred."

"Move up here?" She couldn't keep the happiness out of her voice.

"Well, I heard a whisper that the man with the rag-and-bone round here is finishing and going to stay with his daughter in Bristol. It could be a chance for Fred to join me in the business instead of mudlarking."

"Is that true, Gloria? Have you heard the same?"

"You must mean old Mr Picard. He's been talking about giving up his rag-and-bone round for at least three years. The poor fellow can barely get in and out of his cart, his knees are so stiff." Gloria clapped her hands together, and her eyes sparkled. "That would be wonderful if you and your family came to live at Thruppley. I'm sure Maisie misses you when you're away," she added, giving them both a mischievous smile."

Maisie busied herself with taking her shawl off so that Jack wouldn't see the blush on her cheeks. She was slightly disappointed that he didn't comment on what Gloria had just said other than to thank her again for the offer of staying at the lockkeeper's cottage.

"I'll go and make a pot of tea, and there's some bread, ham and pickles on a plate for supper. You must be famished." Gloria hurried away again, leaving them alone.

"I'd better get going then," Jack said briskly. "If I hear anything about Abigail on my rounds tomorrow, I'll come and tell you."

Maisie stifled a yawn, feeling almost too tired to stand, let alone eat supper. "I'll keep asking around as well. It's all I can do for now, but I don't want to get behind on my work for Gloria."

Jack put his hands in his pockets and shuffled his

THE RUNAWAY SISTER

feet, not quite meeting her eye. "Is it true that you miss me...I mean, us?"

"Yes." She saw surprise in Jack's eyes and wondered if she'd spoken out of turn. "Fred used to make me laugh, and Ava knew Ma so well, she was a link to my past, I suppose. But Gloria is a good friend now, and I'm slowly meeting new folks here."

"It must be strange finding you have all this family." Jack shrugged awkwardly. "I'm glad for you...but don't forget about us if we end up staying in Frampton."

"I'd never forget about you." Maisie wanted to say more but bit her tongue. Talking about work felt like a safer option. "Gloria has been very patient, and she doesn't mind me taking time away from my sewing, but I don't want to take advantage of her kindness. She already said to me that she would be more than happy for Abigail to live with us upstairs."

"That's probably for the best. Well, g'night." He gave her a cheerful wave as he walked away, and Maisie stood on the doorstep in the gathering darkness for a moment, trying to let her thoughts settle. Candles flickered in windows as people got ready to go to bed, and other than the occasional burst of laughter from the pubs, the village was quiet.

A bat squeaked, flitting overhead, and the first stars shimmered like tiny pinpricks in the inky mauve sky.

There was a crescent moon over the hills, and Maise sighed and wondered whether Abigail might be looking up at that same moment and seeing the moon as well.

"I'll never give up looking for you, Abigail," she whispered. "I just hope it's not too late to find you. Good night, my poppet. I love you, and I always will." The moon blurred as her eyes filled with tears, and she wiped them away with the back of her hand. Tomorrow was a new day, and perhaps it would bring fresh news.

* * *

HORACE LEANED back in the mahogany chair behind his desk, and his gaze wandered around the room he used as his office in the Rodborough Hotel. The desk, with its ornately carved drawers on one side, had belonged to his father, Edward, as did all the leather-bound books on the shelves which lined the wall on his right. "These will remind you of how far we've come," Edward had said, happy for Horace to continue the family business traditions.

Since his papa had retired, Horace preferred to base himself at the hotel instead of at Nailsbridge Mill. The hotel was his business, and the ledgers in front of him showed that all his hard work and risks setting the place up were starting to pay off.

As long as Dominic doesn't ruin everything. The thought felt like acid burning his stomach.

He laced his hands behind his head and looked up at the ceiling, but there was no inspiration to be had in the ornate coving, so he turned to look outside instead. Two doors opened out onto his private flagstone veranda with urns containing tall grasses and trailing flowers, and the bees buzzing in the soft summer sunshine soothed him briefly. Beyond the veranda, the gardens sloped down to the river, and he could see two swans serenely gliding across the water.

His long-term plan was to create terraces for the wealthy hotel guests to stroll along on summer evenings, but it would take a while to get the grounds how he wanted them. All his money and focus had been on getting the hotel open, but he knew he needed to get on with the gardens soon if they were to match the elegant interior, which had been painstakingly designed by one of his friends from London, who had a great eye for interior design. So far, the hotel was doing better than he'd hoped. His friends and acquaintances from London were eager to travel to the West Country to take in the country air. The high-society wives adored Lillian's effortless style with how the rooms had been dressed with flowing curtains and the latest fashions in upholstery and bed linens, and word had soon got around in wealthier circles that the Rodborough Hotel was the place to be seen. Although he was a modest person in his private life, when it came to business, he was happy that his hotel was boasted about when guests returned to London.

But Dominic might get tongues wagging for all the wrong reasons. A surge of irritation at his feckless brother made him restless. He jumped up and thrust his hands in his pockets, pacing backwards and forwards in front of the windows, barely seeing the beautiful views that usually gave him so much pleasure.

It was two days since he and Lillian had managed to persuade Constable Redfern to let Maisie and Jack go, and his mind hadn't stopped whirling since. When Mr Eckleton, the family solicitor, had visited a week ago, wringing his hands with concern, to inform him that he had news about Dominic being back from America, Horace had shooed him away. He had been in the middle of entertaining two guests from London, who he hoped would invest in his new business venture, another hotel near Bath, where people would be able to bathe in hot springs and take the waters for all manner of ailments. The soonest he had managed to visit Mr Eckleton's office had been straight after getting Maisie and Jack out of jail, where he learned with a sinking heart that Dominic had indeed brazenly visited Mr Eckleton in broad

THE RUNAWAY SISTER

daylight. Dominic had tried to persuade the man to go against all his morals and give him a sizeable sum of money from their papa's savings.

Mr Eckleton had told Horace with a pained expression that Dominic even threatened to spread false rumours about him if he didn't oblige.

"I've worked with your father for over thirty years, Horace. Edward took me on when I was still just a clerk, learning law, and he helped pay for my education." The staid solicitor had blinked nervously behind his wire-rimmed spectacles. "I haven't done the dreadful things that Dominic is threatening to tell people about. I'm a happily married man, and I would never cheat on Mrs Eckleton, I swear. I sent Dominic packing, but he seemed desperate. I thought that the American woman he married was the wealthy heiress, but perhaps she doesn't have enough money for their lifestyle."

Horace could still hear Mr Eckleton's hurt and shock in his head two days later, and he ground his teeth thinking about how cruel his brother could be in his hedonistic pursuit of an easy life.

He had assured the poor, bemused man that he wouldn't let any false rumours spread about him and that Dominic had slunk off to Paris anyway.

"Can I come in, dear?" His office door opened, and Lillian bustled in, carrying a tray with two tea cups and his favourite lemon cake. Martha, one of the maids, followed her, carrying a pot of tea and milk.

"Just on the side will be fine; thank you, Martha." Lillian waited until the maid had left the room and then brushed a kiss on Horace's cheek.

"I was hoping you might join me for afternoon tea," Horace said. He looked down into Lillian's serene blue eyes and shook his head. "I still pinch myself every day that you agreed to marry me. I really am a very lucky man."

"How could I resist when you were so apologetic about what Dominic did? It took a lot of courage to tell me he was behind the burglary at Dudbridge Manor, and a lesser man would have pretended not to know, let alone coming to tell me in person." She poured out two cups of tea and put one on his desk for him. "Will you sit down and take tea with me, or are you going to carry on pacing?"

Horace gave her a rueful smile. "I feel too angry to sit down, but for you, my dear, I will." He sank into his chair again and sipped his tea while Lillian cut him a slice of cake.

"I don't need to ask what you're angry about. You were muttering about that wretched brother of yours in your sleep last night."

Horace rested his chin in his hand for a moment, then pulled a face. "I honestly thought we'd seen the last of him, Lillian. You'd think that trying to set fire

THE RUNAWAY SISTER

to the mill and then the burglaries would have been enough. God knows it aged Papa ten years. At one time, I even thought Dominic's terrible behaviour would put Papa into an early grave."

"Are you going to tell Edward about Dominic visiting Mr Eckleton to try it on again?"

"No!" Horace's tone brooked no argument. "It will only prey on his mind and make him ill again. My selfish brother won't get a single penny of the family's money, it's what Papa wants, and he told me he won't change his mind about it. He still hasn't forgiven Dominic over how he would have carelessly jeopardised everything Papa worked so hard for all his life, just for his own financial gain and greed."

"What about Abigail? She's your papa's granddaughter," Lillian said softly.

"I don't want to tell Papa about Maisie and Abigail until we help Maisie find her." His gaze softened, and he slipped his arm around Lillian's waist. "We'll have a baby of our own soon, I'm sure of it, my darling. Papa has always said how nice it would be to have grandchildren."

Lillian nodded. "I agree. We don't want to raise his hopes only for them to be dashed again if we don't manage to find Abigail." She brushed another kiss on Horace's cheek. "And I know our time to have children will come, my dear." She smiled again. "Perhaps sooner than you think."

Horace's eyes widened with surprise. "Are you saying—?"

Lillian pressed a finger to his lips. "It's a little too early to tell, but if we are having a baby, I'll make sure you're the first to know."

There was a tap at the door, and it creaked open. Martha peeked into the room. "Are you busy, sir? There's someone –"

Horace groaned and waved her away. "Not now, Martha. I'm not in the mood to deal with the guests today." He went to stand by the window again, feeling too agitated to be still for long.

"Why does my brother manage to ruin everything, Lillian? Time after time, he has brought shame to this family; I'm not sure we can survive another scandal."

Lillian sipped her tea, looking thoughtful. "Part of me wonders whether we should warn the woman he has married. He's probably only with her for her money, and if that's not enough for him, who knows what he might do."

Horace shrugged his shoulders. "I don't care if this sounds like I'm hard-hearted, but we must think of ourselves in this matter, Lillian. Maybe she does deserve our help, but I'm not prepared to give it to her. It will probably end up causing the ruination of all of us; I'd lose this hotel...we have our good family name to think of...we have to be selfish for once."

THE RUNAWAY SISTER

Lillian suddenly noticed that the door was still ajar from Martha's interruption, and she hurried across the room to close it. The last thing they needed was the maids gossiping about their affairs below stairs. She heard footsteps running away and peered out into the hallway. "Martha? Is that you? Was someone with you?" The retreating back of the young woman looked like Maisie Griffin, but she had vanished before she had a chance to call her back.

"You're right. Dominic and his American wife can take care of themselves. What matters most now is helping Maisie however we can. Dominic might not have treated her well, but we must make up for it."

Lillian topped up Horace's cup with more tea and added a dash of milk. "I thought that was her just now, but she's gone."

"Maybe you could visit the dressmaking shop tomorrow? She might feel more inclined to confide in you." Horace felt happier now that he had talked things through with Lillian. She always helped him see reason when his dislike for Dominic clouded his judgement. "Abigail is my niece, and Maisie didn't deserve to be treated so badly by my wretched brother. I only hope we get Abigail back, and then she can be part of our family if that's what Maisie would like."

He drew Lillian into his arms again and looked

into her eyes. "Imagine Papa's delight if he finds out he has not one but two grandchildren."

Lillian rested her cheek on his shoulder momentarily, and her hand drifted down to her waist. She was fairly certain there was new life deep in her belly, but it was too soon to say for sure, so she hugged the knowledge tightly to herself and hoped that she would have good news for Horace very soon once she had visited the family doctor.

* * *

MAISIE STUMBLED SLIGHTLY as she hurried down the narrow back corridor that led away from Horace's office, her ears still ringing with what she had just overheard...

...We must think of ourselves in this matter...maybe she does deserve our help, but I'm not prepared to give it to her...it will probably end up causing the ruination of all of us...we have our good family name to think of...

Part of her regretted coming to ask for Horace's help, but another part of her was not surprised by the words she had overheard from his office. It was only this morning, after the shock of being in jail had worn off, that Maisie had realised she had overlooked something.

She had been talking to Gloria about the fact that Dominic had said his debt was due to losing a card

THE RUNAWAY SISTER

game, and Gloria had asked where the card game had been held. "Of course, why didn't I think of that," Maisie said. "I should have thought to ask Horace when we were walking by the river, but it never occurred to me."

After letting her finish work early, Gloria had urged her to go to the hotel to rectify her mistake. An hour later, she was waiting in the hallway outside Horace's office, nervously admiring the gilt-framed oil paintings hanging on the wall, while Martha, the maid, enquired if Horace had time to see her.

I should have known better, she thought bitterly. In spite of being a nice person, obviously, Horace's loyalties would be to his family first. Her instincts that he would not want a scandal brought upon the Smallwood family name had been correct.

"Are you alright, miss?" Martha had bustled away to welcome some guests to the hotel, but her face creased with worry as she spied Maisie standing in the laundry doorway. "If you don't mind waiting a little while, I can try the master again. He ain't usually so short with people, but I fancy he seems to have a lot on his mind at the moment."

Maisie shook her head. It seemed simpler to leave rather than hear more empty promises. "No, thank you, Martha. I don't want to put you out. There's no need to tell Mr Smallwood I came to see him. As you said, he's a very busy man."

As she walked away from the hotel heading back into the village, it was hard not to feel disheartened. She had hoped Horace and Lillian Smallwood would be her allies, but it wasn't to be. It was understandable, she thought to herself. Dominic's actions had almost ruined the family once, and it sounded as though Edward Smallwood was not in the best of health.

She squared her shoulders resolutely. She would find Abigail with or without help from the Smallwood family. Her ma had raised her to be resilient in the face of adversity, and she hadn't survived all those years at the Jolly Sailor to let something like this set her back.

CHAPTER 24

The sound of raucous laughter drifted out from the Black Lion Tavern, and Maisie paused on the corner of the village square. She had always assumed the card game Dominic had lost would have been played at a gentleman's club or perhaps a private gathering of wealthy friends. But what if that wasn't true? Dominic had mentioned to her once that he drank at the Black Lion. For someone of such wealth and influence, he seemed to enjoy rubbing shoulders with poorer folk, so perhaps her assumption was completely wrong. She walked a few paces closer, wondering if she was being foolhardy. Joe and Jonty had offered to ask around in the local pubs and taverns, but she had told them to wait a little while. *I don't have time to keep waiting.*

Overhearing Horace's reticence to help had left

her feeling spurred on with a new sense of purpose. Abigail was her daughter, so she would have to be courageous. If nothing else, she might find someone who knew more about Dominic's acquaintances. Just a name would be a start.

Before she could lose her nerve, she marched along the lane and pushed open the door, holding her head high.

"Well, ain't you a welcome sight, sweetheart." A burly man with a paunch was just leaving, and he grinned as they came face-to-face. "I've seen you out and about in the village once or twice. If you fancy some refreshments, why don't you let me buy you a tot of gin?"

"No, thank you. That's not why I'm here." Maisie neatly sidestepped him and pushed her way past several other men to get to the bar.

A red-faced barmaid in a frilly white blouse that revealed just enough cleavage to keep the men drinking eyed her with surprise. "You're the new woman at the dressmakers, aren't you?" She leaned her brawny arms on the counter and raised her eyebrows. "What's your tipple, love?"

"She looks like she'd appreciate a glass of sherry," a skinny man perched on a barstool called. He picked up his tankard and lifted his little finger daintily as he drank a mouthful of ale. "We don't often get la-di-da folk like her in here, Beryl. Are you trying to make the place more gentrified?"

The barmaid rolled her eyes and gave Maisie a friendly smile. "I am Beryl Dawley. Ignore him, love. He's just teasing you; we accept all customers from all walks of life in here." Maisie's cheeks started to burn as she felt everyone's gaze upon her.

"I'm trying to find out something about a man who used to drink here," she said quietly.

"Speak up, maid," an old man said from his chair in the corner. He cupped his hand behind his ear and gave her a rheumy smile. "You're one of the prettiest ladies we've had in here for a while. Are you going to entertain us with a song, perhaps?"

"Mind your own business, Frank," Beryl bellowed. She picked up a cloth and started polishing glasses with a slightly wary expression. "Sorry, love. Who is it you're asking about?"

Maisie leaned closer and lowered her voice. "Dominic Smallwood. I'm trying to find out the name of a gentleman he lost a game of cards to. Do you know anything about that? Did they play cards here?"

Silence had fallen in the tavern, and Maisie was painfully aware of everyone straining to listen to the conversation.

"Oh, him." Beryl didn't bother to talk quietly and screwed up her face. "Yes, I know who you're talking about."

"Dominic Smallwood?" The burly man who had been leaving strolled back to the bar, shaking his head. "I ain't seen him for a while, but if you find him, tell him Jerry O'Connelly is still waiting to be paid what he's owed."

"And me," Frank piped up querulously from the corner. "Last time I saw him, I bought him a pint of ale. The scoundrel never bought me one in return. A man of his wealth, too." His hand shook slightly as he sipped his rum, and he scowled. "He's run away to America, and good riddance too. We don't want his sort in here."

Beryl shrugged, and her ample bosom wobbled. "That about sums it up, I'm afraid, love. He hasn't been in here for a while and certainly not to play cards. I can't say I know of anyone other than the locals who Dominic used to drink with." She gave Maisie a sympathetic look. "Has he wronged you, ducky? I wouldn't put it past him."

"It's nothing I want to trouble you with," Maisie said hastily. She didn't want to be gossiped about, even though everyone was eager to hear more.

"You don't want to be bothering with a man like 'im." A thickset man in a farmer's smock with lank hair and stained teeth stood up from a nearby table and stumbled in her direction. "I'm looking to find me'self a wife. Come and sit on my knee, and let me tell you all about my farm." He swayed slightly and

THE RUNAWAY SISTER

grabbed her by the waist, enveloping her in a blast of beery breath.

"Get off her, Claude," Jerry O'Connelly growled. "I saw her first. Anyway, what's a lady like her going to want with an old codger like you? You ain't had a proper wash since Christmas, and she's far too pretty to be looking after 'em stinking cows and pigs of yours." He clamped a hand, the size of a shovel, on the farmer's shoulder, and they eyed each other belligerently.

Beryl caught Maisie's eye and nodded towards the door. "Best to leave now, love, unless you really are staying for a drink. These two are no strangers to a fight, and you don't want to get caught up in that, trust me."

Maisie wriggled out from between the bar and the two men and rushed away just as she heard the first punch make contact. A cheer went up, and the last thing she saw before the door shut behind her was Beryl striding out from behind the bar, brandishing a broom to break the men up.

"Sounds like you had a lucky escape there," an old woman said as she scurried past Maisie in the lane.

"I reckon so." She gave the woman a bright smile, even though she felt far from cheery inside.

"What now?" she muttered to herself. It was

DAISY CARTER

another false start, and another day passing without getting any closer to finding Abigail. Her fears were changing and starting to solidify into something she hardly dared to put into words. *What if Abigail isn't missing me as much as I think and prefers her new family? What if looking for her is the wrong thing for me to do?*

She started walking across the village square, deep in thought. If only she was closer to Frampton, she would have visited Ava. The wise old woman would have been able to quell her fears and suggest what she should do next; she was sure of it. Now that the idea had come to her, she had an urge to do it immediately, but that wouldn't be fair to Gloria. She would ask Jack if perhaps he would take her to Frampton on her next day off, as long as it didn't inconvenience him. She was surprised by a sudden pang of homesickness for her old village and even for people like Elsie Clatterbrook. She knew it would pass within a few minutes, and it wasn't that she didn't like Thruppley. It was more her sense of frustration from being no further forward in finding Abigail.

As if her thoughts had summoned him, Maisie's spirits lifted as she spotted Jack down Drapers Lane, which led off the square. "Jack!" she called. A breeze had picked up, and it carried her words in the opposite direction so he didn't hear her. She quickened her pace. "Jack, over here!" Just as she was about to call again, she realised he was not alone. Florence Porter was standing in the shadow of a beech hedge, gazing up at him with a wide smile.

Maisie felt a sickening lurch of despair as she watched Jack pull Florence into a hug. Although it was brief, even from a distance, she could tell there was genuine happiness in it, and their laughter drifted towards her. Tears pricked the back of her eyes, and a sense of desolation swept over her. She felt very alone. She had always known that Jack had a soft spot for Florence, but part of her had secretly hoped that it was nothing more than friendship and that one day he would notice how much Maisie adored him.

"What a fool I am," she muttered, turning around. Horace and Lillian didn't want to help her. And Jack was probably eagerly making new plans for a life with Florence as his wife, only humouring her in helping to look for Abigail for old times' sake.

Tears filled her eyes, and she walked blindly past the market stalls and turned into Broad Street, hurrying back to Gloria and her sewing. Perhaps a quiet life making beautiful dresses for other people was all she could hope for. The tears rolled down her cheeks, and she wiped them away. She had made a mess of everything.

"Maisie! Wait!"

The sound of running footsteps on the cobbles

behind her grew louder, and she spun around. In spite of what she had just seen, her heart still beat faster as she realised it was Jack. *Will I ever stop loving him?* She would have to if he was betrothed to Florence.

"Didn't you hear me?" he said, smiling. "I called you when you were crossing the square, but the drayman's wagon went past and—" He stopped abruptly, looking concerned. "Is something wrong? You look as though you've been crying."

Maisie took a shaky breath. "It's nothing...and everything." She shook her head, reminding herself that she had no hold on Jack's affections. She should be happy for him. She *would* be happy for him. "I saw you with Florence just now," she said, attempting to sound bright and cheery. "Congratulations. She'll be very lucky to have you as her husband."

Jack tipped his cap back and scratched his head, looking puzzled. "Have me as her husband?" he echoed.

Maisie shrugged, suddenly feeling awkward. "I wasn't spying on you. I wanted to tell you about my visit to the Black Lion. I just happened to see you both... I saw you and Florence embracing."

Jack guffawed with sudden laughter and shook his head. "You had me worried for a minute there, Maisie. I thought you must have been imagining things."

THE RUNAWAY SISTER

She bristled, feeling hurt by the way he was joking. "I did see you embracing. But that's your business. I just want to say...I'm very happy for you. You've known Florence for years, and I'm sure you'll make each other very happy."

Jack's expression changed in an instant, and he put his hands on her shoulders and looked deep into her eyes, making her heart thump harder in her chest. *Doesn't he know how much I love him? Why is life so unfair?*

"I was hugging Florence because she just told me some good news," he said gently. "Mr Fisher and Florence are engaged to be married."

"They are?" Hope flickered again.

"Yes, that's why she's in Thruppley today. She heard that Gloria makes wonderful wedding gowns, and Mr Fisher sent her here in his carriage. She was lost, so I was telling her where your shop is."

Maisie frowned, feeling like a fool. "You mean Edmund Fisher, the coffee merchant? Her master? I never knew she was sweet on him." She blushed and looked down at the dusty toes of her boots. "I always thought she was sweet on you."

"She was years ago," Jack said easily. "But I told her she could do a lot better. I saw how fond Mr Fisher was of her when I used to call for rags, so I mentioned it to her one day. They're hoping for an autumn wedding, and Mr Fisher is the happiest I've seen him in a long time. I just gave her a hug because she's so excited."

"Oh. So, I was mistaken. I'm sorry I jumped to conclusions." Maisie was suddenly aware of the fact that Jack's hands were still resting lightly on her shoulders. She wished the moment would last longer.

"I suppose now that we're on the subject…" Jack cleared his throat and stepped back from her, seemingly lost for words.

"On what subject? Florence's wedding?"

Jack whipped his cap off and attempted to smooth down his hair, but it sprang up again in its usual way, which Maisie found so endearing. "No, the subject of engagements." He gave her a peculiar look, twisting the cap in his hands. "You know…"

Maisie chuckled. "Has anyone ever told you that you speak in riddles, Jack Piper? If Fred was here, he would tell you to spit it out. What exactly are you trying to say?"

Jack gave her a lopsided smile, and her breath caught in her throat. "My heart has only ever belonged to you, Maisie. I've been wanting to tell you for ages, but what with everything that's been going on, I couldn't seem to find the right moment. I suppose what I'm trying to say is—"

"There you are, maid. I thought I saw you walking across the village square earlier." Mr Bagley came up behind the two of them, hobbling in a determined

THE RUNAWAY SISTER

fashion. He had a bunch of flowers in one hand and a basket of apples in the other. "I can't be away from my stall for long, but I was wondering if you would give these to Vera on your way back home? Also, I've got news for you…about that little girl you were asking me about t'other day."

Optimism surged through Maisie's veins, and Jack's eyes lit up. "Do you know something about Abigail?" she asked hastily.

"I do, maid." Mr Bagley handed Jack the basket and flowers, trying to catch his breath. "Sorry," he gasped. "I ain't as nimble as I used to be, and I didn't want to miss you, Miss Griffin."

"Thank you…it's so kind of you." Maisie waited patiently for his breathlessness to subside, even though she felt as if every nerve in her body was tingling with anticipation.

Mr Bagley thumped his chest and smiled again. "That's better. Now, where was I? That's it, I saw a well-to-do couple driving through the village in a smart carriage a few days ago. There was a young girl in the carriage with them who looked a lot like you. Green eyes, light brown hair in ringlets." He twirled his fingers by his head to show her. "She was wearing a posh velvet dress by the look of it, but her face was just like yours, maid. The spitting image of you."

"Don't be shocked, but she's my daughter, Mr

Bagley," Maisie blurted out. She wasn't ashamed of it anymore, and she wanted people to know.

"I know, maid," Mr Bagley said, patting her arm sympathetically. "I could tell the minute I laid eyes on her."

"So, do you know who the couple are?" Jack's question was short and laden with urgency.

"I asked around. I ain't sure of their names, but they're renting a house in Lower Stanley. It's a village just yonder, where I get my apples from. They'm living at Yewtree Villa next to the church. I think that's where your daughter is, Miss Griffin."

"Thank you! Thank you!" Maisie threw her arms around his broad shoulders and smacked a kiss on his wrinkled cheek, making him blush.

"Don't be telling Vera you kissed me, or she'll get jealous." He touched his cheek, chuckling and then shooed them away. "Hurry up, maid. If you're quick, you'll get there a'fore dark. Mind yer fellow goes with you, though. They might not take kindly to giving up such a bonnie little girl."

CHAPTER 25

"Finally! This is the news I've been waiting for."

Jack heard the relief in Maisie's voice and grinned at her. "Granny told me the cards showed your fortune would change." With one last wave of thanks to William Bagley, they ran down Broad Street and through the narrow lanes back to the shop.

Gloria looked startled as they burst through the door. "What is it? You look as though you're being chased by the devil." She eyed the apples and flowers. "Are you making apple pie?"

"Mr Bagley knows where Abigail is," Maisie exclaimed happily.

"He does? That's wonderful news." Gloria hastily put the gown she was sewing aside and stood up.

"Where is she? Has she been in Thruppley all this time?"

"No, Mr Bagley found out she's with a well-to-do couple living in Lower Stanley. They're renting a house by the church; that's all he knows."

Gloria grabbed her shawl and threw it over her shoulders. "We must go to the hotel and tell Horace. And then get Dolly and Joe." She jammed her bonnet on her head and started tying the ribbons under her chin. "What about Constable Redfern? He should probably come as well in case there is trouble."

Maisie lifted her hands and shook her head. "No, Gloria. I know you mean well, but I think that is something I should do alone. If we all go there, it will only antagonise the people who have her. I just want to explain to them that Abigail is my daughter. It's Dominic who did the wrong thing, not them. I think they'll be less likely to talk to me if we rush in, accusing them of being criminals and looking as though we want to snatch Abigail back from under their noses."

Gloria paused, looking alarmed. "You can't go alone, Maisie. Verity and Dolly would never let me hear the end of it if something bad happened. And you're one of us now. We look after our own."

Jack always wanted to be on Maisie's side, but this time, he was inclined to agree. "Gloria is right, but I can see your point as well, Maisie. Why don't you at least let me come with you? It's too far to walk, and Duke is grazing up on the common, not far from here. I'll take you to Lower Stanley in the cart, and when we get there, you can decide if you want me to come into the house with you."

"I suppose that would be a good compromise." Maisie looked around the shop and then hurried over to the table where she usually sat to do her sewing. She picked up the soft green shawl, which was draped over the back of her chair and folded it up. "I knitted this for Abigail last winter. Maybe if the couple can see that she knows this is hers, it will go some way towards proving that I'm her mother."

"That's a good idea," Gloria said. "Don't you think Horace should come as well? It sounds like the people who have Abigail are wealthy and well-connected. They might respond better to a man of Horace's influence, Maisie. It's not that I don't think they will believe you, but Horace wants to help. The Smallwood family name carries a lot of weight around here."

Jack was surprised to see Maisie's mouth turn down and her eyes darken with disappointment.

"No," she said bluntly. "I haven't had a chance to tell you, Jack, but I went to the hotel earlier to ask Horace if he might know where Dominic had played the game of cards. I didn't get to speak to him, but I overheard him telling Lillian that he isn't interested

DAISY CARTER

in helping me...all he cares about is protecting the family name from another scandal."

The shock on Gloria's face was evident, and she gave Jack a worried glance. "Are you sure you're not mistaken, Maisie? I've known Horace for years, and that doesn't sound like him at all."

"I heard it with my own ears. I don't want his help." There was a stubborn, uncompromising tone to her voice, and she walked towards the door. "Can we go now, please, Jack? I'm frightened something might go wrong. I won't rest until I've spoken to Abigail, even though I have no idea how things might work out."

He picked up the basket of apples and bunch of flowers again and nodded. "We have to go past The Lilacs to get to the common so we can give these to Mrs Venn on our way."

Maisie hurried back out into the lane, keen to get going, but Jack held back for a moment. As soon as she was out of earshot, he lowered his voice to speak to Gloria. "I don't like to go against Maisie, but it's true; you have known Horace Smallwood for much longer than us."

Gloria resumed tying her bonnet, still looking puzzled. "Horace always wanted to do the right thing in the past when Dominic caused such havoc. I can't believe he wouldn't want to help Maisie. Abigail is his niece...it makes no sense."

THE RUNAWAY SISTER

"Perhaps he's thinking of the hotel?"

"He's not like that, Jack. Why would he have taken on Constable Redfern if he doesn't care?" This time, it was Gloria's turn to look stubborn. "I have to tell the others. Maisie doesn't know what she's taking on going against Dominic. What if he's at the house as well and hasn't gone to Paris yet? What if the people who have Abigail are just like him?"

Jack nodded slowly, hoping he wasn't making a mistake. "I think you're right. Maisie is high-spirited and as strong-hearted as a lion, but we have no idea what sort of people they are."

"Exactly." They shared a conspiratorial smile. "Promise you'll both be careful and leave everything else to me."

* * *

MAISIE LEANED FORWARD on the cart seat as she willed Duke to go faster. He was already trotting at a lively pace, and the first few cottages on the edge of Lower Stanley had just come into view. But even so, it felt like the dreams she often had where she was trying to run, but her legs felt leaden.

"What are you going to say to them?" Jack frowned with concentration, making sure that they didn't hit any ruts in the road. The last thing they needed was for a wheel to fall off the cart or Duke to lose one of his shoes.

Maisie crossed her arms tightly across her chest. "I don't know. I've had the conversation a hundred times in my head, but I was always afraid I would never get the chance to meet them." She shrugged. "I suppose I'll just speak what comes into my mind." Her gaze flicked across to look at him, and her heart warmed as she took in his strong profile and kind, brown eyes. "About what you said to me in the village, before William Bagley spoke to us—"

Jack reached across and squeezed her hand like he had done a dozen times over recent weeks. But this time, it felt different. Maisie's nerves tingled, and she felt something elemental shift within her, like watching a lightning storm gathering force in the night sky. She stole another glance at him, allowing herself to wonder for the first time whether their future could lie together.

"This isn't the time to talk about that, Maisie," he said, squeezing her hand again before putting his focus back on Duke's reins. "All that matters now is Abigail."

They rumbled past a farmer rounding up his cows in the field with a collie nipping at their heels and then past two thatched cottages. A wooden sign at a fork in the road showed Upper Stanley was two miles away, and they had arrived in Lower Stanley.

THE RUNAWAY SISTER

"Look, there's the church spire." She pointed ahead, and her stomach churned with hope mingled with fear. They rode on in silence for a couple of minutes before Jack murmured something to Duke, bringing the cart to a stop in front of a grand Georgian house.

"This must be it," he said. There was a gnarled yew tree at the side of the house. It had probably been in the church grounds at some point, but now it was in the house's garden, just beyond an ornamental pond and a well-manicured rose garden. He tied off the reins and turned to look at Maisie. "Ready?"

"I'm just going to go straight up to the front door. I might not be well-to-do, but I'm Abigail's Ma, and I'm not going to creep around to the servants' entrance as if I don't belong with her." Maisie fingered the soft shawl in her lap. She could still picture Abigail wearing it in her mind's eye, chattering excitedly as they walked to church last Christmas Day. It gave her courage. "That's the right thing to do, isn't it?"

"Absolutely." He gave her an encouraging smile. "I suppose you're going to tell me you want to do this by yourself?"

Maisie chuckled. "You know me too well." Their eyes met for a beat, and she took a deep breath. *This is it. This is the moment I get my daughter back, and I won't accept anything less.*

She jumped down from the cart and pushed the ornate iron gate open, hurrying up the wide flagstone path. The house had a pleasing symmetry, with tall windows on either side of the imposing front door and long flower borders on either side of the path. Bees buzzed lazily, drifting from flower to flower, and a flock of doves flew overhead, bright white against the blue sky, cooing as they started roosting in the dovecote by the garden shed. In any other situation, it would have been a perfect summer evening, but Maisie's heart was racing, and she barely noticed the beautiful surroundings.

She gazed up at the windows, hoping to glimpse Abigail looking out, but the sun glinted on the glass, so the outside view was reflected back at her, making it impossible to see inside. She ran lightly up the steps and ignored the slight tremble in her hand as she grasped the heavy brass knocker and rapped sharply on the door.

The seconds ticked by, and she leaned closer to the door, waiting to hear the sound of footsteps crossing the hall. There was nothing but silence, and a sense of disappointment and foreboding started to creep over her. She glanced back over her shoulder to where Jack was waiting in the lane. He made a rapping motion with his hand, telling her to do it again.

"Is anybody in?" Maisie called out loudly this time

and hammered the door knocker again. The sharp noise echoed around the garden, sending two blackbirds skittering out from under the rose bushes, chink-chinking loudly in alarm.

Just as Maisie was about to knock again, she saw a small movement out of the corner of her eye. The curtains in the window on her left twitched. "I know you're in there," she called, louder this time. She rapped the door knocker again for a little longer, not caring if it sounded rude.

This time, she was rewarded by the shuffling sound of ponderous footsteps from inside and bolts being dragged across the inside of the door.

"What do you want?" The door opened barely an inch. "Who's making such a dreadful racket loud enough to wake the dead?" A bright blue eye regarded her beadily through the crack. "There's nobody here." The voice sounded nervous, and the door started to close again.

Maisie hastily jammed her toe in the gap and pressed her hands against the door to stop it from being slammed shut in her face. "I don't mean any harm," she cried. "I just want to talk to you, that's all."

The door creaked open a couple more inches, and a wizened old lady with grey curls and a starched mob cap and apron was revealed.

"Are you the housekeeper?" Maisie softened her

voice as the old woman's eyes darted suspiciously, looking her up and down.

"I might be." She sucked on her teeth and tried to peer beyond Maisie, but she barely came up to her shoulder. "Who's asking? Did the bailiffs send you?"

"No, I promise I'm nothing to do with the bailiffs." Maisie took a deep breath and decided that all she could do was be completely honest and hope she could get past the woman's prickly defences. "This is probably going to sound very strange, but I'm begging you to hear me out."

The old woman sniffed and then opened the door wider. "You'd better come in. You never know what busybodies might be passing in the lane, and I don't want Mr Boulter's business being spread about the place."

Maisie followed her into the hallway, and her heart sank. The furniture was covered in dust sheets, and it was clear the place was not being properly lived in. Her gaze was drawn up the sweeping staircase to the landing above. *Is Abigail up there? In one of the bedrooms?* It took all her resolve not to push straight past the old woman and run through the house, but she knew she had to show restraint.

"What's your name?"

"Maisie Griffin."

A nod and a gleam of interest in her blue eyes. "I'm Pearl Evans, the housekeeper. Go on."

THE RUNAWAY SISTER

"My daughter, Abigail, was taken from me by a gentleman called Dominic Smallwood. He gave her to a childless couple to repay a debt, but I want her back."

If she had expected the elderly housekeeper to look shocked by this revelation, Maisie soon realised that wasn't going to happen.

"I thought t'was something like that," the old woman harrumphed. "I never liked that scoundrel who brought the girl here. There was something shifty about him, and he was rude about my chocolate sponge cake." She gave Maisie a beady look. "Just because I didn't like him doesn't mean I believe you though. Who's to say you're telling the truth?"

"You have to believe me. Please..." Maisie suddenly felt overwhelmed by how the odds were constantly stacked against her, and her shoulders slumped in despair. She had been so certain that this time they would find Abigail, but she was facing failure again. "My name is Maisie Griffin, and Abigail thinks I'm her older sister, but I'm not. It's a long story, but I'm her ma. Please, I beg of you, can you tell me where she is?"

The old woman shrugged, and for a moment, it looked as though she was going to turn away, but to Maisie's surprise, two tears trickled down the woman's lined cheeks, and her mouth worked as though she was trying to hold back her emotions.

"Aye, alright. I heard the little 'un asking Master Boulter when her sister, Maisie, would be coming to fetch her." She pulled a voluminous handkerchief from her apron pocket and blew her nose. "I shouldn't be telling you this, but I know what it's like to have a child taken. It happened to me when I was about your age, and I still think of my little boy to this day." She wiped another tear away and shook her head. "The matron at the orphanage gave him to a more deserving family, but I never stopped loving him."

Maisie's heart went out to Pearl. "I'm sorry that happened to you." They shared a moment of understanding...two mothers yearning for their children. "I never had the chance to say goodbye to Abigail. I hope she wants to be with me, but I'll never know unless I can ask her. Perhaps she will have a better life with the people you work for, but—" Her voice trembled, and she felt as though the emotions were choking her. "It looks as though I'm too late anyway," she finished dejectedly.

Pearl shook her head, suddenly galvanised into action. "No, dear. Don't say that." She shuffled across the hall and pulled the dust sheet off the sideboard, opening one of the drawers. "Mr Boulter has inherited a spice plantation in India. He and his wife, Susannah, are going to live there. They're heading to

THE RUNAWAY SISTER

Bristol docks, and they'll be setting sail at the end of the week."

"You mean they're leaving England? Forever?" A fresh wave of anguish swept over her.

"Yes, dear. This is the name of the ship they're going on. They've not long left, and I'm just minding the house until the next people come to rent it." The old woman's eyes were bright with urgency. "If you go now, you might catch them up. I heard the mistress telling Abigail that they were going through Nailsbridge on the way."

Maisie grabbed the piece of paper from her, not even looking at it. "Thank you for telling me, and bless you for your kind heart. I'm forever in your debt."

"I'm not promising that they'll give her up," Pearl warned. "The mistress is very fond of the little 'un. She's been longing for children for years, but it never came to anything." She gave Maisie a steady look. "At least you'll have a chance to say goodbye to your little girl before she goes to India. Or maybe Susannah Boulter will agree to give her back. Good luck, dear."

Maisie ran out of the house and back down the path, scrambling into the cart again. "Nailsbridge…" she gasped. "They're going that way to Bristol docks. We have to catch them up, Jack; otherwise, I'll never see Abigail again. They're setting sail for India at the end of the week."

Jack picked up the reins and slapped them on Duke's broad back. The horse's tail swished, and he sprang into a fast trot, his hooves drumming loudly as they left Lower Stanley.

"What if we don't get there in time?" Maisie clenched her hands together.

"We can't think like that," Jack said. "You belong together, and Granny told me the cards are never wrong. She said you would find a way to be together again."

As they rumbled along the dusty road, Maisie could only pray that he was right.

CHAPTER 26

Smoke drifted up from the mills ahead, and the honey-coloured cottages glowed softly in the last of the evening sun. Maisie stretched and yawned, feeling stiff from sitting on the cart seat for so long.

"We've made good time, but I'm going to have to rest Duke now." Jack gave Maisie an anxious smile. "I know you just want to carry on until we see them, but Duke will go faster tomorrow morning if we let him have a feed and rest now that we've reached Nailsbridge."

"Of course. I don't want to run him into the ground. Besides, it will give us a chance to speak to a few people in the village. Hopefully, someone will remember seeing them and might even know where they headed to next."

DAISY CARTER

"There's an inn on the far side of the village." Jack gave her a rueful smile. "I don't have much money, but maybe they'll take pity on you and give you a cheap room for the night. I'll be fine sleeping under the cart."

"What would I do without you?" Maisie knew very well that without Jack's support, she would never have got this far. "Do you really think the cards your granny reads hold any truth? That she sees me with Abigail again?"

He nodded with a simple certainty that reassured her. "Whether it's because they give you faith in what you're doing or it's the cards themselves foretelling the future, all I know is that Granny wouldn't say something like that if she didn't mean it."

Dusk came quickly, and the inn was a welcome sight when Maisie spotted it ahead of them. The windows were ablaze with oil lamps, and she could hear the tinkling sound of a piano. The sign above the door creaked on its metal bracket, and there was a picture of a fox, wearing a top hat on it, looking at a duck.

"Here we are, the Fox And Duck. Owned by the Wallace family, purveyors of excellent meat pies and good ale." Jack gave her a wink as he turned Duke off the lane. "I came here on the way up from Frampton one day, asking after Abigail, but they didn't know anything."

THE RUNAWAY SISTER

Maisie was surprised by how busy it seemed. She could hear laughter from inside, but it didn't sound as raucous as the Black Lion. Two young women were strolling down the lane towards them, talking about what food they would have for dinner in the parlour behind the bar, which heartened her. Clearly, they catered to ladies and gentlemen so she wouldn't feel too out of place.

As she climbed down from the cart, she noticed a carriage ahead of them. Two tousle-haired boys were unharnessing the horses to take them through the archway into the stable block for the night.

"Take care, they're fine horses, and I want them looked after properly." A tall, smartly dressed gentleman was watching them closely. "I think the mare has thrown a shoe on her front near side. I don't want to travel with her any further and risk her going lame."

"Very wise, sir," one of the lads piped up. He patted the mare's neck and ran his hand down her leg. "Her fetlock isn't hot, so you've done the right thing, stopping here. Our pa will sort you out with a nice room as well."

An elegant woman appeared from behind the carriage, fluttering her fan in front of her face. She wore a fitted blue velvet dress with a bustle, and her hair was twisted up in an elegant chignon with a small hat perched on top. "Do you think it will be safe to stay here, my dear?" She fluttered her fan again and looked startled as a roar of laughter erupted from the bar.

"I don't think we have much choice." The man smoothed his moustache and gave her a reassuring smile. "Don't worry, dearest, I'll make sure they give us the best room."

The taller of the two boys gave them an apologetic grin. "I would ask George, the farrier, to put a shoe on your mare tonight, but he's been drinking all afternoon."

"Oh dear." The woman stepped closer to her husband and frowned.

"Don't worry, missus. He's the best in the village, and he'll sort your mare out before sunrise. You'll be on your way soon enough."

"Do you think these people might know the Boulters?" Maisie whispered to Jack. She watched the stable boys lead the horses away and wondered if she could ask them or if the gentleman would be irritated by the intrusion.

"Let's go inside and ask the landlord if they have a suitable room for us, Susannah," the gentleman said. He pulled a gold pocket watch out of his waistcoat and looked at the time. "Has she woken up yet?"

Maisie's skin prickled with excitement. "Did you hear what he just said, Jack? He called her Susannah. That's what Pearl, the housekeeper, said Mrs Boul-

THE RUNAWAY SISTER

ter's name is." Her pulse quickened, and she felt breathless. "I must speak to them now before they go inside."

Just as Maisie started to approach them, the elegant woman opened the carriage door and leaned in. "Come on, Abigail. Something a little different is happening on our big adventure. One of the horses has lost a shoe, so we're staying at this quaint little inn for the evening before we start travelling again tomorrow morning."

Maisie gasped as the woman lifted Abigail down the steps. "It's her, Jack, my Abigail," she said hoarsely, scarcely able to believe it. She started to tremble as she watched Abigail hold hands with Susannah Boulter and look up at her trustingly as she skipped alongside her.

"Abi—" The word died on her lips, and suddenly, Maisie was filled with doubts. Abigail looked happy. She was wearing a frilly dress made out of the same blue silk that Susannah was wearing, and her hair had been coiffed into ringlets with a colourful ribbon to complete the outfit. She carried the doll she so adored under her other arm. "Abigail," Maisie whispered again. It was as if she had lost her voice now that the moment of their reunion had come. *They look as though they belong together...one big happy family.* The thought felt like a leaden weight in her chest.

"Wait!" Jack called. He reached for Maisie's hand

DAISY CARTER

and squeezed it. "Don't doubt yourself now, Maisie. She belongs with you. We'll get a little cottage together, and I'll work every hour of the day if it means you can have your daughter back again."

"Maisie?" Abigail stopped in her tracks and turned to stare. "Maisie! Jack! What are you doing here? I've missed you so much," she cried. She slipped from Susannah's grasp and ran towards Maisie, throwing herself into her arms.

"We've been searching everywhere for you, my sweet," Maisie said, half laughing and half crying as relief swept over her.

"I kept asking when you would visit me, but they said you didn't want me anymore. Is it true?" Abigail's chin trembled, and tears rolled down her cheeks. "Those horrible toffs who came to the Jolly Sailor pretended to be my friends and then shouted at me when I cried. The man said you don't love me anymore. He said you and Jack were going to have your own family, and I was better off without you, but I didn't believe him, Maisie."

Without looking up, Maisie could sense Mr Boulter and his wife hurrying towards her and knew she only had a few seconds to explain. "You're right, Abigail, Dominic is a horrible man. He took without me knowing, but I promise I've been looking for you every day ever since." She knelt down in

312

THE RUNAWAY SISTER

front of Abigail, and her heart swelled with happiness as she looked into the little girl's face, which was so dear to her. "There's something I need to tell you, my poppet. I'm not your big sister; I'm your ma. It doesn't change anything between us. In fact, I love you even more because of it."

The little girl's eyes widened, but she stuck her thumb in her mouth and nodded solemnly. "I like you being my ma, Maisie. I never had a ma before...but—" She glanced between Maisie and Susannah Boulter, her large green eyes clouding with confusion. "Does that mean I have two mamas now, Maisie?"

A shadow fell over them, and Maisie straightened up, still holding Abigail's hand tightly.

"What is the meaning of this?" Mr Boulter barked. He glanced over his shoulder towards two men who had just staggered out of the inn and lowered his voice. "I don't know who you think you are, but this little girl belongs to my wife and me."

Maisie lifted her chin defiantly, even though her heart was thudding so hard in her chest she felt sure he must be able to hear it. "I'm Maisie Griffin, Abigail's real mother. Dominic Smallwood took her without my consent."

"Nonsense," Mr Boulter snapped with a frown. "I trust Dominic implicitly. He told me Abigail was a runaway, and that you were her sister, and that you

313

didn't want her." He stepped closer and pulled himself up to his full height as if he wanted to intimidate Maisie into submission.

"Jeremy, look at them," Susannah said softly. She placed her hand on her husband's arm, looking rather forlorn. "You can see how similar they are and how Abigail ran to her. Of course this young lady is Abigail's mother. And why would someone who didn't care come looking for her?"

"But… but," Jeremy blustered. "My dear wife has already grown very fond of Abigail. Dominic told us the little girl had nobody to care for her, which is why we wanted to raise her as our own child." He took a long breath and shook his head, patting his wife's hand. "I don't want to upset Susannah."

"I didn't even have a chance to say goodbye to her," Maisie explained, willing them to understand. "I might not be wealthy like you, but it doesn't mean Abigail isn't cared for. I've loved her since the day she was born. Through good times and bad."

Jack nodded firmly. "I can vouch for that, Mrs Boulter. Maisie is as good a mother as any little girl could wish for, and they're both very dear to me. I'll work my fingers to the bone to make sure that Maisie and Abigail have a roof over their heads and food on the table. Things haven't always been easy for them, and they deserve a happy life."

THE RUNAWAY SISTER

Maisie's heart, which was just returning to normal, thumped again, but this time for a different reason. *Dearest Jack...he loves us both.*

Susannah took a lace handkerchief out of her reticule and dabbed it daintily on her eyes, turning aside slightly. "Jeremy, you know as well as I do that Dominic Smallwood is not the sort of man we would usually trust. We believed him because we wanted to...we were desperate to. But you've heard the rumours about what he did to his own family." She sighed and dabbed more tears away. "Abigail did keep asking about Maisie. Perhaps we should let her decide who she wants to be with?"

Maisie's heart soared with sudden hope, but it was short-lived as Jeremy Boulter turned back to her with a stubborn expression. "We would give your daughter a good life. Isn't that what you want for her?" There was an edge of desperation in his voice.

"Jeremy, I know you want me to be happy," Susannah said. Her voice wavered as she tried to quell her disappointment. "If what this young woman is saying is true, think how bereft we would feel if someone took our child away from us under false pretences."

"I promise I'm telling the truth. You can ask anyone who knows me—"

The sound of galloping hooves suddenly inter-

315

DAISY CARTER

rupted the conversation, and Maisie watched in disbelief as Horace Smallwood reined his horse to a halt and vaulted off. Lillian was riding sidesaddle next to him, and her horse was lathered in sweat as it pranced beneath her.

"We've been on a merry chase trying to find you," Horace said. He tugged his riding gloves off and strode confidently towards Mr Boulter, shaking hands with him in one easy movement. "You must be Jeremy Boulter? I'm afraid there's been a terrible misunderstanding, and it's all down to my wretched brother, Dominic. I'm Horace Smallwood, and this is my dear wife, Lillian, daughter of Lord Shaw."

"Dominic's brother?" Jeremy could barely speak, he was so surprised. "And your wife is…Lord Shaw's daughter?"

"Indeed," Horace said, giving him a beaming smile. "I understand you're in a rush to get to Bristol docks. Why don't you step over here with me for a moment, and I can explain everything."

"What's happening, Jack?" Maisie whispered. "How did they know to come here?" She glanced at him, and his eyes glinted with mischief. "Did you tell Horace?"

"Not exactly. I asked Gloria to. I had a feeling we might need his help."

One of the stable lads had scurried over to hold Lillian's horse, and she dismounted and linked arms

THE RUNAWAY SISTER

with Susannah. "I do feel very sad for you, Mrs Boulter, but I'm afraid Abigail should never have been separated from Maisie." She gave Susannah a warm smile as she led her away. "Dear little Abigail was never a runaway. She should be with her real mama, don't you agree?"

Jack suddenly pulled a handful of coins out of his pocket and hurried after Horace and Mr Boulter. "We don't want to do you wrong," he said. "I know it's not much, but I'll happily give you all the money I have on me to make up for what Dominic owed you."

For a split second, Mr Boulter looked affronted, but then he shook his head and smiled at Maisie for the first time. "It was never about repaying the debt from the card game, Miss Griffin. Dominic was a fool if he thought it was. My wife and I have longed to have a child for many years, and when Dominic offered us Abigail, it seemed as though our prayers were being answered. She truly is a delightful little girl, but no, keep your money. We offered Abigail a home because I wanted to make Susannah happy."

Maisie's throat thickened with emotion, and she lifted Abigail onto her hip, adoring the feeling of her little arms around her neck as she clung on. "You're a good person, Mr Boulter. And you too, Susannah." Her eyes misted with tears, and she blinked them away. "If I could do anything to give you the happiness of having your own child, I would in a heartbeat. I will never forget your kindness and understanding."

"We shall miss Abigail," Susannah said. She smiled sadly, and Jeremy hurried to her side and put his arm around her shoulder. "One day, our time might come, but truly, I'm glad that you have been reunited with your daughter."

"Wait." Maisie suddenly knew what she had to do. "Take this, Susannah." She pulled the wooden charm that Ava Piper had given her from her dress pocket and pressed it into Susannah's hand. "A wise woman gave it to me a while ago. She told me it would bring my daughter back to me and that it helps women who want a family."

Jack smiled with understanding. "My granny is never wrong about such things. You probably think it means nothing, but keep it on you. Who knows what may happen?"

As the Boulters walked away, Maisie smiled as she saw Susannah tuck the charm inside her gown pocket and pat it.

"Is it too late to go back to Thruppley, please?" Maisie asked Jack. "I know Duke's tired, but I just want to go home to our family."

Horace walked over to them. "I have a few details to take care of with Mr and Mrs Boulter to make up for my brother's wrongdoings," he said in a low

THE RUNAWAY SISTER

voice. "But I think you should leave now rather than make the parting any harder for them."

"How did you know we were here?"

Horace looked awkward for a moment. "Don't be cross, Maisie, but Gloria came to find me as soon as you left for Lower Stanley. It seems you overheard me saying I didn't want to help?"

She nodded. "I'm sorry I doubted you."

He chuckled, shrugging her apology away. "I was actually talking about Dominic's wife, Genevieve. Lillian was worried that Dominic might not treat her well if her inheritance runs out, but as far as I'm concerned, they deserve each other. She should have stopped Dominic from taking Abigail, but she went along with his cruel plan without a thought for anyone but themselves."

"We're going to head back to Thruppley now," Jack said. "Duke's a sturdy horse. If we take it steady, it won't take long. Poor Abigail is exhausted, and Gloria must be waiting on tenterhooks for us to return."

Horace strolled away to talk to the Boulters again, and Jack helped Maisie settle Abigail on the cart seat between them.

The stars were just starting to come out in the night sky as they clopped out of Nailsbridge. The air was heavy with the scent of wild honeysuckle and dog roses, and Maisie tucked the green shawl around

DAISY CARTER

Abigail's shoulders as she drifted off to sleep, leaning against her.

"That was quite some day," Jack said quietly.

Abigail's eyes flickered open again, and she looked up at Jack, then Maisie. "Did you mean what you said about us living in a cottage together?" she asked sleepily.

Maisie's heart fluttered with hope and longing. Did he mean it? Or had he said that just to help her cause with the Boulters?

Jack reached across Abigail and took Maisie's hand in his. "Perhaps now, I'll get my words out," he said, giving her a lopsided smile. "Will you marry me, Maisie? Can the three of us make a home together?"

"Say yes, Maisie…I mean, Ma…" Abigail giggled to herself as she snuggled against Maisie and fell asleep again a moment later, lulled by the rocking motion of the cart.

"Yes, dear Jack," Maisie said. "I thought you'd never ask."

They shared a smile over Abigail's head. "Well, we have been rather busy."

"Nothing would make me happier than for us to be together, wherever that might be. And with Fred and Ava as well. We'll be one big family."

Jack chuckled and adjusted the reins in his hands. "Granny saw that in the cards as well, I just didn't tell you until today."

THE RUNAWAY SISTER

A barn owl glided silently across the lane in front of them, and a fox barked in the distance. Maisie put her arm around Abigail and sighed happily. She might have been lonely and felt as though the world was against her at times, but things had worked out just as they should in the end.

EPILOGUE

*S*ix Months Later...

GLORIA SHOOK out the creases on the small train of Maisie's wedding gown, stood back and gave her an approving nod. She had been making the alterations for weeks, and she looked like a proud mother hen. "You look beautiful if I say so myself."

Maisie blushed and smoothed her hand over the ruby-red velvet stole around her shoulders. "Are you sure it's not too grand? I don't want people to think I'm getting above myself."

Verity bustled towards them, overhearing what she had said. "Don't be silly, Maisie. Horace was quite insistent on Dolly having a new gown made for her wedding, and Gloria has adjusted it just enough to make it look different for you." She tweaked the stole and smiled. "We've been through a lot, all of us, one way or another. Why shouldn't you have the treat of a nice wedding to celebrate better times ahead? Besides, you and Jack have been betrothed for almost six months. You can't keep him waiting too long."

Abigail came skipping through the lychgate of the church, holding hands with Dolly and Joe as Amy and Billy walked behind. "Look at me, Ma," she called excitedly. Her cream muslin dress fell in frills to her ankles under a short cloak for warmth, and her hair ribbons were made of the same red velvet as Maisie's stole. She twirled as she reached them.

"Are you all ready to come in now?" The vicar beckoned from the church porch, and his cheeks reddened as everyone turned to look at him. He was new to the village and still finding his way through the maze of who was related to whom. All he knew was that Verity Webster could be formidable, and he didn't want to get on the wrong side of her.

Maisie felt a fizz of nerves in her stomach and took a deep breath. She would be a married woman before the hour was out. Mrs Jack Piper.

"Allow me to escort you in." Joe gave her a kind smile and tucked Maisie's hand in the crook of his arm. He squeezed her hand. "Your ma would have been very proud of you today, Maisie. And of every-

THE RUNAWAY SISTER

thing you have achieved...rescuing Abigail...starting a new life in a village away from where you grew up."

Maisie touched the locket at her neck and felt her nerves melt away. "This belonged to my ma. Pa gave it to her for their wedding, so wearing it today makes me feel close to them."

"Don't forget, you still have all of us as your family," Dolly said.

The vicar cleared his throat again, and Verity shooed everyone into the church. "Come along, I've got a huge spread of food back at the lockkeeper's cottage for afterwards. We'd better let this poor vicar conduct the service before he gets tongue-tied." She gave the vicar a wink and nudged him with her elbow. "I'm only teasing," she chuckled. "You'll soon get the measure of all the Thruppley folk, and I trust you'll be joining us at the cottage to eat with us after the ceremony?"

The vicar nodded eagerly, then hastily adjusted his expression to be more serious as he remembered his duties. "I wouldn't have it any other way, Mrs Webster," he murmured. "Now, would you be able to get your family to take their seats?" He smiled nervously. "Please?"

As Joe walked Maisie up the aisle and the organist gave an enthusiastic, if slightly tuneless, rendition of Medelssohn's Wedding March, she fixed her gaze on Jack, who was waiting for her at the front of the

325

church. He turned to smile at her, and her heart beat faster, as it always did.

"Remember to enjoy yourself," Joe said quietly.

Jack and Fred were wearing smart morning suits, which had been lovingly repaired and pressed by Gloria. Even their unruly hair had been tamed into submission.

"I was worried you might have changed your mind," Jack whispered as he took her hand. They turned to face the vicar, who glided serenely to take his place in front of them, holding his bible.

"Never," Maisie whispered back. Her heart melted as he gave her a lopsided smile, and she could see Abigail and the rest of her family settling themselves in the front pews of the church out of the corner of her eye.

"Welcome to Saint Joseph's Church, on this auspicious day, for the wedding of Maisie Griffin and Jack Piper," the vicar said. He smiled beatifically at the congregation, and the ceremony began, his deep voice echoing off the ornate vaulted ceiling of the old church.

THERE WAS a nip in the air as they emerged from the church soon afterwards to cheers and clapping. Maisie could barely believe that so many of the villagers had turned out for her wedding, but Verity had told her to expect it. Thruppley was a tight-knit community where people looked out for each other and enjoyed any excuse for a celebration.

"I reckon we'll have snow a'fore the day is out," Bert said, glancing up at the grey skies overhead.

Fred and Joe were swinging Abigail between them as they walked towards the lychgate, and she laughed delightedly. Maisie thought it was one of the sweetest sounds she had ever heard, especially as she reflected on how close she had come to losing her darling daughter forever. As she looked around at the gravestones, a shiver of regret made her pause.

I'm sorry you're not with us today. She still had no memory of Abigail's twin, the baby she had lost at birth. She could only hope that Abigail would not feel the loss during her life.

Ava Piper hobbled over to join them and fell into step next to her and Jack. "Don't be sad for the other little 'un," she said, looking up at her knowingly. "Everything happens for a reason, and just because the baby is not with you in this realm doesn't mean its presence is lost forever. There may be times when you sense the child's spirit nearby, and Abigail might even imagine she's seen them, t'is common with twins. Enjoy those moments and give Abigail all your love...plus your future children." Her eyes twinkled as Jack laughed.

"I don't think we need you reading the cards to

tell us about future children we might be blessed with, Granny. Some things should be left to nature."

Just as they got to the lychgate, Horace walked briskly after them and called Maisie.

"Congratulations to both of you. Lillian sends you her best regards. She would have come, but she's not feeling very well at the moment."

"I hope she's not overdoing it," Maisie said. "You must be very excited that she's expecting a spring baby."

Horace couldn't hide his delight and smiled broadly. "Now that you mention it, I can't wait to become a papa."

"Will you join us at the lockkeeper's cottage for a celebratory glass of sherry, Horace?" Dolly asked.

"It's kind of you to invite me, but I don't like to leave Lillian for too long." Horace turned his attention back to Maisie and Jack. "I hope you don't mind me asking today of all days, but it's been on my mind for a while. I desperately need a new head gardener for the Rodborough Hotel. I remember Maisie mentioned that you wanted to work as a gardener. Would you perhaps consider it?"

Jack's eyes lit up. "Would I consider it? I'd love nothing more."

"Really? Oh, thank goodness." Horace shook hands with him, looking relieved. "Lillian said I should ask you. The only reason I didn't do it before

THE RUNAWAY SISTER

is because I've been so busy, but you can start next week if that suits you. I'm not sure what you might do about your rag-and-bone round?"

Fred appeared next to them and gave Jack a cheeky grin. "I happen to know someone who's itching to get his hands on a rag-and-bone round. What about it, Jack? You always said I had the gift of the gab to persuade people to give us their best things."

Jack slapped Fred on his shoulder and nodded. "As long as you promise to look after Duke properly, it's all yours."

"There is just one other thing," Horace said. He shot Maisie an apologetic smile. "I know you're eager to get on with your wedding celebration, but while I'm here, it seems prudent to ask."

"What is it? And don't be silly; you're not delaying us at all. Verity will have us celebrating until the small hours, I expect. And I'm not too sure about Bert's homemade wine," she chuckled.

"Dolly told me you and your family have been renting a small cottage for the last few months in Thruppley, Jack."

"Yes. It was better for my rounds, and Lord Pickering put the rent up in Frampton. Granny and Fred like it here, although Fred's not having much luck with the mudlarking."

"Well, I have an empty cottage in the hotel

329

grounds. It's rather rundown at the moment, but with a bit of work, it could be nice. It's not far from the lockkeeper's cottage either, Maisie, to be near the rest of your family."

"Oh, Horace, that would be wonderful!" Maisie beamed at Jack. "But I hope you won't take this the wrong way...we would only move if there's room for Ava and Fred. Ava's not getting any younger, and she'll always have a home with us. She's like a second mother to me."

"Of course, my dear. There's plenty of room for all of you, plus a growing family. I know you've been through a lot because of Dominic, so it's the least I can do. It means Lillian and I will see plenty of little Abigail. We've grown very fond of her."

They strolled under the lychgate and out into the lane. "Abigail is part of your family too, Horace." She gave him a warm smile. "Dolly told me when I first arrived in Thruppley that you're nothing like Dominic, and she was right. If he comes back from Paris, I'll never agree that Abigail can see him, but I'm pleased that she has you, Lillian, and your papa in her life."

Horace's expression darkened momentarily. "He won't come back here, Maisie, I can promise you that. I wrote to him and said that if he dares to show his face, he'll be arrested and thrown into jail. Like

THE RUNAWAY SISTER

most bullies, he's a coward at heart. You don't need to fear him causing problems for you again."

Verity came hurrying back towards them, her cheeks red from the sharp winter wind. "Are you lot coming, or what? We've got mulled wine, roast turkey with all the trimmings, and a syrup sponge waiting to be eaten. I fancy a bit of a knees-up." She flicked her petticoats, making the vicar blush, and jigged her way back to Bert.

"I'd better get home, myself." Horace tipped his hat and unhitched the reins of his horse. "Oh...I almost forgot to give you this." He pulled a letter out of his pocket and handed it to Maisie. "It was delivered to the hotel; I think it's from Susannah Boulter, sent from India."

Maisie and Jack followed everybody towards the towpath, walking arm in arm.

"You read it, Jack," Maisie said, handing it to him.

Jack broke the wax seal on the back, pulled out a piece of paper, and read aloud.

"Dear Miss Griffin,

I hope my letter finds you well. We have just arrived in India, and it's very different, but I'm sure we'll get used to it. The journey was interminable, and I shall be very happy if I never have to do it again.

I think of you and Abigail often. You might be

wondering why I'm writing to you, but I thought you would like to know our news. During the journey, one of the maids on the ship sadly died in childbirth. She had no other family with her, and the ship's captain agreed that Jeremy and I could adopt the baby. Little Flora is absolutely delightful, and we have never been so happy.

Jeremy said the charm that you gave me was nothing but a trinket, but I believe it did what you said it would and helped our family become complete, and for that, I owe you my heartfelt thanks.

I wish you and Abigail well. I hope you do marry that fine young man who clearly cared so much for you.

With best wishes,

Susannah Boulter."

Maisie sighed happily, and Jack slipped his arm around her shoulders. Everyone they loved was together now, and they had the security of Jack's new role as head gardener at the hotel and a bigger cottage to go with it.

"I'm so pleased for them," Maisie said. "She really did care for Abigail, and I felt terrible for dashing her hopes of being a mother."

"Has anyone ever told you how kindhearted you are, Maisie Piper?" Jack stopped and turned to face her. "Thank you for trusting me to become Abigail's pa. It means a lot to me."

"You'll make a wonderful father and the best

THE RUNAWAY SISTER

husband I could ever wish for. I love you, Jack." Maisie stood on her tiptoes, and they shared a tender kiss.

As they parted a moment later, the first snowflakes of winter drifted down from the sky, landing in her dark hair like shimmering crystals. "Christmas is just around the corner, and I can hardly believe that so much has happened since last year."

"Our first Christmas together," Jack said softly. He tucked a lock of her hair behind her ear and kissed her again.

Abigail came running back towards them, her dark ringlets flying out behind her. "Look, Ma...look, Pa...it's snowing!" she exclaimed. She threw her head back and twirled, with her arms wide, and Maisie knew at that moment she had never been so happy. They had their whole lives to look forward to together, and this was just the start.

READ MORE

If you enjoyed The Runaway Sister, you'll love Daisy Carter's other Victorian Romance Saga Stories:

The Snow Orphan's Destiny

As the snow falls and secrets swirl around her, Penny is torn between two worlds. Does a gift hold the key to her past, and will her true destiny bring her the happiness she longs for?

Penny Frost understands that she's had an unusual start in life. Taken in by a kind-hearted woman, she becomes part of the close-knit Bevan family of Sketty Lane.

Poverty is never far away, but they manage to scratch a living working for the miserly Mr Culpepper in the local brickyard.

READ MORE

Penny dreams of something better and never feels as though she quite fits in. And the fact that her mother never mentioned her own childhood only adds to the mystery of who she really is.

When she is bequeathed a piece of jewellery, Penny wonders if it might unlock the secret to her past. However, before she can find out, a shocking event one dark and snowy night brings her to the attention of the wealthy Sir Henry Calder.

Suddenly she finds herself swept into a world of privilege and comfort, far away from the Bevans and her best friend, George, and it seems as though her future is finally secure.

But not everyone wants Penny to succeed and will go to any lengths to get their own way, even if it means leaving her destitute.

Will the mistakes of the past be repeated and snatch Penny away from her true destiny?

Can she reclaim what is rightfully hers even though the odds are against her?

Torn between two very different worlds, Penny must decide whether to follow her heart or put duty first if she's to have a chance at love and happiness...

The Snow Orphan's Destiny is another gripping Victorian romance saga by Daisy Carter, the popular author of Pit Girl's Scandal, The Maid's Winter Wish, and many more.

READ MORE

* * *

**Do you love FREE BOOKS? Download Daisy's
FREE book now:**

The May Blossom Orphan

Get your free copy here: https://dl.
bookfunnel.com/iqx7g0u0s7

Clementine Morris thought life had finally dealt
her a kinder hand when her aunt rescued her from
the orphanage. But happiness quickly turns to fear
when she realises her uncle has shocking plans for
her to earn more money.

As the net draws in, a terrifying accident at the
docks sparks an unlikely new friendship with kindly
warehouse lad, Joe Sawbridge.

Follow Clemmie and Joe through the dangers of
the London docks, to find out whether help comes in
the nick of time, in this heart-warming Victorian
romance story.

Printed in Great Britain
by Amazon